Kabbalah of Stone:
A Novel

Irene Retí

Juniper Lake Press
P.O. Box 7467, Santa Cruz, CA 95061
http://juniperlakepress.com

ISBN: 978-0-9843196-0-2
This book is also available as an e-book from http://www.smashwords.com/

Cover photograph by Toni Verdú Carbó of Girona, Spain. See Carbó's Flickr site at:
http://www.flickr.com/photos/tonivc/

Black and white illustration of the tree is by Bettianne Shoney Sien. See her website at:
shoneysien.wordpress.com

For Gloria Evangelina Anzaldúa
1942-2004
mi comadre in writing

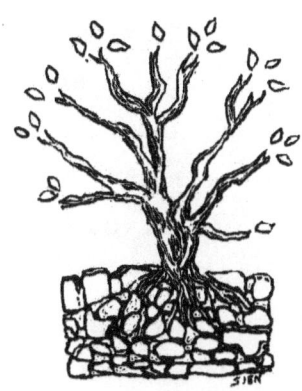

Acknowledgements

As a writer I am blessed with an unusually large circle of friends and colleagues who helped bring this work to fruition. Most of all thanks to Rabbi Lori Klein, my brilliant and gifted life partner and true love, for accompanying me on every step of this spiritual and literary journey and for her deep rabbinical imagination and keen editorial eye.

Thanks to my parents, Andy and Ingrid, both Holocaust refugees, who gave me both a love of words and a visceral understanding of hidden Jewish identity and the *converso* experience; to Gloria Evangelina Anzaldúa, my "comadre in writing," housemate, and friend, whose theories and spirit are integral to this book; and to physicist-philosopher Karen Barad, whose friendship and theories about entanglement are entangled in these pages and in the stones.

Several other rabbis generously read versions of this manuscript, enriching it greatly. (Of course, any errors of fact and interpretation that appear here are the writer's responsibility!) Special gratitude to Rabbi Nadya Gross, whose spiritual direction through Soul Memory and gifts as an editor and thinker blessed both the conception and the unfolding of this work. Thank you to the members of Reb Nadya's "Wisdom School" (2007–2008), which included Rabbi Victor Gross and many other astute thinkers of the Jewish Renewal movement. In the heady atmosphere of Colorado's high mountain country we wrestled with ideas of gender and Kabbalah; those discussions helped midwife this novel. Appreciation to Rabbi Eli Cohen of Chadeish Yameinu, both for his incisive editorial advice and for the spiritual work we did together in Girona; to Rabbi Leah Novick for several close and thoughtful readings of this manuscript, her teachings on the *Shekhinah*, and her support; and to Rabbi Elisa Klapheck, who shared my journey to Girona, grappled with the painful legacy we found there, and discussed Huldah with me.

Thanks to Silvia Planas i Marcé, Director of the Institut d'Estudis Nahmanides in Girona, for her warm welcome and substantive help with library research in Girona and to Margarita Alburnà with the Guia de Turisme de Catalunya for her inspiring, in-depth Jewish tour of Girona's *call*.

My heartfelt thanks to Susan Reddington, longtime writing partner, who read more drafts than anyone else and helped cook up plots and characters over three years of stuffed potatoes and deli sandwiches. To Bettianne Shoney Sien, one of my best editors and best friends. To Sarah

Rabkin and Jenny Kurzweil, the sharp and perceptive members of my writing group, who asked all of the right questions. And to Ellen Setteducati, longtime friend, poet, and skilled editor, who carefully labored over the final version of this book and entered into its vision.

Many other friends and colleagues have been an essential part of this writing in smaller but important ways too numerous to detail here. Thanks to De Clarke, Ellen Farmer, Jeanne Freebody, Philippa Gamse, Hannah Good, Holly Blue Hawkins, Jerry Hull, Lisabeth Kaplan, Alisa Klaus, Diane Tiferit Lakein, Andrea Lowgren, Kathy Miriam, Beth Remak-Honef, Daniel Reti, Steve Reti, Debbie Rifkin, Rabbi D'vorah Rose, Leslie Smith, Ahouva Steinhous, and the members of Capitola Book Café's fiction writing group and Emily Mitchell's Novels-in-Progress class at Stanford University.

And finally, thank you to the Jewish Renewal movement, particularly Chadeish Yameinu of Santa Cruz, which has gifted me with spiritual and intellectual community.

Prologue

In a sacred grove of terebinth trees high on the Mount of Olives, water rose through a crack in stone and gathered into a pool. Huldah dipped her gourd in the spring and mounted a platform holding the ancient altar of Asherah, Queen of Heaven. She poured water from her gourd and then wine from her goatskin bag on the dark soil, libations for the Divine Mother. Tall and carved from pale stone, Asherah guarded her leafy grove. Her eyes gazed peacefully down at the earth. Her hands held her heavy breasts as if to offer them to a nursing child. Below her waist, her figure tapered into a smooth pillar.

Huldah walked over to the fire burning in a circle of rocks. She removed a twig and lit the incense cupped in the horned altar at Asherah's feet. She had taught her students to prepare this incense of tree sap, myrrh, frankincense, saffron, and wine. She was old. Now it was their task to clean and fill the bowl, stoke the fire. They knew when to respect their teacher's need for solitude in the grove and had quietly left when they saw her approach.

Spicy smoke curled over the platform sheltered by trees. Huldah opened her flask of olive oil and anointed the stone pillar standing by Asherah's side. Finally, she removed a round cake of freshly baked bread from her satchel. This too she placed at Asherah's feet. Fruits of the earth, water, fire, air, stone—she offered these to the Queen before asking for prophecy.

The grove was quiet, its shadows filled with the presence of the Queen of Heaven. Huldah circled the grove, greeting each familiar tree. Some trees had already shed their leaves, though the autumn rains were late this year. One terebinth, said to be older than the Temple, clung to the edge of the mountain, its roots cupping rock. This tree would serve as her oracle. Huldah placed her age-spotted hands against the oldest terebinth tree's knobby trunk and closed her eyes. "Tell me," she said to the tree, "tell me what the future holds."

The sap of the tree pulsed under her palms. After a few moments, Huldah could no longer distinguish between the tree's blood and her own. The terebinth took her on a voyage through time. A sapling emerged from a fissure between rocks. Wind blew through spindly branches hundreds of years ago, long before her people planted olive groves on terraced lands and named this mountain ridge with three peaks the Mount of Olives. There was no Temple below the ridge, no Jerusalem, only a small village.

The tree divulged to Huldah all it witnessed as it matured. High on the Mount of Olives, beyond walled cities and invading armies, terebinth trees recorded the history of the people in rings. The Temple rose as if in a day, though it took seven years to build. Smoke from the priestly sacrifices swirled into the sky. The streets of Jerusalem filled with beggars and traders, priests and prophets. The sound of the ram's horn resonated against the hills. The people shaped terra cotta figurines of Asherah, the agricultural goddess, and placed these magical talismans on their hearths, in hopes that their animals would multiply and remain in good health, their harvests would be plentiful, and they would be blessed with many children. On hilltops, they created shrines in her honor and marked them with wooden poles and standing stones.

Huldah and the tree reached the present moment, the year 3140 in Jewish time, or 621 BCE as the Christians later counted the years. Huldah felt her arms wrapped around the mature tree at the edge of the mountain. She enjoyed the tree's solidity, the spicy scent of cinnamon. Logs cut from cinnamon trees warmed the hearths of Jerusalem and enveloped the hills in fragrance.

Suddenly, a searing in her legs — someone had chopped the tree down near its base. She flung herself away from the trunk just as it fell onto the earth amid other severed trees. The tree had shown her its future: a stump in a graveyard of stumps lodged in thick mud. No shrine now, no statue of Asherah. Below the skeletal trees, the city of Jerusalem smoldered in ruins.

Huldah's spirit took the form of a stork. She soared down the Mount of Olives into the destroyed city. Blood marked the streets and stained her wings. She opened her stork mouth, sounded a cry of mourning across the Kidron Valley.

She awoke from her trance sprawled beneath the living tree, her tunic soiled. She sat up, brushed herself off, and shook her head. But the images remained: exploding stone, the Temple in flames, vultures feasting on dead bodies abandoned in the streets, a mourning king. She cupped her cheek to think. Her vision had not shown her King Josiah but some other king she did not recognize.

The grove darkened. It must be late afternoon, time to return home. Huldah bent to tighten her sandals. In the month of *Tishri*, the turtledoves departed for warmer lands; terebinth trees shed red leaves. Sheep and goats grazed terraced fields beneath the olive trees, though the grass was short and dry this late in the year, leaving not much for them to eat. They, like the farmers, longed for the first rains of the season. As she descended the mountain, she looked at Jerusalem framed in olive trees, its yellow stone buildings spreading down the ridge from the sacred Temple of Adonai, which had graced the mountain for almost four hundred years. All of this would be destroyed.

Years passed, and on the last afternoon of her life, Huldah sat in the weak sunshine by the spring, listening to the water bubble amid golden rocks. The old terebinths had been chopped down and their stumps remained, just as she had been shown in her vision. Some of the younger terebinths still stood, but they looked naked, their thin trunks fragile in the mountain wind, unprotected by their older relatives. The altar, the statue of Asherah, the horned incense holder—all had been pulverized. But the Temple was not yet destroyed. Jerusalem stood. It was her people who had done this, not strangers.

She stretched out on a golden boulder warm from the midday sun, listened to the sad song of the water, and drifted into sleep. The slow beat of stone caught Huldah's breath as it stilled. She entered the stones of Jerusalem, the walls of the Temple itself.

A resonant voice said, "Well done, Huldah."

"Who are you?"

"The Angel Gabriel."

Gabriel stood immense, over seven feet tall, surrounded by the yellow light of Jerusalem stone. Shimmering orange butterfly wings sprang from a dark, muscular back. The angel looked at her through black, serious eyes. "Look," Gabriel said, and on the wall of stone Huldah saw an image of her husband and son burying her bones near the place where her students had sat at her feet.

"I am dead."

"Yes," the angel said. "They received special permission to bury you within the gates of Jerusalem. Your body is buried near your school, but now your spirit inhabits the stones. There is wisdom to be found in this realm. You are still a prophet."

Chapter One

Eighteen centuries after Huldah's vision on the Mount of Olives, on a rainy evening in Girona, Spain, the great Rabbi Moshe ben Nachman, Nachmanides, sat in his study in the synagogue, which faced east toward Jerusalem. He was calculating the period between creation and redemption. "Each day of creation represents one thousand years of history," he wrote in what later became his *Book of Redemption*. "I believe we near the seventh epoch, the generation when the Messiah will come." Still young, Nachmanides was only beginning to conceive the texts that would distinguish him as one of the most renowned rabbis of all time.

As he mused on that blustery night, Huldah spoke from the spirit world through a crack in the wall. "Rabbi, you are not the first to think the end of times draws near, nor will you be the last. Obsessing about the Messiah is a dangerous distraction, which is why the rabbis in the *Talmud* warned:

'May the bones be blown away of those who calculate the end.' You, of all people, should know better. There is no map of creation, no predestined path."

Nachmanides peered into the blue light emanating from the crack in the building he called home. He closed his eyes to resist its pull. "I did write that in every Jewish year we begin again," he answered. He was not surprised a spirit spoke to him, for he frequently encountered spirits in his meditations. But this outspoken female voice was new. "I distinguish between the ongoing creation through the fire of the Hebrew letters, in which there is no before or after, and the orderly unfolding of history, which will be completed with the resurrection of the dead. You have not understood my argument."

"Your prophecy centers on the world of the human, on the history of the Jews, on human personifications of the Divine," argued the voice. "Here in the foothills of the Pyrenees you live among bear and wolf, fig and oak tree, hawk and butterfly. Do you think an oak tree lives according to Jewish ideas of history, human notions of time?"

"Spirit, are you a pagan?" demanded the rabbi.

Outside, the rain grew heavier, but the spirit's voice lifted over the pelting water.

"No. But like many men and women in Jerusalem before the destruction of the First Temple, I honored both Asherah and Adonai. We asked the Lady Asherah to bless us with children and with soft rains to water our crops. We kneaded dough and shaped it into round cakes for the Queen of

Heaven, wove splendid garments, and draped them on her figure, which sometimes graced the Temple itself."

"You speak of Asherah. How did you honor Adonai?"

"I taught *Torah* and the holy language in my school inside the southern gate of the Temple."

"As a woman?" Nachmanides cupped his chin in thought. Something about the story this spirit told seemed familiar.

"There is much that might surprise you about your ancestors, Rabbi. Educated by my father and my uncle, I fell in love with the sacred texts. Most people could not read or understand the scrolls that were their heritage. I took it upon myself to teach them. However, I also loved Asherah. Adonai's *Torah* as recorded by the priests speaks little of our love for the Divine Mother."

Nachmanides rose from his chair to peer into the fissure from where this candid female voice spoke. "How did you come to be in the wall of my synagogue?"

"The Romans shipped some building blocks of Jerusalem across the sea. They used a few to construct Girona, including this holy building in which you pray, study, and teach. My spirit lives in these stones, though I sometimes travel beyond them."

He needed to be sure that this was not a demon. "What is your name, Spirit?"

"They called me Weasel."

She had never been pretty. Her neck was too long, her nose pointy, her ears small and rounded, her eyes black against her white face. Her mother had named her Weasel.

"Does this name trouble you?" her students had asked.

"No, it is a gift from heaven," she had told them. "A weasel is clever and fearless and burrows beneath the everyday surface of things. Weasel is a good name for a prophet."

Nachmanides' quick mind scrolled to the correct passages in the book of Kings and the book of Chronicles. Like all rabbis of his time he knew the texts by heart. "Huldah?" he asked in wonder. "I thought you advised King Josiah to destroy Asherah."

The light from the stones flared hot blue. Nachmanides shielded his eyes.

The High Priest Hilkiah and his men had summoned her to authenticate a scroll they had discovered while remodeling the Temple. Its words were hard to decipher on the worn vellum. Hilkiah had twisted his fingers as he had waited for her answer. Finally, she had pronounced, "This is a very old copy of the fifth sacred book of the Law, the book of Deuteronomy."

"The scroll is not a good omen," Hilkiah had told her. "Shaphan the Scribe discovered it open to the text of curses describing God leading Israel and its king into exile. Shaphan read it to the King, who demands to know its significance." The High Priest had watched Huldah's face.

She had closed her eyes. She could not think with men staring at her.

"What does this mean?" Hilkiah's voice had cracked like dry rock. "Tell us."

"Please. Silence," Huldah had murmured.

She had never liked Hilkiah. He did not believe in Asherah. He had declared there was a place only for Adonai in the Temple, though it had not always been so. Even King Solomon had honored Asherah, as had many other kings of this land. Hilkiah and his cohorts would like to erase this history. However, she had never heard Hilkiah sound so vulnerable. That day they had been simply two leaders concerned about the fate of their city. She must describe her vision of the destruction of Jerusalem. To withhold this information might endanger their people.

She had opened her eyes and looked directly at Hilkiah. "Tell the man who sent you they found the scroll in this position because He sends a message to us: Calamity will befall this place and all its inhabitants."

Hilkiah had looked at Huldah with disdain, destroying the moment of rapport. "You dare refer to King Josiah as 'the man'? The King rips his clothes in grief even as we speak. Now I understand why you are named Weasel."

"I am sorry. I meant no disrespect. I only meant that we must have compassion for King Josiah as a man, a man with human frailties." The eighteen-year-old king must hear this terrible prediction and then lie awake during the night like her.

"You are reputed to be a more compassionate prophet than your cousin Jeremiah. We hoped you would go to Adonai on our behalf."

"Perhaps I can speak to Adonai and ask for his mercy, though I fear it will not change the future. Please accept my apologies, Hilkiah. I am not myself. This knowledge wears on my soul. I have not slept well. I have revisited the high places several times to check the accuracy of my prophecy."

"The high places," Hilkiah had scoffed. "It would be better to rely on Adonai's texts."

"You know I do not choose between them."

"Weasel," Hilkiah had muttered. "So do you have any other words for the King?"

What comfort could she offer? "Hilkiah, please assure King Josiah neither he nor I will live to see Jerusalem in ruins. My visions show me a different king of this land. Perhaps Adonai will show mercy for Josiah, who already reveals his agony over this prophecy. The destruction will not happen for some time. I believe by then Josiah will be gathered to his fathers in peace."

Hilkiah had addressed his men instead of her. "We must give the King some reason for this impending devastation. King Josiah will want to believe something can be done to avoid catastrophe. We will tell the King the Israelites shall be punished because the people make offerings to Asherah. When he returns to Jerusalem, Jeremiah will concur with this interpretation."

"No!" She could not allow her message to be distorted. She had tried to keep her voice calm, respectful. "Hilkiah, it is not our task to figure out God's reasons. Perhaps God has a new destiny for us, one we cannot yet understand. We have not cared for the poor of our city. We have not followed the path of righteousness. You and I know this has nothing to do with Asherah."

She had been dismissed, betrayed.

"Huldah?" Nachmanides' voice transported her back to the synagogue in Girona. "Are you still here?"

"I never agreed with the priests who forced us to choose between the Queen of Heaven and the Divine Father," she told Nachmanides. "You may ask why the priests allowed me to run a *yeshiva* within the First Temple. Perhaps they tolerated me because I descend directly from Joshua, student of Moses, who led our people into the land and ended their exile in the desert. I also descend from Joshua's wife, the prostitute Rahab of Jericho, a Canaanite woman who assisted the Israelite spies by hiding them from the local authorities. I might add that Rahab knew how to speak to stones, and she helped Joshua bring down the walls of the city but protected her own house."

Nachmanides groped frantically for his quill. He must write down the prophet's words.

"No," she ordered. "My story is not yours to record. You have your own books yet to write. However, I do have an interesting prophecy for you. It has nothing to do with the Messiah. Shall I tell you?"

"Speak."

"There is an older kabbalah, one spoken by stones and trees. We must learn once more how to listen to its language."

"This still sounds like paganism," the rabbi replied.

"No, even our ancestor Jacob understood this kabbalah. You know this story. Long ago, *Even Hashetiyah*, the foundation stone of the world, emerged from the primordial waters of creation and gave birth to the mountain now above Jerusalem. When the ancient Israelites entered the Holy Land, they received kabbalah from stone. Jacob absorbed this kabbalah as he slept, his head resting on the navel stone of the world, which grew soft as a pillow. He dreamt of a ladder to heaven upon which angels ascended and descended. The next morning, Jacob took the stone he had used for a pillow, set it upright as a pillar, and consecrated it with oil that rained down from the sky in the morning light. He understood that this mountain formed a gate to heaven. In time, King Solomon built his Temple over Jacob's stone."

Nachmanides nodded. "How do I study this text?"

"Place your hand on the stone wall, here, by this crack from which I address you."

Nachmanides placed his hands on the stones and listened. Huldah never spoke with Nachmanides again, but soon he wrote "The Holy Letter," in which he argued that the bodies of human beings are as divine as their souls.

Huldah's spirit did not freeze within those golden stones shipped across the sea from Jerusalem and embedded in the synagogue's walls in Girona. Huldah's spirit suffused the stone and altered it, and it changed her. The stone became Huldah; Huldah became stone. Huldah immersed herself in the kabbalah of stone, which flows from the first lava that solidified out of the fires of creation, gathers all that it touches and hears and sees, and continues to the present day.

When she had spoken with Asherah on the Mount of Olives, Huldah had begun to comprehend this kabbalah. It is not an accident that there are many names for stone in the sacred language of Hebrew — *even, tzur, sela, tzror, tzuk, kaf, barad,* and more — for Jews are an ancient people who long ago spoke the language of stone. Stone records the voices, the weeping, the laughter, the songs that emanate from the most sacred or the most profane places. Stone remembers all.

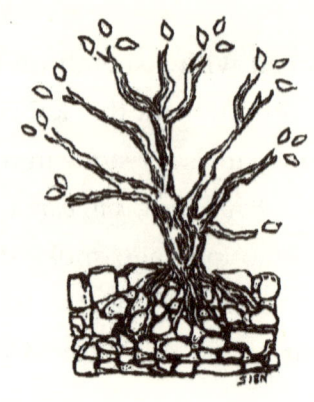

Chapter Two

More than two centuries later, on a warm afternoon in Girona in the month of Nissan 5251, or March 1491 as the Christians and the conversos counted the years, Domingo Fontclara argued with his mother.

"Please, I can't imagine marrying Nuria."

Domingo had met Nuria Costa when they were children. The Costas and the Fontclaras had planned a match: Domingo would marry Nuria when she turned sixteen and he became a journeyman scribe. Now he had spoiled everything.

"You don't want to marry Nuria. You're too good for her? You're so handsome with your huge hands and feet, your messy hair?" his mother said.

"Nuria is graceful and kind. But it wouldn't be right."

His mother smashed the clove of garlic for the Friday stew. She always used the same ingredients—lamb, chickpeas, eggs, and chard. Then she stirred in rosemary and thyme. She cooked enough to last until Saturday after sundown. When Domingo had lived at home before his apprenticeship to Roca, the scribe, he had grown tired of this meal. Now he appreciated his mother's finely spiced stew on those Friday nights when she invited him for dinner.

"So many men in Girona would love to marry Nuria. She's devout, beautiful. What am I supposed to tell Doña Costa?" Caterina turned back to the fire. The garlic burned while she listened to her son throw away the future she had planned for him. She scraped the scorched mixture into a pail, pried another clove of garlic from the bulb, and began to chop it. She swiped at the smoke spreading over the room and began to peel and chop an onion.

"Let them marry her," Domingo said. Years ago his best friend, Pau, had confided to Domingo that his sister Nuria loved Andreu Gras, the shoemaker. An honorable man, Andreu respected the arrangement Nuria's family had made. Well, now Andreu and Nuria could marry and be happy; Nuria would have someone who could be a true husband. And he would be free, at least until his mother and uncle began to pressure him to marry some other girl.

He could not confess to anyone, not even Father Santos, that he felt no desire for Nuria. Two years ago, when they were eighteen, he and Pau had visited Maria, who worked at the tavern. Men called her an expert. He remembered Maria's laughter following him as he had fled that back room. A demon must have crept into his genitals during his infancy. Perhaps it had seized Pau separately or possessed the two of them together when they played in the forest as young boys, for they desired only each other.

Pau had found a solution to this pressure to marry. Always religious, he had easily discovered safety in the Church. He had studied at the Cathedral school since the age of nine and become an excellent scribe. Pau was still an acolyte, responsible for lighting candles during Mass. He handed out bread to the poor at the almshouse, tended to the lamps of the Cathedral, and carried the Host in a linen bag to the priests. But soon the bishop would examine and evaluate him for the priesthood. If Pau passed the examination, he would take the vows of poverty, chastity, and obedience, a promise to God. After that, Pau could be cloistered. They might never see each other again.

"Come be a priest with me," Pau had proposed.

"But I'm not meant to be a priest. I have too many doubts," Domingo had told him.

"And you think priests never doubt?" Pau had laughed.

Domingo had loved Pau his entire life. He could not bear the thought that they might soon be separated.

"If only I felt for Nuria the way I do for—" he ventured. Pau had covered Domingo's mouth with his slender hand.

Now his mother dropped chunks of lamb into the pot. They sizzled amid translucent onions. "It smells so good, Mama," Domingo said. She ignored him, busying herself with cooking. Her eyes looked red. He stood behind her and put his hand on her bony shoulder.

Her body stiffened.

"I'm sorry, Mama."

Usually his charm would soften her, but she kept her face turned away.

The stew would not be ready for a while. He left his mother's house in search of comfort.

The stones held warmth from the afternoon sun, though the courtyard behind the synagogue lay in shadow. Domingo stood in front of the wall and pressed his palms into its mosaic of different-sized stones. Some were yellow and rectangular. His uncle had once told him these dressed stones scattered throughout Girona's buildings were of Roman origin, but from what quarry he did not know. Perhaps they arrived on a ship from Italy or even from across the Mediterranean. The rest of the stones in the wall were irregular and looked as natural as those Domingo encountered on his rambles through the hills. He fingered a tree root working its way into the wall. The fig trees that shaded the courtyard drank from the stones just as he did when he sought sustenance here. How old *were* these stones?

"The stones are as old as the floor of the sea that birthed them, Domingo," he heard the woman's voice respond. Here she was, the one who offered comfort, who always seemed to know his thoughts. "Notice the shells of sea creatures embedded in the rock."

Domingo fingered round shapes. How could sea creatures come to reside in the walls of Girona? Perhaps they
were a remnant of the biblical flood. He had never seen the
ocean. He placed his ear against the chalky rock, thinking
perhaps he would hear the sound of the sea. Instead, he
heard her voice again.

"It does not matter if you do not understand how they
came to be here," the voice soothed. "I am glad the stones
interest you."

"Who are you?" He glanced around to see if anyone was
watching. The courtyard behind the synagogue was empty.
He had asked her this question before, but she had refused
to answer.

"Who do you *think* I am, Scribe?"

"I don't know. Perhaps I hear the voice of God."

He heard a chuckle. A chunk of stone crumbled and
shed powder into the cooling air. The sea creatures trapped
in the rock glowed in the late afternoon light; they seemed
to pulse, grow flesh. He shrank back. Perhaps a demon
lived here, a demon who tormented Christian boys who
dared visit this sacred building of the Jews. But her voice
always sounded kind. He leaned in again and pressed his
ear against the wall to listen.

He had not told Pau about the voice. He had also
heard human voices raised in song inside the synagogue,
but music had not lured him here. For as long as he could
remember, Domingo had searched for God in the Cathedral—in the wafer, in the candles, in the sermons Father

Santos gave each Sunday. The familiarity of the rituals he had known since childhood pleased him. The contrast between the Cathedral's white exterior walls and plaza and the cavernous dark interior dazzled his eyes. No building in Girona came close in grandeur. When he was a small boy, the stained glass windows, the painting of the Virgin Mary with Infant, the sepulchers of Bernat of Pau, Bishop of Girona between 1436 and 1457, and countless other monuments to martyrs and clergy impressed him. His mother had had to prevent him from fingering the shining crosses rendered of fine enamelwork, gold and silver, and natural pearls that hung on the wall of the chamber. Later, he and Pau had come to the Cathedral to admire the sumptuous Tapestry of Creation embroidered in the eleventh century. When he had become a scribe, he had marveled at magnificent rare manuscripts cradled in carved boxes. The Cathedral remained rich in symbols. But Domingo did not hear God's voice there.

If only he could tell Pau he had discovered God in the most unexpected place. He didn't even know what had urged him to visit the *call*, the Jewish area of town where he and Pau played as children. Only a few weeks ago, he had found himself at this back wall of the synagogue, pressing his hands against these stones. They softened under his fingers, like the belly of a cat hungry for touch. A voice had spoken to him. "Domingo, you are lonely. You have a secret. Tell me. You can tell me anything."

At first he had felt afraid, but then he had confessed what lay in his heart. She had listened to everything without judgment. Now he leaned into the wall. Today it seemed a current of thick warm water he might swim into. "I told her. I told my mother I cannot marry Nuria. Please. What will happen to me?"

She did not answer.

A cream-colored cat, exactly the shade of the stone, studied him from the top of the wall.

Chapter Three

Pau hovered next to Domingo's desk in the shop. "Domingo, I'm concerned about your mother. I saw her enter the gate of the *call* several times this week. A good Christian woman should not visit that neighborhood."

Domingo concentrated on copying the complex manuscript of the Latin version of Ptolemy's *Almagest* on his desk. The ancient Greek astronomer's tome consisted of thirteen books. Domingo now labored over books four and five, which described the motions of the moon.

Pau rested an ink-stained hand on Domingo's slanted writing desk. Domingo looked up at him. Pau's bald crown shone where the priests had shaved it, leaving only a fringe of black hair to circle his head. His face looked pale and worried. "Domingo, please find out why your mother keeps visiting the *call* just before sunset."

What *was* his mother doing there? He studied Pau's pinched face and gestured at the page he had worked on for the past four hours. "Later, I promise. After I finish this."

After Pau left, Domingo refilled his ink horn, determined to keep working. He loved his trade. His master, Roca, had a steady business arrangement with the university in Barcelona to provide the students with copies of books about science — works by Thomas Aquinas and William of Ockham, and of course Ptolemy's *Almagest*. Pau worked only on liturgical manuscripts as part of his training for the priesthood, but Domingo had the opportunity to read these astounding scientific texts.

Usually he looked forward to Pau's interruptions. When Roca traveled to Barcelona, if there was not too much work to do, he and Pau climbed the stairs to Domingo's room, past the fresco Roca had painted in the hallway of Jesus's *Miracle of the Loaves and Fishes*. Pau admired that painting. "If only a miracle like that would happen when I pass out bread to the poor," he had once lamented. "We never have enough for everybody." But last week he had averted his head as they had passed. "I feel Jesus's eyes on me when we walk to your room to sin together," Pau said.

Domingo lifted his cap and pulled at his curls. He wished he could yank his desire for men out of his body. Pau must be upset because by not marrying Nuria, Domingo had shamed Pau's family. Of course, Domingo's mother felt distressed too. Her only child refused to marry the girl she had picked for him. And she always wandered the streets when she pondered her problems. Still, the *call* was no place for a Christian woman. Pau was right. He should go find her.

Domingo went upstairs to wash his hands in the basin in his room and put on his cloak. He walked the short distance to his mother's house but hid in an alcove near the doorway. He felt odd and disrespectful spying on his mother. She emerged a few minutes later dressed in her best blue cloak, her expression serious, intent.

He followed her through the streets of Girona. They crossed the wooden footbridge over the Onyar River, whose waters ran high with spring snowmelt from the Pyrenees. Tall and broad-shouldered at twenty, Domingo could no longer run through the town unnoticed the way he had when he and Pau had chased each other up this hill as boys. When he journeyed to the building he loved, he took a secret passageway below ground, careful not to be seen. But now his mother openly entered the oldest part of the city built in the shadow of the Cathedral. She looked exactly like other women in these streets, mothers rushing home at sunset to prepare the evening meal.

Trailing his mother up the Carrer de la Força, Domingo nearly collided with a donkey pulling a cart packed with vegetables for the market the next day. "Clumsy young man!" the cart owner yelled, and his sickly dog bared his teeth and growled. A somber cat watched him pass.

A butcher in a stained apron stood in front of a shop, his burly arms folded. He scowled as Domingo rushed to keep up with his mother. She moved quickly through narrow alleys formed by tall buildings. The smell of baking bread wafted from the Jewish bakery, reminding Domingo he had forgotten to eat dinner.

There. A flash of blue disappeared around the corner onto Carrer de la Sinagoga. She vanished into the synagogue. Domingo hesitated by the wooden door shut against the gloom of the street. Far above, the sky held sunlight, but here in the stone canyons of the *call*, night already swallowed day. Feeling frightened for the first time, he considered retreat. But he was worried about his mother. He opened the outside door, walked across the courtyard, and pressed his ear against another door. Faint voices chanted inside.

He pushed the heavy door open slowly, but still it creaked. Inside a candlelit chamber, a dozen men swayed back and forth. He glimpsed a raised wooden platform in the center of the room; nearby, a lamp shed a steady glow. This simple, intimate room looked nothing like the grand Cathedral. His mother stood close to some women on the other side of a wooden partition. She didn't notice her son standing in the doorway. One of the women hugged her. He looked at his mother's face, marked with tears. He should go to her. But he couldn't, not in front of all of these people. He turned quickly and walked out the door; it closed behind him.

He circled to the back of the building, slumped against the wall in the courtyard, pressed his face into the familiar stones. "Domingo," he heard the voice murmur. "My beloved young man. Why are you in despair?"

"Why? Why is she here? Why is my mother inside the synagogue?"

"Come," the voice answered. "You know why. You have always known. Why do you return to speak with me? This is your tradition."

He rested his forehead against stone. His mother kept secrets. She startled when he entered the kitchen, sang in a strange language as she stirred soup. She refused to answer questions about his father's death. Once in a while, she left the house on Saturday mornings and would not tell him where she was going. Finally, he let himself see the truth. His mother was a Jew.

He did not know how to name all he felt in this moment: relieved, because he could explain his mother's behavior; angry, because so much had been withheld from him; terrified, because he grasped his family's vulnerability. Beneath the terror, he felt excitement, hope. If he was a Jew, perhaps that explained why his faith felt weak during Mass. Here he might better pray to God. But he knew nothing of Jewish prayer.

He pushed his face into the stones for comfort. They had grown cold. The voice remained silent; the sun had set. He should leave. But his legs were heavy and he could not rise.

Some time later, a hand touched his shoulder. He squinted up into the candlelit face of a red-bearded man.

"Come," the man offered. He reached out and helped Domingo up from the wall. His arm felt thin but strong. Domingo's legs had stiffened in the dark. He wobbled. As he swayed in the courtyard, he recalled how the men had swayed while they had prayed inside the room.

The man steadied him. "Your mother's all right, Domingo."

"How do you know my name?"

"I know your mother. She's gone home. She is in grief over her cousin."

"Her *cousin*?"

"That's when they return to the *call*, when someone beloved dies. She has come every night this week to say prayers for Judith."

"I had a cousin here?"

"You must be upset. Would you like to come inside? It's getting late. Our voices will wake people nearby."

Domingo looked up at the tall buildings with their tiny windows. Eyes probably watched them from the darkness. A long moment passed in which Domingo felt the buildings, the town of Girona, even the night sky pause as if they waited for his answer. "Who are you?" he finally asked.

"Rabbi Raphael Halevi."

The rabbi of the synagogue of the talking stones. Domingo followed him through the back door of the synagogue, down a narrow hallway, and into a room dominated by a table piled with books. The rabbi moved two stools so they faced the hearth. Domingo sat and rubbed his legs. The warmth felt good after the damp air. Rabbi Halevi remained quiet. Domingo didn't know what to say or ask and looked at his feet, which he had placed as close to the fire as he dared.

"So you are Caterina's son," the rabbi finally said. "You look like her. I recognized you immediately. She speaks highly of you, her good son the scribe, who helps support her."

Domingo looked away from the rabbi and into the fire. He thought he saw robed figures dance in the flames. Then he looked back at Rabbi Halevi, whose compassionate eyes disarmed him. Suddenly he wanted to confess his troubles. "I am not a good son. I am a disappointment."

Rabbi Halevi sat calmly, waiting for him to continue.

"What is it, Domingo? You can tell me."

"I've hurt two families." His cheeks burned. "I will not marry Nuria Costa."

"Marrying a Christian could protect you from the Inquisitors. You don't like Nuria. Find some other girl."

"I can't."

The fire crackled loudly as the largest log caught flame. Domingo quickly pulled his feet away. "I have been to this building before," he confessed.

"I know. I've glimpsed you through my back door. I knew you meant no harm. What brought you here?"

"God talks to me through your stones. I long for God. This is the only place I can hear Him. I cannot find Him in the Catholic Mass, where others can. Pau finds Him there." He did not tell the rabbi that he heard a woman's voice.

The rabbi nodded. "I hear the voice of God here as well. It does not surprise me God speaks to you through this building. Once great mystics wandered these streets and chanted within these stone walls."

Domingo's stomach growled. He pressed his hands against it and blushed.

The rabbi smiled. "Can I offer you some bread? My daughter, Miriam, baked it and brought it by today. She takes good care of me."

"I'm sorry," Domingo said. "I never ate dinner because I trailed my mother here."

"Come," the rabbi said as he rose. "The bread is in the other room. I don't use the cooking hearth, but that's where I keep the food Miriam brings me. It is not good to eat in the same room where one keeps sacred texts, don't you agree?"

"Of course," Domingo replied as he followed the rabbi down the hallway and into a larger room. He sat at a small table in the icy room while the rabbi sliced bread for both of them. No fire burned in this hearth. How unlike his mother's house this place felt and looked. Her hearth was warm, the room scented with drying herbs hanging from the ceiling, rich soups and stews bubbling in iron pots suspended over the fire. She lined her shelves with jars of chickpeas, almonds, and honey, with baskets of onions and garlic. He gazed around this bare room and at the rabbi's thin, bearded face, so unlike his uncle's plump, smooth cheeks.

The rabbi noticed his expression. "Miriam brings me meals every day. She is a good daughter. My wife cooked well, but—"

"What happened to her?"

"A Christian mob killed her, crushed her face with stones. I have been alone a few years now."

"A mob. I think that's how my father died—" Domingo began.

"Yes, I remember when Diego perished, though it was many years ago."

"I was eight."

"Yes," the rabbi said. "Your mother came to the *call* to mourn."

"But she didn't bring me with her."

"No."

"You also knew my father?" Domingo asked.

"Not as well as your mother. He came to pray, but he never stayed to eat with us. He always said he had to work, even on the Sabbath. This attitude did not win him friends among the men of the *call*. But I heard he was a gifted scribe."

"Yes, I feel him in my hands when I work," Domingo said. "Do you miss—"

"I miss Leah every day," the rabbi replied.

The two men looked at each other in silence. The rabbi got up to wash his hands in a nearby basin. Domingo watched his lips move in what must be silent prayer. Then the rabbi cut each of them a slice of bread. He held his own portion up and said, *"Baruch atah Adonai Eloheinu Melech ha'olam, hamotzi lechem min ha'aretz. Blessed are you, Lord our God, King of the universe, who brings forth bread from the earth."*

"How sweet this bread tastes," Domingo said.

"My daughter uses honey."

"So does my mother." After a few chunks of bread, Domingo felt more alert, stronger, full of questions. "Why didn't she tell me we are Jews?" he asked.

"She wanted to protect you, Domingo. Some of us still hide from the mob that one hundred years ago lit Girona's Gate of the Jews on fire, stormed into the *call,* and murdered forty men, women, and children, most of them by beheading. Priests stood nearby ready to convert us. You know the Roman tower up on the hill?"

"The Torre Gironella."

"Yes. The city fathers locked up the Jews who survived the massacre up there to protect us from further violence."

Girona was a small town. Domingo had grown up hearing this story but had never understood it. "Why were they concerned about what happened to the Jews?"

The rabbi raised his red eyebrows ironically. "Mind you, they did not care for our lives. The King ordered them to do this because we Jews are his property, his private source of revenue. Through our governing body, we pay him large sums in taxes. The Jews of Girona fund the remodeling of royal buildings, royal weddings, and coronations and, of course, campaigns against the Muslims."

"I have heard that a ghost in the Tower of Gironella wails for her lost children," Domingo interrupted. "Is it true?"

Raphael nodded. "Some say it is the spirit of Tolrana, who refused to convert to Christianity in 1391. Her husband gave in and allowed himself to be baptized. He climbed up to the tower to beg her and their two children to accept Christianity. 'Never,' she swore. She cut her children's throats and then killed herself. If you enter the tower and press your ears against the stones, sometimes you can hear her moan. On windy nights, they say, her wails emanate from the stones of the *call*."

Domingo shuddered. "How long were the people in the tower?"

"Seven hundred remained over four months. Even there, the peasants attacked them. These were the ancestors of the people of today's Jewish community but also of those forced to convert to Christianity, the *conversos*. Your great-grandmother was one of them."

"My great-grandmother? You know much about my family, more than I do."

Rabbi Halevi rubbed his blue eyes, bloodshot in the firelight. "I am sorry, Domingo."

Outside, the wind came up. A pine tree rubbed dry branches against the window.

"I was taught to hate Jews. Now I discover I am one. Why do Christians hate Jews so much?" Domingo asked.

"Domingo, I could speculate, but I truly don't understand why. The violence against us comes and goes like the seasons. My teacher, Rav Chaim, passed these stories down to me when I told him I would serve as the rabbi of Girona. In 1348, they blamed the plague on us; they burned us alive with the corpses of our dead. When the Tower of Gironella fell in 1404, they held the Jews responsible. In 1409, they locked us behind a wooden barricade in the Plaça Sant Domènec like cattle and forced us to listen to sermons from the fanatical preacher, Ferrer."

A gust of wind pierced a crack in the wall and extinguished one of the candles on the hearth. "Ay, this old place is full of drafts." The rabbi got up to relight the candle. His back to Domingo, he kept talking.

"In 1418, priests broke into this synagogue and tore up half of our library in retribution for something. Now the Inquisition draws on the hatred of Jews to unify Spain as a Christian nation. It is families like yours, *conversos*, who pose the greatest threat to that purity, especially those who secretly keep their Jewish customs, like your mother."

Domingo looked at the rabbi's back. A long thread hung off the bottom of his tunic, and a small hole at the collar exposed part of his pale neck. His mother could easily mend that hole. He could offer to take the tunic home. But how could he think of mending now?

The rabbi returned to the table and regarded the distraught young man in front of him. "Domingo, I know Caterina lives a simple life and your uncle struggles to support your family on a bookbinder's wages. But not all *conversos* — "

"I give them most of my wages." Domingo interrupted. "My master, Roca, takes good care of me, so I do not need much money for myself."

"I know you are a good son," the rabbi said, smiling. "I am trying to explain the hatred of *conversos*. Unlike your family, some *conversos* have a lot of money. Their families have secured high government and church positions. They even serve in the court of the King and Queen. They extend credit, form guilds, marry only each other. They claim to be Christians, but they hold themselves apart. All of this threatens the Christians, so now they persecute the *conversos*."

"But isn't it harder to be a Jew? You have to wear that badge."

The rabbi glanced at his cloak hanging on a hook over the door. A yellow circular badge was sewn on the chest. He shrugged. "Yes, we must wear these badges whenever we leave the *call*, although sometimes the rule is not enforced. Lately it has been. Our twenty remaining families leave through one guarded gate during the daytime. At night there are curfews. More and more of us depend upon the charity of the Almshouse, which only stays open because of donations from one or two wealthy families that remain here. No, it is not easy to be a Jew in Girona." He looked at Domingo thoughtfully. "Nor is it easy to be one of the *conversos*. You pay a high price. Inquisitorial spies search for suspicious behavior. One thoughtless remark can endanger a whole family."

"Is that why my mother kept this secret from me?" Domingo asked.

"Yes, many *conversos* wait until their children are mature enough to understand the need for discretion, for silence."

"I am no longer a child," Domingo said sadly.

"Of course not. But you must understand how fear impairs the judgment of parents in these times."

Domingo helped himself to another slice of soft bread. He looked at the rabbi who was taking time in the middle of the night to answer his questions. "I wish I'd met you before," he said as he dropped crumbs on the rabbi's floor.

The rabbi smiled. "I met you once. Your mother brought you into the *call* to meet your cousin. You were a baby. Only a few decades ago you would have grown up coming here regularly. Once we mixed freely. *Conversos* came to the *call*. Your mother and I are both old enough to remember a time when Jews and *conversos*, usually from the same families, danced at the same weddings, attended a *brit*, feasted together, and mourned their dead as one extended community. But now the Christians fear we Jews will influence *conversos* to return to our faith. This conversation in which I, a rabbi, speak about Judaism to a *converso* might be enough to have me condemned to the stake."

Domingo looked at the rabbi in alarm. "Why did you invite me in to talk, if it is so treacherous?"

"Because I must. It is my task to teach *Torah* not only to the Jews but also to the *conversos*, who need me perhaps even more than the Jews."

Cathedral bells tolled the midnight hour. They rang so loudly that the rabbi stopped talking. For the first time, the bells sounded ominous to Domingo's ears—dull, metallic, out of tune, not at all pretty. To live here in the *call* would be to live under the crushing weight of this all-powerful church, its commands cutting through the very air.

"I try to carry on the traditions of my predecessors," the rabbi continued after the bells had ceased, though the room still vibrated. "I have inherited their books, for despite prohibitions from their master, Isaac the Blind, the Gironese circle wrote down the secrets of Jewish mysticism, which we call Kabbalah. 'A book which is written cannot be hidden in a cupboard,' Rabbi Isaac warned his disciples in an angry letter from Provence. He thought Kabbalah should remain oral tradition. I have believed him overly cautious. But perhaps Rabbi Isaac was right. How shall we protect these precious texts from those who would burn them?"

"I am a scribe. I believe in books. Wisdom must be written down."

"Yes. I couldn't agree more. The *Bahir*, the *Zohar*, Rabbi Ezra's commentaries on the Song of Songs—how glad I am to have these texts to study. I guard my scrolls and books as if they are living beings."

"You know, there are some who build shelves for collections so large, instead of stacking them on tables, where they may fall and be damaged," Domingo commented. Then he blushed. He dared to tell this rabbi how to store his books.

"Shelves. This would be a good solution. I spend much time looking for a book. My arms grow tired from sorting through my piles."

I could build you a bookcase, Domingo wanted to offer, but that seemed bold. Besides, he had other questions he needed to ask. "My mother?" he ventured. "How often does she come here?"

"Caterina has attended services on the Sabbath sporadically for years to seek spiritual solace. Lately, she has not visited as often. But she came to mourn your cousin Judith."

"Do I have other relatives here as well?"

"A few distant relations, I believe. Domingo, your mother wanted to tell you the truth. 'He'll be so hurt that I kept our history from him,' she once said to me."

Domingo rubbed his eyes. "She was right. I am hurt. But what shall become of me now? Am I Jewish?"

"You are one of the lost ones. I know others like you. Some return to us; others remain Christian. Some, like your mother, walk a middle road. That road can be treacherous to the soul as well, wandering between faiths, between worlds. I believe you already know this." He reached across the table as if to stroke Domingo's head, but he seemed to think better of it and instead rested a hand on Domingo's shoulder. "God will tell you what path is to be yours. Perhaps he will address you through the stones."

The rabbi rose to his feet. "We have spoken long enough. Soon it will be light. You must not be seen here. You should return home, Domingo. Do you know how to leave this place unseen?"

"Yes. I know about the secret passageway, the one behind the building. It leads under the river to my neighborhood. I found it a few months ago. It is how I came here without being noticed, except by you, of course."

"Good. That passageway also connects to a staircase inside the synagogue. It is better for you to use this more discreet entrance concealed behind a false door in the hallway. Let me show you."

They descended a spiral staircase to the passageway below the synagogue. Domingo walked a few steps into the darkness and looked back at Rabbi Halevi standing in a circle of candlelight, watching him leave.

Chapter Four

I worry about you alone in that drafty place," Doña Falco
had said last week as she had sent him home with half a
stewed chicken. "A rabbi with no wife. Why do you not
remarry?"

Raphael could not sleep after Domingo left. Doña
Falco was right. He should look for a wife. Only he and his
daughter, Miriam, remained to carry the memories of their
family. Raphael's father, Abram, had been the doctor at the
Jewish hospital in the *call*. He and Raphael's mother had
died during an outbreak of smallpox ten years ago.

His father had expressed pride when Raphael had
become a rabbi. But he did not deserve his father's respect.
He could not protect his people or even offer them much
comfort during these times. But still they wanted him,
trusted him. The Jewish council, the *aljama*, begged him to
remain their rabbi, though they could pay only room and
board and a small stipend. He did not feel fond of some of

the council members who received bonuses from the Catalan counts and stayed wealthy while most people in the *call*
went hungry and wore shabby clothes. Still, some members
of the *aljama* were generous with acts of charity.

So he remained, caring for this sacred building and
the people whose ancestors' prayers were imprinted in
its stones. For six hundred years the Jewish community
had survived here at the confluence of the Onyar and Ter
rivers, near the border of France. But now, were it not for
the generous Falco family, who had been silversmiths and
moneylenders for generations, there would not be enough
oil to keep the lamp in the sanctuary lit. Last night rats had
scuffled near his bed. He must repair that hole in the wall,
if only to save his beloved texts from their gnawing.

Still unable to sleep, he turned his mind to the problem occupying the *aljama* these days: how could the Jews
afford to pay the additional tax King Fernando demanded
to fund his war against the Muslims? The *aljama* had been
meeting more often than usual. Next week they would
convene with the nearby towns of Besalu and Olot. The
smaller *aljames*, as usual, would resent Girona, which, with
its much larger Jewish population, dominated affairs and
collected taxes from all of the *aljames* in the region. Alas, the
usual arguments would break out about who should pay
what share. The eldest members of the council still remembered two members of the *aljama* killing each other in some
political battle. As rabbi, he was expected to prevent or at

least mediate these kinds of feuds. Raphael sighed. His neck hurt; his body felt old.

The work of a rabbi could be overwhelming, his teacher, Rav Chaim, had warned him years ago. He must prepare teachings from the *Torah*, perform weddings and funerals, maintain meticulous records of births and deaths, serve on a rabbinical court, teach at the Jewish school. But Rav Chaim had never faced what Raphael faced now. Rumors held that the King and Queen might expel the entire Jewish community from Spain, though others said this was unlikely because the Crown found the taxes the Jews paid too valuable. The Jewish population of Spain, including *conversos*, numbered in the hundreds of thousands. Raphael tried to imagine that many Jews departing the country in mass exodus. Jews were part of the economic backbone and culture of almost every city and village. But this calamity had happened throughout Jewish history. Other countries in Europe had expelled their Jews. Where had they located shelter? Soon he might need to find the Jews of Girona a new home.

But what obligation did he have as rabbi to those who were no longer technically Jews, the New Christians, *conversos*, over whom the Inquisition now claimed jurisdiction? Between the seventeenth of *Tammuz,* a fast day to remember the breach of the walls of Jerusalem, and the ninth of *Av,* which commemorated the destruction of the Temple, Spanish Jews recited *kinot*. These elegies recounted the terrible events of 1391 he had related to Domingo that evening. Raphael deliberately had not told Domingo about these verses that blamed the *conversos* for their current problems, claimed that God punished the Jewish people for the desertion by the *conversos* of the Jewish faith, and proclaimed that the *conversos* were sinners.

A vision of the young *converso*'s vulnerable face floated in front of Raphael. He could not accept the harsh judgments of the *kinot*. The forced ones, the lost souls, were also his flock, not just the Jews who remained in the *aljama*. Raphael's concerns included the young man who had ventured through the door of the synagogue during evening services. Domingo seemed so full of longing.

As soon as the wild-haired youth had appeared in the synagogue doorway during the standing prayer, Raphael had noticed him through his back window. He had watched the young man press his hands against the courtyard wall and cock his head as if he were listening to someone. The first time, he had almost called out to him, but the desire in Domingo's face had been so intense and private that Raphael had not wanted to interrupt. Tonight he realized Domingo looked so familiar because he had inherited Caterina's features. Before Raphael could welcome him inside to join the congregation, Domingo had fled.

He gave up trying to sleep, sat up, and poured a cup of cold water to ease his dry throat. He felt he ought to spill it over his head to quench the heat in his body. Domingo would surely return with more questions. If he helped Domingo, the young scribe who loved books and learning, it would arouse his own *yetzer hara*, the impulse toward temptation. This was not the first time Raphael had found himself in such a predicament. Domingo had hungry eyes. He reminded Raphael of Isaac, a fellow student he had loved when they had been in the *yeshiva*. Since that time, he had resisted, buried, and denied his attractions for men.

But now he must consult a certain book, if only to feel less alone with his desire. The text contained ideas and images he dared discuss with no one. Raphael lit a candle, left his bedroom for the adjoining study. He shuffled the piles of books until he found the fragile volume of poetry passed down in his family for over three centuries. Judah Samuel Halevi of Castile was his direct ancestor. Some said Halevi loved both men and women. Raphael opened the book to a poem by Halevi that sang of a man's honeycomb lips. He traced his own lips with his finger, felt his body respond. He would like to imagine Domingo's lips on his. Were Judah Halevi's poems really about men, or did the poet simply sing of his passion for God? The words felt so physical. When Jews dwelled among the Arabs in Southern Spain, such acts were not uncommon, were even accepted. But some of Halevi's poems sang of love between men and boys. That he could not abide. Domingo was a grown man, but still, Raphael was old enough to be his father. He had even met the boy when he was an infant. No. He could not abide any of it. He was a rabbi, responsible for upholding *Halachah*, the Law, which included prohibitions against love between men. His actions with Domingo must remain rabbinical, fatherly. God, I have known such desires to linger in my blood. My God, forgive me. Purify me. And please guide me to help Domingo. Raphael prostrated himself on the floor and waited for an answer.

Huldah hovered over the rabbi's bed that night, intrigued. Here was a man with a passion for justice. As with Nachmanides, his devotion to mysticism would make it easier for them to talk across worlds. He was not learned like Nachmanides. But perhaps that was for the best. Rabbi Halevi did not have his own books to write. And his world was cracking apart. She could feel the shift even here in the walls of Girona. He might be able to comprehend the kabbalah of stone.

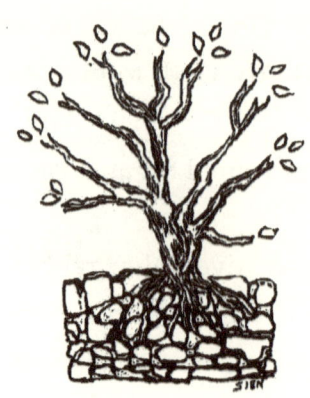

Chapter Five

"This will be your holy work," Father Hidalgo instructed Pau and the row of other young acolytes who kneeled before him. He held up a piece of parchment. "Here is a list of those *conversos* we suspect are unfaithful to Christian tradition. Each of you will be assigned to one or two of these families. I will count on you to gather whatever information you can about their heretical practices. This will be your final test before your examination for the priesthood. The blood of *conversos* is unclean. It stains our country's soul. You can help purify our land." He smiled at the young men who kneeled on the floor. His handsome smile and his charisma made them yearn to please him.

Father Hidalgo stopped in front of Pau and leaned down.

"Pau," the priest whispered in his ear, "I know your sins. I will inform Alfonso de Espina."

Pau sat in shock. He had thought he could continue to meet Domingo without suspicion because they were both scribes and would have legitimate business with each other. Alfonso de Espina was the Inquisitor General. Pau had glimpsed the jovial-looking Espina from a distance as he went about his tasks in the monastery, where the Inquisition had opened a regional office last summer after plague had swept through Barcelona killing over three thousand people. Some people welcomed the Inquisition's relocation to Girona, while others disliked its presence but were afraid to say so. The Inquisition provided employment for lawyers, carpenters, rope makers, and scribes and brought prosperity to inns and taverns.

"I have a special assignment for you, Pau," Father Hidalgo said. "See me after class in my office."

Outside Father Hidalgo's window, it began to pour; the witch gargoyle spat streams from her mouth. It was said this gargoyle memorialized a real witch who had lived one hundred years ago, a pagan woman who had thrown stones at the Cathedral until she herself had petrified. The priests had hung the stone witch high on the Cathedral wall as a warning not to engage in sorcery.

"Girona is a small place. I know where you go, whom you meet under a certain tree, and what abominations you perform. Surely you are aware that such offenses are punishable by death. You could be castrated and then stoned to death or hung."

Pau's eyes traveled up the highest spire of the tower. Heaven lay beyond the black clouds. God watched from there, knew his sins. Pau rubbed the bald top of his head. He had the honor of tending the lamps in the Cathedral, despite his sins of the flesh, this grand Cathedral, a fortress of God built to withstand violent winds. He passed out bread at the almshouse, looked into the holy faces of the people. He held the Host for the priest during Mass. He was trusted, and he performed his duties with great heart, even though he was a sinner. He had hoped his sincere intentions would redeem him. But he had been a fool to think God would not punish him. This priest must be a messenger of God, of salvation.

"Father, I beg your forgiveness," Pau began in a hoarse voice. "I know this is a sin. I want to purify myself. Please help me. What can I do? I will do anything to become a priest."

The priest studied him with a sad smile. He extended a well-groomed hand and patted Pau's shoulder. "My son. You have always been a good student, a meticulous scribe. There is something you can do to redeem yourself in the eyes of the Lord. But it is very difficult."

Pau sat up straight. "Father, I have wanted to be a priest since I was a small boy. I cannot imagine life without the priesthood. I love God more than life itself. What can I do?"

"Tell me about Domingo's family, the Fontclaras," the priest ordered. "We suspect they are not the pure Christians they claim to be, but we need more evidence to prosecute them. Then we will see if hope remains for your future in the priesthood."

Huldah hovered over Pau as Father Hidalgo gave him instructions. She wanted to caution this earnest and decent young acolyte not to take the path offered to him. She remembered another betrayal.

Hilkiah had cleverly twisted her prophecy. He had known the words would sway people in the kingdom if they believed they originated from Huldah, Prophet of Asherah, who had now renounced her idolatrous ways and turned completely to teaching Torah. They had named a gate in Jerusalem for her, near her yeshiva, honored her as one of the women prophets in the holy texts, and credited her for the destruction of the Asherah.

She remembered King Josiah standing on a platform in front of a rapt crowd, reading the words from the scroll found in the Temple—the warning about the impending destruction of Jerusalem, followed by a reminder of the covenant Moses and all the Israelites made with Adonai. The king had renewed this promise for the entire nation: "We will walk in the way of Adonai, keep his commandments and laws, with all our heart and soul. We must purify the land of idolatry."

King Josiah had enlisted the people to help the priests purge the land of Asherah. In a frenzy of destruction, they had ransacked the groves, destroyed the carved images and the images of

Asherah, broke her altars, and chopped down her terebinths. They had ground the stone pillars into chalk and scattered the chalk to the desert wind. They had murdered the priests and priestesses who tended the altars and groves, pulverized their bones, and strewn their ashes on the earth.

After the destruction, she had wandered, brokenhearted, up to the high place on the Mount of Olives where the shrine to Asherah had stood. The spring had still flowed, and beside it the sacred stone had lain toppled on its side—all that remained of Asherah's holy place. The winter cold in those hills had burned her skin, but she could not bear to remain in the city.

She had closed down her school. Her former students had avoided her eyes when she passed. Some had been afraid to be seen talking to the prophet of Asherah in a time when priests were persecuting or even killing her followers. Others had believed Huldah had betrayed Asherah, and they could not forgive her. So she had returned again and again to the fallen shrine. It was there that she had died, met Gabriel, and entered the stones.

Now as she watched Pau plunge down the hill below the Cathedral and into the Valley of Sant Daniel, she saw that violence would repeat itself for the same tangled, misguided motives.

Pau ran, panting, past the abandoned Benedectine monastery. He sought purification in the sweat soaking his white tunic, in the sun burning away the clouds from the morning storm. Oh, let this sun extract the sin from me, he prayed. God, grant me release from these perverted desires that have plagued me since boyhood. He cast his eyes up to the pine trees crowning the conical peaks. Did God see him now?

He passed the tangle of aged oaks along the Ter River, the cool shadowy nest where he and Domingo had discovered each other's desires and still met to gratify them. They told each other they rendezvoused to gather oak galls to make the ink they needed as scribes, but both knew what they would do in this secret place. When Domingo looked at him sideways through long eyelashes and pulled him down with big and urgent hands, Pau could not resist. No more, he vowed. Domingo had gone too far by refusing to marry Nuria. She had been their protection. If only Pau had already been a priest cloistered in the Cathedral when Domingo had made this foolish decision.

Now he climbed up the other side of the valley, pushing his legs until the oaks along the river squatted far below like dwarves. The shadow of a hawk passed between Pau and the sun. He shoved a boulder over the edge of the cliff and listened to it break far below.

The sound of shattering rock sobered him. He bowed his head in prayer. God, please help me. I cannot betray Domingo and his mother and uncle. But I have studied so long to become a priest. Must I help the Inquisitors? Is this the price I need pay for your shelter? Please, I beg you. Help me discover another path to serve you.

He turned and walked the dusty road back to Girona in despair, unable to feel the presence of God.

Chapter Six

Why didn't you tell me? I could have known my cousin."

"Shush. You were a child, Domingo. No child can be trusted with such secrets." His uncle looked nervously out the window.

"I am twenty years old now, a journeyman."

"I know, but your mother fears you will return to the Jews and risk your life. She wants you to start a Christian family."

"Where is she? I want to talk to her."

"She is at the butcher's. She'll be back soon. But I'm glad we are alone. My sister might not approve, but it is time you knew everything." Uncle Fernando rose to bolt the door and draw the curtains. The floor creaked under his heavy steps as he returned.

Domingo picked at a sliver in the oak table carved by his father long ago. Suddenly he felt afraid to hear his uncle's words. He wanted to escape, to dash out of the house, run through the forest, and plunge his face into the cold waters of the Ter River. But he also wanted to know the truth.

"For one hundred years our family has lived with this secret," his uncle began. "My grandparents kept the Sabbath by lighting candles in the cellar, and they celebrated Passover down there as well. Such rites seem meaningless to me, foolish. Why take risks? We will only bring trouble upon ourselves. Your mother was wise to marry your father, a successful scribe. But he still practiced Judaism, got up early to say the morning prayers."

Domingo stopped hearing his uncle's voice. He was eight years old. His mother sent him to fetch something from the root cellar. There he discovered his father wrapped in a white cloth, reading from a small book in a low voice and swaying back and forth.

"Papa, what's wrong?" Domingo cried.

His father turned and saw him. He placed his finger across his lips and then gathered Domingo to him under the smooth cloth. Domingo felt safe next to his warmth. His baritone voice rose and fell rhythmically as he prayed in a language Domingo did not understand. Over the next few weeks, his father invited him down to the cellar several times to be with him again under the magic cloth. Domingo began to look forward to these soothing moments.

Domingo pressed his knuckles into his eyes. He had forgotten his father's prayers.

Uncle Fernando was still talking. "Your mother and father — they were always drawn to the *call*. For many years it was not so perilous to return to the *call* for weddings and funerals, to keep the customs that meant much to them. But then, twelve years ago, while praying in the synagogue during Easter Week, your father was killed in a riot against the Jews. The priest had delivered a sermon blaming the Jews for the death of Christ. The congregants left Mass and stormed into the *call*, armed with rocks."

Domingo remembered Uncle Fernando arriving home with two other men carrying his father's body. His mother climbed into bed with the corpse. When it came time to wash Diego, his uncle pried Caterina's arms away from her dead husband's body. She did not see Domingo standing behind her. So it was true. Stones had killed both the rabbi's wife and Diego, his father. And yet the voice of God spoke through the stones of the synagogue. Stones could become weapons or hold sacred teachings.

Uncle Fernando reached out a hand to smooth Domingo's hair.

"I remember how you grieved, hunched silently in the garden. I felt glad Pau stayed by your side. He's been a good friend. Your cousin Judith, may her memory be for a blessing, gave comfort to your mother, so your mother could not stay away from the *call*. She visited, heedless of all warnings. At the same time, she hid her Jewishness from you, to protect you."

His uncle shook his head. "It has not been easy for Caterina. Perhaps now you understand your poor mother better, bless her soul. Like many *conversa* women, she keeps the ways of our religion secretly, in her home. But, Domingo," he said, looking at his nephew sternly, "You must never speak of this to anyone except your master."

"I may speak with Roca?"

"He was your father's best friend. Diego trusted him, and I too find him trustworthy. Domingo, we have been good *conversos* for so long. We have created a safe identity for you. Don't throw your life away." He leaned forward. "Do you understand me? Not a word to anyone else, not even Pau."

"But Pau is my best friend, just as Diego trusted Roca."

"Yes, but Pau's greatest wish is to become a priest. Please, Domingo. You must obey me."

Domingo nodded. And he would not tell his uncle about his conversation with the rabbi of Girona. He rose. His uncle waved at him to sit down.

"One more thing, nephew. When you were born, we dared not circumcise you. We named you Domingo because you were born on a Sunday and it is a good Christian name in honor of their Sabbath. But we did give you a secret Hebrew name. Your name is Amos."

Soon after Domingo left, Caterina came home from shopping to hear about her brother's revelations to her son. "He's old enough for the truth, Caterina. We couldn't keep it from him forever. The boy followed you into the *call* a few days ago; he saw you at evening services."

"I glimpsed him standing at the door, staring. He disappeared before I could talk to him. I wish you had revealed it to him more slowly. I wanted to comfort him."

"He needed to know." Fernando savored the warm bread she had brought from the bakery. "He's a man now. He can bear the truth, Caterina. When he was twelve, thirteen, even fifteen, it made sense for us to protect him. He seemed too volatile a boy to be trusted with such dangerous secrets. But every *converso* child in Girona knows by the time they are seventeen. Twenty is far too old."

"Domingo is not like other sons. He is inquisitive, thirsty. He will venture into the *call* in search of deeper knowledge."

Fernando sucked in his breath. "We must forbid that."

"Forbid him?" Caterina sighed. "You can't forbid Domingo to do anything," she said almost proudly. "Willful, stubborn —"

"Just like his mother. We must caution him of the risks, teach him to be wily. But there is something else I told him."

Caterina raised her eyebrows at her brother.

"I told him his Hebrew name."

That afternoon, Caterina stood in the doorway looking across the valley at the dark clouds resting on top of distant hills. It would rain soon. She must work in the garden before it grew too muddy. Caterina wrapped herself in her oldest cloak and made her way around to the back of the house and her kitchen garden. She felt proud of this patch of land, all hers, where she grew the vegetables that nourished her family. This time of year it was mostly greens: lettuce, chard, spinach, spicy cilantro, white bulbs of fennel. Later in the summer, eggplants and melons would ripen in the heat and she could cook Domingo's favorite dish: stuffed eggplant casserole with garlic, celery, apples and pears, rosemary and sage.

If only Domingo would marry Nuria. She and Judith came up with this plan years ago as a way to protect Domingo. Domingo seemed so much like his father: passionate and opinionated, brave but sometimes impulsive. Diego had insisted upon going to services to pray. Easter was always the worst time. If she had not stayed home to take care of Domingo, she too might have died amidst the mob with their knives and stones. She felt grateful that her brother had supported them these past twelve years. A good man with a lucrative business binding books of administrative records for the city of Girona, he had grown to love Domingo in his own way.

Caterina squatted on the soft black earth and weeded between the chard plants. Something had nibbled the young spinach leaves, turned them into green lace. She pulled a leek from the ground, spraying her cloak with moist soil. Now the boy knew every family secret. She remembered the synagogue door opening that evening, her son's shocked face. She had sought comfort in the arms of the women of the *call*, mourning Judith, who had taught her how to plant and care for her garden long ago, before the divisions between Jew and *converso* had made it hard for them to visit each other.

Judith had cried in joy when Caterina had agreed to marry Diego Fontclara. "But promise you will come to us here in the *call*."

Caterina had nodded.

"Be careful. There are those who loathe the *conversos*. When you have children, you must consider when to tell them the truth."

Caterina had imagined a small version of Diego standing with the men in the synagogue. But Domingo had never stood in that building until a week ago. He had only met Judith once, when Caterina had smuggled him in her cloak as an infant into the *call* so her cousin could see her child. Judith had given Domingo his Hebrew name. She had studied Domingo's face. "He has the soul of a prophet. Longing eyes," she had observed. "A father who is a scribe; the eyes of a prophet. Let's call him Amos."

Diego had held up Domingo's tiny hand. "He has a scribe's hands," he had boasted. "And someday he shall be one. I have already spoken to Roca about an apprenticeship."

Judith's eyes had teared as she had looked at the baby Caterina had held in her arms. "Amos also means 'to bear a burden.' I am afraid this too may lie in his future."

"Come, Judith. We must not speak of such things in the presence of the baby. Who knows what his soul might already understand." Caterina had stroked her cousin's arm, while inwardly she had trembled. Judith had sometimes possessed the gift of seeing the future.

Roca had been a good master and guarded their secret. Of course, he and his wife were also *conversos*. Roca had acted like a father to Domingo, had given him a spacious bedroom above the shop and bought him *frutas* and *empanadas* and other treats.

As the laws became more stringent and the penalties more severe, Judith had said it was too risky to bring Domingo into the *call*. Caterina had gone alone.

Maybe it was her fault. If she had told Domingo marrying Nuria might save his life, perhaps he would have married her. He was, after all, a pragmatic young man.

Exhausted, Caterina smoothed over the dirt where she had pulled up a bunch of cilantro, and she gathered her harvest into her cloak. Her head felt light when she stood up.

She had felt relieved when Domingo had chosen Pau as his best friend. Of course their customs would not permit Domingo to be in the company of Nuria alone, so she felt pleased that Pau, as Nuria's older brother, could act as their chaperone. But then Pau and Domingo had spent all their time together without Nuria. Domingo had spoken only of his adventures with Pau in the hills beyond Girona. He had come home glowing and excited. As he had grown older, he had shown no interest in Nuria or in any other girls in Girona. There was something strange about how Domingo spoke of Pau. She had shared her concerns with no one but Judith. "Is he handsome?" Judith had asked. "Do the girls look at him?"

"*Very* handsome. That's not the problem," Caterina told her cousin. "I've seen girls watch him walk down the street. You should see his dimples, that charming smile. And those dark eyes—no, if anything he's too handsome or, rather, too pretty."

Now Caterina watched rain clouds blow in from the Pyrenees. Maybe she could tell Doña Costa that Domingo was still too young, that he wanted to establish himself in his trade so he could take better care of her daughter. At sixteen, Nuria was young enough to wait. Perhaps this was a solution.

But the broken match was only the beginning of her problems. Domingo knew everything now. Caterina brushed the dirt off her tunic and went inside to fetch a thick cloak to protect her from the rain. She must warn Roca that Domingo knew the truth.

Roca massaged his temples after Caterina left. Caterina had been distraught about her son. It seemed unkind to remind her that he too had warned that keeping this secret from Domingo would become more difficult as the boy grew into manhood.

Roca lay down on his bed and closed his eyes. What could he tell the young man, that all of their lives were a lie and had been for over a century, that most days he and Fernando and Caterina felt neither Christian nor Jewish—just numb or terrified by the growing power of the Inquisition?

Diego had been daring. He had savored the adventure of crossing between worlds and dodging stones thrown into the *call* on Jewish holidays. When they were young, Diego had made rude faces at the priests behind their backs. He had never been caught. "I will not live afraid," he had told Roca. "Can't you see? We can have the best of both—the freedom of the Christian world, *and* the family and traditions we celebrate in the *call*."

"There will be a price to pay," Roca had warned. He had looked up from the work of Thomas Aquinas he was copying. He had put in long hours in the shop in those days, many more hours than Diego. But Diego had remained the faster, more skillful scribe, a master of perfection.

"Then I'll pay the price," Diego had announced as he had put on his cloak and prepared to walk out into the icy March streets of Girona. That Saturday morning he had been off to the *call* to pray. Roca had lifted his hand in farewell, worried that if he rose to embrace his friend he would smudge the ink on the page. And that had been the last time he had seen Diego alive.

It had taken Roca a full year to recall what his best friend's face had looked like before his attackers had smashed it with rocks. In truth, the horror of that day had never left him. He still cast his eyes anxiously about as he walked through the streets directly under the Cathedral, wondering when stones would rain down on him. If nothing else, Diego's death had convinced him and Fernando that brazen openness brought nothing but danger. Only Caterina continued to return to the *call*, insisting that she would not be separated from Judith. Now that Judith was dead, he hoped Caterina would cease these risky journeys.

Roca had painted *The Miracle of the Loaves and Fishes* in his upstairs hallway, trying to fill his house with Christian imagery. He wore a crucifix around his neck for protection. Then one day when he attended Mass he looked at the figure of the gentle man on the cross, the light caressing his tormented face, and felt moved by Jesus's love in ways he had never expected. Jesus had endured torture on the cross in the name of love. Would he, Roca, choose such an honorable death for the sake of those he loved?

Basking in his newfound awareness of Jesus, Roca decided to study the Christian gospels. His Latin was fluent enough. His friend Nicolau in Barcelona found him a copy. Perhaps Roca felt more Christian than Jewish in his heart now. Or he had simply lost himself, abandoning his Jewishness even though he could never fully become Christian.

Soon Domingo would burst through the front door, complaining about his mother as he often did. "Why is he always so rude?" Clara had asked when Domingo first came to live with them. "And loud. He clumps around the house like a young bear with that sullen look on his face. When I ask him what is the matter, he scowls at me."

"Beneath his anger is the grief of a young boy who has lost his father," Roca had explained, stroking his wife's hair.

"In you he sees a father. In me he sees only a rival for your affections. And he has his own mother, though he does not appreciate her."

"I know you long for your own child, Clara. So do I. We will pray God gives us this gift."

"Perhaps Adonai punishes us for forsaking the religion of our ancestors," Clara said. "Perhaps taking Diego's son as your apprentice will only make Him angrier with us."

"Diego was far more faithful than I am," Roca had argued.

"True."

"Please, Clara." Roca kissed his wife on the cheek. "Try to be kind to the boy and patient with his moods. In time he will grow calmer. I will ask him to be more considerate of you. And he will prove to be a gifted scribe, of that I am sure."

His head ached from thinking about Domingo. Roca walked over to the washbasin and splashed water on his face. Clara had put mint in the water to give it a good scent. She made ordinary life more pleasant. The cold water felt good. Diego, your son is so much like you as a young man — passionate, intense, gifted with his hands, a magnet for women, opinionated, stubborn. If only you had lived to see him. He still spoke to his friend in his heart every day.

71

The memory of Domingo as a small boy standing over his father's still form haunted Roca. The boy had refused to eat for weeks. If it hadn't been for Pau, his spirit might have left his body. The two still spent hours together in Domingo's room. Pau always seemed to lift Domingo's mood.

Domingo was the son Roca had never had. He and Clara were growing old. They would never raise the seven sons and daughters they had dreamt of. A vision of seven sons and daughters gathered around a Passover table tantalized him for a moment, but then he laughed out loud, realizing how a short while ago he had been thinking of his love for Jesus and now he was fantasizing about Passover. He hadn't been at a *Seder* for over fifteen years.

Domingo was a talented apprentice. Who else but Domingo would have shown such interest not only in the skill of a scribe but also in the content of the texts they made for the university? Domingo's enchantment with the star map he was currently copying from the *Almagest* far exceeded any he showed for that young woman, Nuria. Whenever Roca asked Domingo questions about his marriage plans, Domingo changed the subject. Roca suspected that the young man had secrets of his own.

Thunder boomed and echoed through the stone canyons outside the shop. He felt relieved that the rain had held off long enough for Caterina to return home without getting soaked. Now the wind picked up. It poured. Roca walked downstairs and stood in the open doorway, peering up the empty, wet street like a worried father, waiting for Domingo to come home.

Chapter Seven

Jucef read the passage from the *Talmud* in a monotone:

Four sages entered Paradise: Ben Azzai, Ben Zoma, Elisha ben Abuyah, and Rabbi Akiva. Rabbi Akiva said to them: "When you reach the stones of pure marble, do not exclaim, 'Water! Water!'" Ben Azzai looked and died. Ben Zoma looked and lost his mind. Elisha ben Abuyah became an apostate. Only Rabbi Akiva ascended in peace and descended in peace.

The four young men gathered around the wooden table at the *yeshiva* seemed to be falling asleep. The rabbi would have attributed this somnolence to warming spring air, but lethargy ruled them in every season. Raphael looked at his students in despair. Behold the remnant of the grand *yeshiva* of Girona founded by Nachmanides, this class of pathetic youth who studied *Talmud* with so little feeling, so little interest. The great lineage of Rabbi Ezra and Rabbi Azriel rested clumsily on these students' mediocre shoulders. Yes, his students read accurately. Their Aramaic sounded fine. But their discussions contained no life, no fire. Raphael blamed himself. He should not try to teach such a difficult passage. Still, he would not give up.

"One sage died. One went mad. One became an apostate. Why did only Rabbi Akiva come back from Paradise safely?" he asked.

"Because Rabbi Akiva's wife, Rachel, remained devoted to him. He had an anchor in this world," Avram replied.

Perhaps hope remained for this one. Raphael nodded. "True, Rabbi Akiva's wife was righteous. She married a penniless and ignorant shepherd but saw in him the potential for a great scholar. Twelve years she waited for Rabbi Akiva while he studied *Torah* with Rabbi Eliezer and Rabbi Joshua, returning to Rachel's home with twelve thousand disciples in his wake. Yes, such a wife would indeed be an anchor."

The young men blushed and snickered in their new beards. Eli leaned over to whisper something to Avram.

Raphael rapped his hand on the table. The students jumped. How easy they were to scare. He was nothing; they should have studied with Rav Chaim. He would force a disobedient boy to immerse himself in the icy waters of the Onyar in midwinter. "Perhaps you have something to add to the discussion?" Raphael asked the gossiping young man.

Eli sank back into speechlessness.

"Avram, since your classmate seems to have misplaced his tongue, perhaps you will share his insights with the class."

Avram cleared his throat. "Ah. He wondered how you know anything about a wife being an anchor, Rabbi."

"I see." Raphael looked around the table, silent. "I do know something of marriage," he said at last. "I was married for many years."

Simon, a scrawny pale boy who had scarcely spoken all year, ventured, "But why aren't you married now, Rabbi? My mother says several women wanted to marry you after your wife died. And you only have one daughter. Shouldn't you obey the commandment to be fruitful and have more children?"

Raphael felt amazed at Simon's impertinence. "No one could replace my Leah," Raphael replied curtly. "Now, enough questions. Let us return to more relevant things." The students lapsed into indifference again in the stuffy room, unmoved by Rabbi Akiva's story. Finally, Raphael dismissed them. He walked back to the synagogue, passing through the door over which the archway read in deeply carved letters: *Open for me the gates of righteousness. I will enter them.* He kissed the *mezuzah* as he entered. Could he count himself among the righteous, he who had no wife now and had fathered only one child, a girl, he who felt attraction for men?

He sank down at his desk and opened the *Talmud* to the page he had tried to teach his students today. The letters blurred under his eyes. He pondered the passage, but he could not grasp its deepest meaning. In the past few months Raphael had read the mystical texts in the synagogue's library, the texts he could not share with his students, who were too young to study mysticism, about *Merkavah*, the Secrets of the Chariot. Rabbi Akiva had meditated on the name of God, the Tetragrammaton, and returned safely from the realms beyond this everyday world. Raphael felt kinship with this sage even though thirteen centuries separated them. If only he could invite Rabbi Akiva for a meal and a flask of wine and ask for his help.

Yes, Rabbi Akiva was brilliant, Raphael thought. But that's not what captivates me centuries later. It is his courage. When the Roman government made the study of *Torah* an offense punishable by death, he continued to teach. The Romans arrested and then tortured him. As they combed his flesh with iron combs, he smiled in joy because his faith in God was so deep. He chanted *Shema Yisrael Adonai Eloheinu Adonai Echad — Hear, Israel, the Lord our God, the Lord is One —* and his soul passed into the other world as he pronounced the word *Echad*.

Raphael lowered his head. God, bring me the courage to be your servant and continue to teach my people. Let me also not forsake the *conversos* of Girona. Yes, even if it means my death, if it be your will, God. Little has changed in all these centuries. Now, across our land, they torture and burn us. The peasants watch the gruesome festivities. The Inquisitors spread poison in Girona. Help me face all of this with Akiva's bravery and be worthy of you.

A knock yanked him from his prayers. Raphael opened the door. There stood Domingo, his arm raised for another knock.

"Rabbi, I must speak with you."

The rabbi peered through the open doorway and blinked. Noon sun bleached the walls of the city. "Domingo, it is dangerous for you to be seen here."

"I took the secret passageway. No one saw me. I just didn't want to come up the spiral staircase inside your house and frighten you."

"Well, you can't stand here now exposed in my doorway. For heaven's sake, come in."

Domingo followed the rabbi to his study, chattering even before they reached the room and the stools before the hearth. "I talked to my uncle. He told me about our family. Now I can't sleep at night. All I do is think." He glanced over at the desk, half covered with the large volume Raphael had been studying. "I have a question. What does Amos mean?"

"What does *what* mean?" Raphael looked at the feverish young man whose eyes devoured his books.

"The name Amos. What does it mean? My uncle told me it is my name. My parents gave it to me, my secret Hebrew name."

"A name is very important. Sit down."

Domingo sat on the stool.

The rabbi continued. "It is good that you know your name. Amos literally means 'to carry.' Amos was a prophet, the first literary prophet, the first to write down his prophecies," Raphael explained. He walked over to the table, sorted through his books, carried one over to his desk, found the passage, and translated: "Behold, days are coming, says God, when I will send a famine upon the earth: not a hunger for bread nor a thirst for water but to hear the word of God."

"Hunger for the word of God," repeated Domingo. He rose from the stool, walked over to the far wall of the study, and placed his ear against the stones with the same longing expression Raphael had seen on his face when he had glimpsed Domingo through the window weeks ago.

Studying the younger man, the rabbi felt shame, for he also felt hunger, not for God but for Domingo's shapely hands. What is happening to me? My God, save me from these impure thoughts.

Domingo walked back over to the desk. "Can I touch the book?"

Raphael nodded. Domingo leaned down to trace the letters with one finger. His hand trembled.

"I want to write these letters, to read this language. Perhaps then I will know this Hebrew God who speaks to me through your building."

Raphael shivered. If only his *yeshiva* students felt such passion for the text.

"Why is the text divided into different blocks and scripts?" Domingo asked.

"Each section is a different commentary on the passage of the *Talmud*."

"The *Talmud*?"

"The Rabbis' discussions of Jewish law, ethics, customs, and history written over a thousand years ago, in the first few hundred years after the Temple in Jerusalem was destroyed. This is when Judaism became a portable religion instead of a religion centered on the Temple."

Domingo touched Raphael's arm. "Teach me, Rabbi. I will come only at night through the passageway. I will be careful. Please."

He could not resist a student with such fervor.

"You must come at midnight or after. Before that hour, the demons rule the darkness. The Kabbalists believe that at midnight light emanates from God to all worlds. Secrets are revealed. It is the best time to study."

"I will come at midnight. Thank you, Rabbi."

And so it was that Raphael agreed to teach Domingo the Hebrew alphabet.

Huldah watched the two men talk, the rabbi and the scribe. Around her the stones murmured agreement.

Chapter Eight

A mos left through the north gate of Girona and climbed the hill he and Pau had explored since they were young boys. He passed through groves of pine trees planted by the Romans, their dusky needles framing the white bulk of the Pyrenees far to the north. Beyond those immense mountains lay France, birthplace of the Kabbalists, the disciples of Isaac the Blind who later came to Girona. Here on the hill of Sant Daniel overlooking Girona, he and Pau shared all confidences. Amos also came here to think.

Amos looked at the Cathedral. It dominated the crest of the nearest hill. Gulls perched on its tower. Hidden below the Cathedral's fortress lay the streets of the *call*. There the rabbi tried to teach him the sacred language he desired. Last night he had received his fifth Hebrew lesson. Nearly a month had passed since their first meeting.

Shin, Bet, Tav. The letters spelled *Shabbat,* the Jewish Sabbath. He tried to picture the letters in his mind. Two of them floated over the branches of a nearby oak tree like birds. *Shin* was easy. It opened its arms in three directions just like this tree. *Bet* looked like an ear. So far, so good. But then he tried to conjure a *Tav.* Its shape refused to materialize. He had learned it last night, but he had already forgotten. He wanted to bang his head on the tree trunk in frustration. Why did such a simple thing become so difficult for him?

He was not usually so stupid, he told himself. In fact, he had a gift for words. Language sheltered him. Diego's spirit had taught him to cherish the intersection of vellum, ink, and text. Roca had taught him how to write elegantly in Latin and Greek. Words poured through Amos's hands with ease. Now those hands hungered for Hebrew. He longed to know them all immediately, the letters. He had expected to put them together effortlessly and within a few weeks read the sacred texts on the table in the rabbi's study. Yet the letters remained elusive.

After a month, Amos had learned only a few words in the language denied him until age twenty. He could not suddenly be a Jew. He wasted the rabbi's time. The rabbi might grow impatient with his slowness. When Amos pronounced the letters, his voice cracked like an adolescent boy's. When he wrote them, his hands shook and he splattered ink like a beginner. The word *Shabbat* should be simple, but it eluded Amos. *Shabbat* represented everything forbidden to him.

Judaism swept through his life like spring floodwaters cascading out of the Pyrenees: a rich and terrible river carrying persecution, death, the debris of history but also wisdom, years upon years of it, extending back to the time before the Romans built the Via Augusta he walked on every day, back to the Holy Land, the time of Abraham. Yet he remained terrified to receive that river of wisdom through the letters. Once he immersed himself in those waters, there could be no return.

Hebrew could open an entire world to him. Despite his fierce yearning for them, the letters washed out of his mind. Now when he crossed the Onyar, he leaned over the bridge, mesmerized by the spring flood. He imagined the bodies of his Jewish ancestors, murdered one hundred years ago, floating in that river. "Amos, forget being a Jew. Save yourself," they begged.

Five times now he journeyed to the synagogue after midnight. Each week he struggled to remember the letters he learned. He practiced silently in bed. But once he left the *call*, it became too perilous for him to inscribe the letters on paper. How could he learn a language if he could not write it, take it into his hands, his body?

His mother did not want him to be a Jew. Uncle Fernando did not want him to be a Jew. Even Roca did not want him to be a Jew. "Jews are being murdered again, especially those devious enough to pass as Christians. If you become a Jew, you will endanger your family," Roca had warned.

"But if I pass as Christian, I could be killed as well. Either way there is danger. Why not follow my heart?"

"You are too young to understand how much your mother sacrificed for you."

"My mother lied to me."

"Have compassion for Caterina. She does not want to lose you the way she lost Diego."

"Christians killed my father. Why would I want to be one?"

"Not all Christians are murderers, Domingo."

Amos flushed. "I'm sorry. I know you're not that kind of Christian. You're different."

Roca's face looked sad. "Jesus loves all of us. He did not preach hatred."

Domingo had spent his life listening to the words of the Christians, worshipping in their awesome Cathedral on the hill. Now he desired to know the Jews' prayers and customs. Amos remembered the rabbi's frightening warning—if the rabbi were caught teaching him, the penalty could be death. He could not learn a difficult language under such peril.

The rabbi suggested he make the shapes of the letters with his body. Last night they had studied the letter *Vav.* "Hold yourself as erect as a tree, your feet on the earth, your head in the heavens. Your spine is a *Vav.* Enter the letter with your body so you can remember it. But, Amos, take care not to do this where anyone else can see you."

Watching Raphael pose in the *Vav* position in front of him, Amos recognized his physical desire for the sweet, red-bearded man who promised to teach him. He must not act on these feelings. It was one thing to enjoy boyhood pleasure with Pau and quite another to seduce a man of God. He surprised himself. How could he feel attracted to this skinny old man with warm blue eyes? Perhaps he felt this way because Raphael offered the comfort of a father. More likely it was his attraction to Judaism itself in the form of the rabbi. He felt such passion for the text, for the letters the rabbi showed him. Last night he experienced desire not only for Raphael's body but also for the letter *Vav* itself. What did it mean to desire a letter, to desire a letter receding from you even as you reached for it?

"Will you call me Amos?" he had asked the rabbi the night before.

The rabbi touched his shoulder. Then he pulled his hand back and stared at it. "Yes, Amos," he nodded gravely. "It would be my honor to call you by your Hebrew name."

Amos returned home late last night to his quarters above the shop and entered stealthily. Thank goodness Roca no longer heard well. When he was younger, Roca would have asked what had kept him out so late.

As he fell asleep that night, he heard a voice call, "Amos." It sounded like the voice who addressed him from the stones. It was weeks since he had journeyed to the synagogue wall.

Amos. The name offered a powerful key to the world he longed to enter.

"Domingo!"

This voice was loud, insistent, interrupting his memories. He looked down from the tree. Pau glared up at him.

"I called and called. But you ignored me."

"I'm sorry, Pau. I was thinking. Come up and we'll talk." Domingo patted the branch next to him, polished smooth from years of them perching here together.

Pau's eyes slipped past him. "No, I just came to tell you that yesterday evening I saw your mother go into the *call* again."

"Oh, Pau. Let it be, my friend. She harms no one by these journeys."

"What! Do you know how suspicious it makes your family look, to have your mother walk the streets of the Jews?"

"I suppose," Domingo replied. He kept his voice deliberately casual. Should he tell his mother about the passageways? "So, how is Nuria?"

Pau picked up a loose branch and whacked it against the base of their tree. "Nuria is humiliated. How do you think she feels? The handsome and brilliant Domingo has refused to marry her, shamed our entire family." He banged the branch against the tree again.

"But doesn't she like Andreu?"

"It doesn't matter right now. She says she must be too fat for you, too ugly."

"Can't you talk to her, tell her it isn't personal?"

"And tell her you don't like *any* girls, not just her? *That's* a splendid idea." Pau snorted. "Besides, she doesn't want to see me. I just remind her of you."

Pau's expression seemed strange, tight around the eyes.

"Are you okay, Pau?" Domingo asked. "You look tired."

"I'm fine."

"Why don't I come down and we can lie together."

"No!" Pau backed away from the tree. "Not that. It's a sin. We can't touch—"

The sound of gravel on the footpath nearby startled both of them. Perhaps someone had heard them. Pau looked terrified. He waited a few moments and then peered through the bushes. He looked back at Domingo, shook his head vehemently, and disappeared.

Amos had entered a landscape of deception, where even his new name was a secret from his best friend. He had always told Pau everything—his nightmares about his father, how he awakened during the night crying like a small boy. Pau had held his hand as they sat in this very tree in the numb weeks after his father's death, Pau with his boy sweetness. Without Pau, he might have thrown himself into the Onyar River.

He remembered his uncle's warning. He must not confide in Pau. Now he kept enormous secrets from his best friend. He had not told Pau about the voice that spoke from the stones. He had not told Pau where his mother had gone the afternoon he had followed her, only that a friend had died and his mother had wandered disoriented and grief-stricken through the town and he had felt worried about her. Pau appeared to accept this answer. Deception seemed so easy. But now his mother had returned to the *call*. Pau might have guessed why. What if Pau had found out about his lessons with the rabbi?

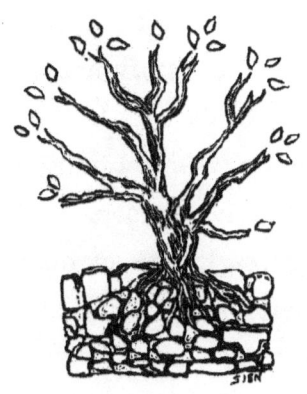

Chapter Nine

Raphael studied Nachmanides' treatise on the Messiah with a mixture of skepticism and admiration for the great rabbi who once wrote in this very room. According to Nachmanides, the creation story in *Bereshit* (Genesis) spelled out all that would happen in human history from the time of Moses's death until the time of redemption, the coming of the Messiah. Nachmanides divided the six days of creation into six thousand-year periods. The rabbi believed the world had entered the end of the sixth day. By the Jewish year 5118 or the Christian year 1358, the messianic age would begin. This was one of the major arguments Nachmanides made in his four-day disputation with the convert Friar Paul Christiani in Barcelona during the summer of 1263. At the end of the disputation, which covered such topics as whether the Messiah had yet appeared, King Jaime I awarded Nachmanides three hundred *solidos* and declared that never before had he heard "an unjust cause so nobly defended." Nevertheless, the Dominicans claimed victory and exiled Nachmanides from Girona at age seventy-two. In Palestine he built a synagogue and founded a *yeshiva*. Living in Acre, he wrote of Girona, "I left my family, I forsook my house. There, with my sons and daughters, the sweet, dear children I brought up at my knees, I left also my soul. My heart and my eyes will dwell with them forever."

Raphael sighed as he read. Almost a century and a half had elapsed since Nachmanides' promised date of redemption. How wrong the rabbi had been, and yet how courageous, how brilliant. Clergy and rabbis from Girona, Barcelona, and other cities witnessed his calm and articulate performance during the disputation. Miraculously, King Jaime encouraged Nachmanides to express his critical opinions about Catholicism freely, and neither he nor the Jewish people were punished for his audacity. But two years later, when Nachmanides presented an account of the disputation written in Catalan to his friend the Bishop of Girona, the clergy turned against him and forced him to leave Spain. Rumor held that he and the Bishop were friends who often drank strong wine together and argued about theology. Surely such friendships, or at least a written record of them, threatened the Church.

Doctor, philosopher, *Talmud* scholar—Nachmanides had mastered everything. He composed commentaries on Jewish law at age sixteen. And yet he defied the *Talmud's* warning "May the bones be blown away of those who calculate the end." Why did the *Talmud* warn against this? Perhaps because those who concentrate on calculating the end of days may become more preoccupied with the future than with the life they live. The time of the Messiah is Adonai's business, not within the purview of human beings. Raphael sat thinking, his hands clasped on the desk. If only he could summon the mind of the brilliant rabbi who once wrote here.

In Nachmanides' day, the *call* was larger. As Jews were murdered or converted, the town seized their houses and streets, forbade them to have windows or doors opening onto the Carrer de la Força. Royal processions and visiting bishops used this street to access the Cathedral. The Jewish remnant in tattered robes and uncut hair must not be visible to these dignitaries.

Rabbi Halevi considered his abilities honestly. He did not have the mind of a Nachmanides or any of the other illustrious rabbis who once studied in this room. Raphael could not write brilliant essays or figure out how to successfully navigate through his community's present troubles. But he must do his best despite his weaknesses. On his worst days, Raphael wondered if God had chosen him to be the rabbi of Girona simply because few men wanted to be rabbis now. Two decades ago, only six men had come to learn with Rav Chaim in his *yeshiva*. Four fidgeted and looked out the window. Only Raphael felt a passion for study and then for the rabbinate. And Isaac. Isaac had felt passion but not for the *Torah*. Raphael smiled to himself.

Those memories lifted him out of his cramped existence. But he must not think of Isaac's lips on his, how they had sinned together —

"Father," a quiet voice said in the doorway.

"Miriam, come in." Raphael looked at his daughter. How long had she been standing there? She had inherited his pale skin and freckles, and although cloth now covered her long auburn hair, he remembered its beauty before she got married, when she had followed her mother around the house and the streets of the *call*. Three children Leah had given birth to, all of them girls, but only Miriam had lived past age three. Leah had been pregnant when she died; she'd believed she carried a son. A son. What would it be like to have a son?

"Father." Miriam approached. "The Falco family sent lamb. Jonas butchered it yesterday. I cooked a stew for you. It's on the stove."

"Lamb! That is truly a miracle, in these times, to bring lamb." Only the Falcos could afford such luxuries. "How generous of them to share with us."

She hesitated, seemed about to say something else, but then kissed the top of his head and left. She probably had someone to visit. He knew the women came to her for help with everything from midwifery to understanding the meaning of their dreams. Miriam always dreamt vividly. He remembered how, when his daughter was small, she had awakened from a dream and begged to touch the *Torah*.

He had carried her into the sanctuary, cradled in his arms like a *Torah*, opened the ark, and held her up so she could touch the wrapped scroll with one small pink finger. For her he had broken tradition, teaching her Hebrew and then Aramaic and *Talmud*.

Now he felt tempted to break other rules. God, save me from my *yetzer hara*. He didn't like the direction of his thoughts. It would soon be dark. He must not think such things on *Shabbat*.

Chapter Ten

M iriam, please come. We need the cure for the evil eye," Rosa Zafria begged.

Miriam let Rosa drag her to the apartment in a crumbling house at the edge of the *call*.

"I don't want her to go to the hospital. Babies die there."

Miriam nodded. "I'll see if I can help." But when she looked at Sara's still body in the bed, she knew little could be done. The spirits of Sara's ancestors hovered around her small form. Ever since childhood, Miriam had felt the presence of spirits who rode the winds above Girona, who hid in the very cod they ate.

"After I fed her tonight, she began to shake. Now she's so quiet. Look, Sara barely breathes."

Miriam rested her hand on the girl's chest. There, an almost imperceptible movement, a tiny breath. She saw more and more sickness lately, especially with the little ones. Doña Pardo's boy had fallen ill two weeks ago. His mother had prepared his favorite delicacies, but he could not sleep and had vomited continuously until he died. The women usually thought it was their fault. "I praised my son's intelligence and forgot to spit and say 'Ojo!' as you taught me, Miriam," Doña Pardo had sobbed.

"Miriam, I spoke badly of my dead father-in-law," Rosa now confessed. "Perhaps his spirit came for Sara in revenge."

Perhaps, Miriam thought to herself. But so many had sickened at once. She pondered her own theories, ideas she could not express to the women, for she would frighten them. What she saw on the faces of the children was terror, terror that scared their spirits out of their small bodies. And it wasn't only the children. Several older people had fallen ill, including Judith, the cousin of the *conversa* Caterina. Girona's Jews suffered from *espanto,* a plague of soul loss caused by terror. The very old and the very young were the most vulnerable to the fear the Inquisitors brought to their city.

"Bring me a bowl, Rosa." She reached into her bag for a pouch of sugar and poured it into the ceramic bowl Rosa brought her. "Here. Put this out in the night air. Sugar to sweeten the disposition of the demons." She fastened a bracelet of blue beads on the baby's wrist. "This may protect her. Let us hope in the morning Sara will awaken smiling. But I cannot make promises."

Rosa's eyes met hers. "Thank you for being truthful with me, Miriam."

After she hugged Rosa, Miriam walked down the stairs to the street. Her legs felt as heavy as her spirits. Her women's cures — putting salt, rue, and garlic in a linen bag under people's pillows — had worked in the past. She had learned these cures from her mother. But she feared they were not strong enough for what ailed them now.

She looked at her hands, the veins prominent, the skin dry and chapped from washing, no longer the hands of a young woman. "You have curing hands," her mother had praised. "And a sweet mouth that speaks only good of others." Leah had kissed her on the cheek. Miriam longed for her mother.

Her mouth had not felt sweet lately. The bells tolled nine times to mark the opening of the market. Outside the *call*, the women of Girona, at least the Christian women, rushed to buy fresh vegetables and fruit. But Miriam knew that by noon, the time she and the other Jewish women were allowed to enter the market, she would be lucky to find some shriveled figs to bring back to her husband.

A few months ago she had sniffed at some cod to see how fresh it was. "Filthy Jewess," the vendor had jeered. "Now you must buy what you touched." She had forgotten, but only for an instant, the new law forbidding Jews to touch cakes, buns, biscuits, cheeses, meat, fresh or salted fish, raisins, dried figs, dates, or fresh fruit, pine nuts, broccoli, cabbages, or spinach sold in the stalls in the Christian market. If they touched those goods, they must purchase them. She remembered the shame she had felt that day as she had drawn her hand back and reached into her satchel for coins to pay the vendor for the smelly cod. The yellow and red badge on her cloak burned her chest. Her fair complexion revealed her shame. She turned and fled into the *call* with nothing from market day but old fish. Only later had she felt anger, which had fermented into bitterness. No, her mouth no longer felt sweet.

"The *mikvah*, Miriam," she heard her mother's voice advise. "That is what the *mikvah* is for, to wash away shame, to remind you that you are pure in the eyes of God."

She felt relieved to find no one in the blue-tiled room below the synagogue but Chava, the old woman who managed the ritual bath. Chava nodded but did not intrude. Immersed in the *mikvah*, even with other women nearby, Miriam sometimes found solitude. She climbed down the tile staircase and lowered herself into the limestone pool fed by *mayim chayim*, living waters rising from a spring below Girona. No one knew the age of this *mikvah*. Generations of women have immersed themselves here, Miriam thought, including grandmothers and great-grandmothers I never met. The silty but clean waters of the pool soothed her. She closed her eyes. The water purified not only her body, as it did each month after her menses were complete, but also her soul.

Huldah called to Miriam from the spring-fed mikvah. *In Miriam she recognized the lineage of women who had followed Asherah and understood the healing qualities of herbs and*

prophecy in kitchens and gardens. Hilkiah and his kind had not
succeeded.

Tears came.

"Miriam—" She thought she heard her mother's voice call her from the spring below the pool. Maybe it was the sound of water talking below the stones.

Miriam's patients had blessed her, feeding her sugared almonds in gratitude for healing their families. But their blessings could not protect Leah, who had perished from rocks thrown by a Christian mob. For a full year after her mother's death, Miriam could not touch healing herbs, lay hands on her people. At the end of one year, Doña Hannah Falco had taken her aside. "Enough. You cannot refuse your destiny. Your mother would not have wanted this." So Miriam followed her mother's path, though she also felt drawn to her father's ways, to Hebrew and the sacred texts. She would not choose between them.

Now these rules of humiliation. Far worse, these dying babies and elders, this *espanto*. Her mother had never prepared her for this. She had gone to see her father, intending to speak with him about this wave of sickness. But he had looked drawn, wan. She did not want to burden him. True, he was a rabbi, but he didn't have the strength her mother had possessed.

"*Refua shelema para todos los hazinos,*" Miriam chanted to herself as she submerged herself a third and final time in the cool waters of life. "Please God, bring cures for all who are sick." She would advise Rosa to change her baby's name so the demons could not find her again. The door to the *mikvah* opened, and Malka and Blanca descended toward the pool, laughing together about their impotent husbands. Miriam felt in no mood for gossip. She dressed and left quickly.

Chapter Eleven

Amos stumbled along the narrow tunnel. He did not dare light a candle. Light could seep through a crack in the passage and reveal his presence to the Christians. "It is the same old story," the rabbi had raged a few nights earlier. "They accuse us of murdering Christian children and drinking their blood. They believe we torch their homes, curse their churches, stab their communion wafers, and flog their crucifixes. To them we are hook-nosed, blood-sucking horned devils."

Amos had flinched when the rabbi had spat out the word *Christian*. He loved Roca, who taught him to be a scribe. He loved Pau, who would soon be a priest. Both of them worshipped the Christian God.

The rabbi had noticed his anguished look. "Not all Christians, true. Forgive my anger. I fear my rage will devour me."

The night he had followed his mother here seemed long ago. He forgave her for lying to him. But now he had more secrets to keep from her. "To teach a *converso* is to put the entire *call* in danger. It is better if your mother does not know we study together," the rabbi had said.

"Why do you continue to take this risk on my behalf?"

"I must," the rabbi had said simply and looked away.

The rabbi had remained encouraging, understanding. He had even suggested they proceed more slowly so Amos could absorb the letters. But Amos had grown increasingly frustrated and impatient with himself. He wanted to read *Torah* now, to master his fear of Hebrew.

Amos stooped and emerged in the corridor inside the synagogue. He tiptoed up the spiral staircase to the study. The door stood open, the room silent. Through the door, Amos saw the rabbi lying on the floor, motionless. The hearth smoked. A candle stub burned on the table. Amos suppressed an urge to cross himself. He entered the room, bent down, stretched out a hand, and then drew it back, afraid to touch. Raphael might be cold, as Amos's father's body had been after he died.

He picked up the candle and shone its light over the form on the floor. The thin chest rose and fell. A carafe of wine stood on the table. Perhaps Rabbi Halevi had been poisoned. Amos leaned over the carafe and took a sniff. It smelled fine, but how would he know?

"Rabbi," Amos whispered. "Rabbi!" He shook the rabbi's shoulder.

The rabbi convulsed. His arms flailed and he knocked the candle out of Amos's shaking hand to the floor, where it expired. He groaned. His legs twitched. Perhaps something possessed Halevi. Amos grabbed his shoulders and shook him again, but the groans continued. Finally he began to sing a melody his mother had sung to him years ago. Soon the rabbi opened his eyes. Perhaps he was drunk. He looked altered. But he seemed to recognize Amos hovering over him. He reached up and touched Amos's cheek.

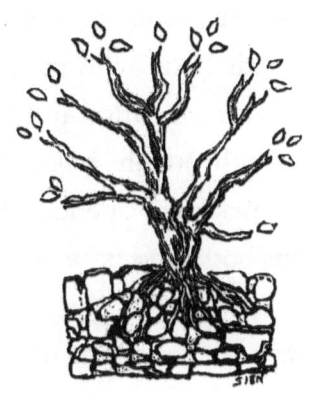

Chapter Twelve

Raphael remained a novice at meditation. In the past few weeks, he had spent time with the texts of the old Kabbalists of Girona. He had also studied Ezekiel's glorious visions of chariots and seven palaces found in *Merkavah* and *Hekhalot* mysticism, ideas first written down over a thousand years ago. He knew nothing of heavenly palaces. He was just a lonely rabbi dwelling within a few streets of stone, sleep-deprived from nights of teaching Amos and from fear for his people, whose lives were imperiled by the Inquisitors. His judgment might not be the best. But an idea came to him, an idea founded in desperation. If he could become an adept enough Kabbalist, he could locate Rabbi Akiva in the World Beyond and ask for his help. Raphael had studied the purification rites, learned the sacred chants. He took his body into short and then longer and deeper trances. Tonight he would attempt to go deeper still.

Breathe. Breathe. Breathing through the crown of his head, *Keter*, he filled his body with breath. It took a while for his body to relax, for his lungs and belly to allow him to receive spirit through breath: *ruach*. Finally the top of his head tingled and prickled, opened like a gate. Breathe, breathe. He forgot his body and became breath, contraction and expansion.

Then he no longer felt conscious of the air in his lungs. He looked down at his own inert form stretched out on the floor. He had journeyed this far once before but had become frightened to see his body lying there as if dead. The moment he registered fear, he had collapsed back into his body, his heart racing.

The candle's flame flung shadows on the white plastered walls of the room. The shadows moved. There must be a draft. This ascent seemed different. He rose higher than ever before, hovered just below the ceiling, and looked down at his study, at the dusty books stacked on the table.

He floated higher until he entered the roof of the synagogue. His spirit mingled with the stones dating back to the Roman era, perhaps to the year when Akiva himself was murdered by that empire. He sensed rough places where the stones touched each other, thought he heard the stones murmur, noting his presence.

Then Raphael floated no longer among stones but in night air. He looked down on the red-tile roofs of the *call*, at the steep moonlit streets below the Cathedral: his shelter and his prison.

He ascended higher. A cloud brushed his face. Then the sky cleared. To the north, moonlight shone on the snow-covered peaks of the Pyrenees. Eastward the Mediterranean glimmered. The Iberian Peninsula stretched out a giant paw. Directly below him lay foothills, black valleys.

He laughed, ecstatic. He had escaped. He could fly. He experimented and soon circled above Girona among the stars. Nachmanides must have flown here too. He felt free. He could journey anywhere: France, North Africa, Jerusalem. He felt drunk. Was this a dream? The moment he questioned what happened, he plummeted toward the earth. Terror. What had he done? He would become as mad as Ben Zoma in the Talmudic story of the four sages who ascended to Paradise.

Desperately he reminded himself, Remember the teachings. Find refuge in the letters. He pictured a large *Yud* in the dark sky. Its soft back broke his free fall. He stretched out on the *Yud* and glided through the night in luxury. Then he conjured an enormous *Hey* hanging near the Pyrenees, brought it toward him, and flew through its doorway. "*Vav*," he pronounced next. The letter materialized, a tall, reassuring tree. He grasped it. "*Hey*," he said again. Another doorway opened. He swung from the *Vav*, the momentum sending him through the gate of the second *Hey*.

Beyond the gate of the *Hey* he encountered light, the sun, whose rays scarcely reached the canyons of the *call*. He rested in its warm lap. He did not want to return to his body, to the dim life below.

"Raphael."

Who spoke?

"Raphael." The voice sounded closer. Was it Rabbi Akiva?

But it was a woman's voice.

"Rabbi?"

A different, resonant male voice yanked him earthward, concerned and then frantic. The rabbi fell through icy air, into sharp stones that poked and complained as he crashed through them, and then back into his body. He groaned. It had been a mistake, this ascent. He must be in the grasp of demons.

"Rabbi!"

A shape leaned over him, singing a lullaby. A demon would not be so kind. He did not feel afraid anymore. He opened his eyes to Amos's face.

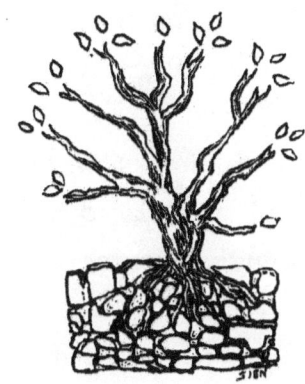

Chapter Thirteen

That summer of 1491 in Girona, a summer of lush grass, deep red poppies, and delicate white orchids flowering in the hollows of the Valley of Sant Daniel, Amos walked through the meadows imagining Hebrew letters in the curled limbs of oak trees. Raphael listened to the ghost of the sea booming inside the synagogue walls and fought his desires. It was a summer of midnight study, a summer of suppressed longing.

"Rabbi, teach me to pray," Amos begged. "How can I become a Jew if I don't know how to pray? You tutored me in all of the letters, but I cannot remember what you teach me. Perhaps it's because I don't know how to pray like a Jew."

"Amos, your heart already knows the language of prayer."

"Please, I want to pray like a Jew, in Hebrew."

"Very well. I will teach you one prayer. It is the first line of one of our most important prayers. You already know some of the words. *Shema Yisrael Adonai Eloheinu Adonai Echad. Hear, Israel, the Lord our God, the Lord is One.* They are written on a scroll and placed inside the *mezuzot* on our doors. You've seen the *mezuzah* on the side of the synagogue's door?"

Amos nodded. "I've noticed that you touch it before you enter. Will you teach me to do this as well?"

"Yes. It is also placed in the *tefillin* men put on each morning."

"*Tefillin?*"

"These are two black leather boxes filled with this and other prayers, attached to long leather straps. We bind one box, the hand *tefillin*, around one arm and hand, and the other box we wear on our forehead, between our eyes, in the place of our deepest sight."

"Can you teach me to put on *tefillin* too?"

"Not so quickly, Amos. It's just like the letters. We must go slowly. You cannot learn all of what it means to be a Jew in just a few months. Let us start with the *Shema*. It is a commandment to say the *Shema* when we wake up, when we go to sleep, and at other times of the day. We say the Bedtime *Shema*—*Kri'at Shema al Hamitah*—before we go to sleep, for protection from demons, and also in case we die before we wake. Sleep is a small death. We practice the *Shema* so we are able to say it at the moment of our deaths."

"*She-ma* . . ." Amos began.

"Wait. Cover your eyes with your right hand. Repeat after me."

Shema Yisrael Adonai Eloheinu Adonai Echad.

As he prayed, Amos felt a deep calm enter his soul.

The stones resonated to the new vibration in the rabbi's study.

"I promise you, it's safe," Amos told the rabbi a few weeks later. "You assured me no one knows about the passageway. We will go by night. I'll lead us into the hills, to the oak forest. We will be there before dawn. We can spend the entire next day hidden until it is night again and we sneak back into the *call*. We must go while it is still summer and the nights are warm. I will tell Roca I want a day off to wander the mountains. He understands I must have adventures now and then."

"What shall I tell my daughter?"

"Tell her you will take the day to rest."

"She knows I never rest."

"Then she will be overjoyed you have decided to rest for once," Amos argued. "She can take care of her husband. Or study. Doesn't she like to study? She might welcome a free day. You must get away from this dank room, the *call*, this prison."

"This is a holy place, the place of the Kabbalists." Raphael did not tell Amos that he too had sometimes felt the *call* was a prison.

"Yes, it's holy. But you also need to feel your feet on the fertile earth. Look at how skinny and pale you are. You need some fresh air."

"That is how you see me? Skinny, pale?"

Amos's eyes were moist. "I'm worried about you. You don't eat. You look tired."

"Now you sound like Miriam. Next you'll bring me stew."

Amos blushed. "My mother makes the best stew. If I could carry it into the *call* without everyone smelling it, I would. Please, Rabbi," Amos begged. "I only want to walk with you under the open sky, to be with you outside of this room."

"But wild beasts live in the forest," the rabbi protested. "What if we are attacked by a bear or wolves?"

"Then we shall say the prayer against wild beasts. Surely our tradition has such prayers."

"I surrender. You will have your wish. In three nights it will be *Rosh Chodesh Elul*. The moon will be dark and we shall go into the hills."

From the stone walls of the synagogue, Huldah listened to Amos and Raphael make this plan. She hoped that this night in the woods would strengthen their love and that their bond would provide a gate for her prophecy.

Raphael breathed cool air as they emerged from the passageway. The breeze tasted of wild rosemary and the last roses of summer. From the east blew the faint salty scent of the sea. His feet stumbled over unfamiliar ground in the darkness. Amos reached out an arm to steady him. God, forgive me my sin, Raphael prayed. I have wanted his arm around me. Now give me the strength to stay pure. I am a rabbi and he is my student. And I am old enough to be his father.

Raphael had not walked so far in a long time. His breath came fast in his chest. *The soul of Jonathan was knit with the soul of David, and Jonathan loved him as his own soul,* he recalled the passage from the book of Samuel.

As they walked through the outskirts of Girona, an emaciated black dog growled, advanced on them.

"Hey! Who's there?" a voice called out from a third-story window. Amos took out the lamb bone he had saved for this possibility and tossed it to the dog. The night grew quiet, save for the dog gnawing bone. In silence they continued.

They climbed alongside the ruined Roman wall near the creek. The path narrowed and Amos dropped Raphael's arm. In places the way was overgrown. Brush tore their cloaks. Raphael's feet kicked a rock that plummeted over the side of the cliff. The rabbi coughed. Coughs echoed down the valley. Something screeched — an owl? The bushes rustled with invisible creatures. How could Amos see the path? The night seemed too still. Raphael heard every sound, even the creek trickling over the rocks below.

Amos had not counted on Raphael's clumsy feet and coughing. He was used to his young eyes with their ability to see in the darkness. But at last they came to the tangled refuge of the oak forest. They crawled into the shelter of its arms. Amos placed his cloak ceremoniously on the grass for the rabbi. "Don't step in the thistles," he advised. "Stay on this side of the glen." Raphael sank onto the cloak, his legs weak. Amos flopped next to him. "Look," Amos said, pointing through the branches framing the sky. "There's the Great Bear, and next to it, the Little Bear. I recognize them from the map in the book I am copying." For once, Raphael became the student, Amos the teacher.

"In the morning you will enjoy sun and fresh air," Amos promised. "We will feast on wild mushrooms and greens. I know just where to find them."

"What a blessing that will be," the rabbi murmured as he fell asleep. "It has been years since I have tasted and felt such miracles. Thank you. *Shema Yisrael Adonai Eloheinu Adonai Echad.*"

Raphael cried out in his sleep.

"Wake up. It's all right."

He opened his eyes. Amos perched next to him. Sunlight streamed through a weave of tree limbs. A squirrel chided from above. It looked so bright. He had forgotten how morning sun lit a forest.

I thank you God, eternal one, for mercifully restoring my soul to me —

"I had a bad dream," he said to Amos after he had finished his morning prayers. He did not tell Amos that in his nightmares he had fled a belching iron monster that had roared across the Jewish cemetery. He had sought safety in the *call*, but it too had appeared strange, its stone houses festooned with red and yellow flowers. Christian songs had echoed in the passageways.

"Well, wake up, Rabbi," Amos crowed. "We have the whole day. Hours and hours stretch before us, like a whole year full of hours if we treasure them. I'm sorry, it is too dry for mushrooms this late in the summer. I should not have promised you mushrooms." He reached into his satchel. "But look, I found berries and greens. Let us feast and give thanks for the blessing of this day, as you have taught me."

From his perch on a neighboring tree, Pau watched them savor their meal and then lie close together, talking and laughing. They were too easy to follow. It had been a long night, sleepless, for he was afraid he would fall from the branches. Now he felt light-headed, starved. His legs were stiff, his neck was sore, and his best tunic was stained with tree sap. He wanted to shout at Domingo. Now he understood why his friend had no time for him. Domingo liked this shriveled, pale Jew. Thin legs stuck out from his tunic like a skeleton's. He snored like an aged dog. Domingo had brought this old man to their secret place. Pau felt sick. Domingo could have become a priest. They might have lived out the rest of their lives in peace, making ink together, safe in the monastery.

He must betray the boy he had loved his entire life. If he did not pay this price to Father Hidalgo, he would have to give up his dream to become a priest, one of Girona's shepherds, one of Jesus's beloved servants.

Chapter Fourteen

L et's go to the tavern tonight," Roca proposed.

"But I haven't finished copying this page."

"Leave it, Domingo. Our trade will be here tomorrow. My birthday comes once a year. I am not getting any younger. Come. Celebrate with me. Tonight we will drink red wine and eat *empanadas* stuffed with lamb, and dove pies. For dessert, maybe they will have warm fritters."

Domingo organized his desk so he could continue his projects in the morning. They left the shop arm in arm on this balmy evening in late summer. Domingo wished they were strolling along the river instead of heading for a noisy tavern, but he could not refuse Roca's invitation. They celebrated Roca's birthday every year. Domingo remembered the first year he had worked for Roca. Nightmares ripped away his sleep and he would awaken screaming to find Roca stroking his hair, watching over him. The next morning Roca would make him an extra cup of steaming tea before work. He never pried into Domingo's affairs, but he noticed everything and understood what it meant for a boy to lose a father.

"You're quiet tonight, Domingo. Anything ailing you?"

"I'm fine. Just a bit tired. My eyes hurt."

"I see. Maybe the light's not so good in the corner. Move your desk closer to the window. And get some sleep. I heard you come in very late last night again. More like morning, actually. You know, it's not good to walk in the dark. One becomes prey for the spirits."

"No, the rabbi says—" Domingo began, and then stopped. He had been about to explain what the rabbi had said about midnight being the best time to study.

"Eh? Who says what?" The older man stopped to peer at him.

"A friend of mine said the same thing," Domingo said. He felt grateful Roca hadn't heard the word *rabbi*. "About the demons. I just like to walk. When I can't sleep, I like to look at the moon."

"No moon last night," Roca remarked, examining Domingo closely. He seemed about to say something else but then thought better of it.

Under the light of the tavern entrance, Domingo saw Roca's face more clearly. Roca looked like he had not slept well for many nights. "Are you feeling well, Master?" he asked.

Roca ignored his question and gestured at the door of the tavern. "Well, here we are. Tavern looks crowded tonight. Shall we go in?"

The tavern was packed with journeymen and apprentices spending their meager wages on carafes of wine or mugs of beer. Few of the men here were masters like Roca, for most masters did not like to be seen with their inferiors. Roca was different. He did not hold himself above these men, so they welcomed him. "Roca, Domingo. Over here!" a voice shouted over the din. Domingo saw Carlos, who worked at the parchment shop.

"Sit." Carlos gestured at two spaces on the narrow bench in front of a wooden table laden with meat pies and carafes of wine. "Busy night."

"What?" Roca shouted, pointing to his ear.

Carlos shook his head, gestured at the men behind them lined up out the door and waiting to eat.

"It's my birthday," Roca beamed. "Domingo and I are here to celebrate."

Carlos leaned close and deciphered the word *birthday*. He patted Roca on the back and smiled. Then he turned to speak to Domingo. For a moment there was a lull in the loud tavern, and he managed to say the word *Inquisitors* before the curtain of sound descended again, making communication impossible.

"What?" Domingo shouted.

"Inquisitors," Carlos breathed into Domingo's ear. He reeked of red wine and garlic sausage. He passed the plate of sausage to Roca.

"Think I'll wait for the dove pie. It's my favorite," Roca said.

"Sausage?" Carlos waved the plate at Domingo.

Pork sausage. He could not visit Raphael later with sausage on his breath. But if he didn't eat the sausage he might be revealed as a Jew. Domingo took a small piece of sausage and nibbled it.

Carlos looked at Domingo strangely. "Never known you to sniff at sausage before."

"What were you saying earlier?" Domingo asked. The bar had quieted down enough that he could make himself heard.

"I hear Father Antonio Rios will speak at the Cathedral on Sunday," Carlos said. "He is to address the problem of *conversos*."

Domingo ran his tongue over the remnants of rich sausage in his mouth. He tried to look nonchalant at Carlos's news. "Oh, really. How do you know?"

"That friend of yours, the acolyte. Pau, isn't that his name? He came to buy parchment for the Cathedral yesterday. Told me the news." Carlos looked around the tavern and lowered his voice. "So, will I see you in church?"

Roca, who had been silent until that point, jumped in. "Of course." His eyes skimmed around the tavern.

Domingo wondered if people could hear them. But it seemed impossible anyone could have overheard amid the raucous conversation and many toasts. They could scarcely hear each other.

"Father Rios is reputed to be an inspiring speaker," Roca said.

"Well, I'll see you tomorrow," Carlos said. He heaved himself to his feet and wiped his greasy face with a sleeve. "I'd best get going. Master wants us at first light tomorrow."

He winked at Domingo. "You have a great job, you know. Best in Girona. Great wages, splendid hours, nice boss."

"I know I'm lucky." Domingo nodded.

After Carlos left, Roca smiled. "Let's forget about the Inquisitors tonight. How about some warm fritters?"

"You're like my son," Roca confided on the way home from the tavern. "Bring me a grandson by marrying a nice girl. Why not Nuria?"

"She can only be a sister to me."

Roca raised his eyebrows. "She's a pretty one with her shiny black hair. Those hips." He'd drunk a little too much wine.

"Nuria will marry Andreu."

"Lucky fellow. But what about you?"

"I'll find someone to love."

"The Bible tells us to be fruitful and multiply."

At Sunday morning Mass, Domingo fidgeted next to his mother and uncle in the pews. Roca sat a few rows behind, with Clara.

It was time to kneel and pray. He sank to his knees on the floor, forced himself to intone the Latin. Around the sides of the vast Cathedral lay the crypts of Girona's most faithful. The sanctuary felt dark, imposing, terrifying. He opened his eyes to see Pau watching him. He stood in his usual place near Father Santos, holding the linen bag containing the Host. He looked so sad. Domingo realized how much he missed his friend. But he could reveal so little now to Pau about his life, about what really mattered to him: the religion he was exploring.

Domingo rose for Communion with the others. "They believe we torch their homes, curse their churches, stab their communion wafers, and flog their crucifixes," he recalled the rabbi saying.

He took the wafer from Father Santos, who smiled at him. He had studied catechism with Father Santos, and Santos had officiated at his father's funeral. Domingo had forgotten how much he had adored this priest. He used to work hard at his Bible studies to earn his praise. All of that seemed long ago.

Domingo sat back down next to his mother, who leaned over to kiss his cheek. He looked at her with a new sense of wonder. His mother was a strong woman. She came here week after week, year after year, serenely reciting these prayers and taking the wafer. Then she returned home to her cellar to chant Jewish prayers and make secret journeys to the *call*. She went to priests for confession, something he had not been able to do since he had learned the truth about his family. But Mass remained inescapable. He had come here since childhood. If he stopped coming, everyone would notice.

Father Hidalgo rose to speak. "There is a conspiracy in Spain, a plot to defile the pure blood of our country. Last year on the eve of Passover a group of *conversos* near Toledo murdered an innocent boy. These same *conversos* claim to be good Christians."

A murmur spread through the congregation. Most people in Girona had heard this story of the Holy Child of La Guardia but didn't believe it. Supposedly one of these *conversos*, Benito Garcia, was imprisoned for this alleged crime and under extreme torture had confessed to plotting to overthrow Christianity throughout all of Spain. But this was no time to question the fabrications of the Inquisition. Domingo stared straight ahead. No expression must show on his face. His mother's leg tensed next to his.

"There's a certain smell," the priest continued, "the smell of a Jew, especially one who hides among us."

Sweat poured from Domingo's armpits and seeped into his tunic. Yes, Father, it's the smell of fear.

"The Holy Office must not tolerate such deception. The trial against Benito Garcia and his diabolical circle of conspirators proceeds. For months we have been hard at work in Girona, preparing to cleanse our citizens of the sickness festering in our midst. Still, many have not been found. Now Father Antonio Rios, a devoted Dominican preacher, has traveled from Barcelona to speak to us about this special challenge we face."

"I hear he is so religious he wore a hair shirt as a young man and refused all meat and sweets," Domingo's mother whispered.

Flanked by ceremonial guards, Father Rios paused to look at the congregation in an extended moment of silence. When he spoke, his deep voice filled the Cathedral and echoed off the high ceiling. "We are engaged in a holy crusade against the infidel. This is a Christian country with a Christian King and a Christian Queen. Valiantly, we battle the armies of the Muslims in Granada in their last stand. Make no mistake. We shall win. All of Spain shall be Christian. We shall cleanse Spanish blood of foreign impurities and build our Christian empire." He clutched the large silver crucifix swinging from a rope around his waist. "The Inquisition will not tolerate sinful blasphemers. Look around. They may be your neighbors, the baker, the carpenter. They may be your parents, even your children." People shifted in wooden pews creaking beneath them, their eyes glued to the floor.

"Here in Girona, the Holy Office has identified the deceitful ones within our midst. We will purify Girona of this stench, these vile creatures who plot against us."

Rios walked down the steps into the congregation, his robes trailing behind him as if he were a king. Domingo tried to avert his gaze, but Rios's magnetic black eyes drew attention. Flanked by four guards and Father Hidalgo, he advanced through the pews, heading directly for the section where Domingo sat. The entourage reached his side. Hidalgo's dark eyes flickered over Domingo, resting there for a moment. Domingo stopped breathing. Then, blessedly, they passed by.

But two rows behind where Domingo sat, the entourage stopped. "Take this one, this treacherous scribe. Take his wife as well," Hidalgo ordered. Domingo turned around to stare. Two guards forced Roca to his feet. They twisted his arms behind his back. Roca's face contorted with pain; wetness spread along the lower part of his robe. Clara rose but then collapsed on the floor in a faint. Domingo started to get up, but his mother grabbed his arm and forced him back down. And so Domingo did nothing as his beloved master, Roca, and his wife, Clara, were led away.

The Inquisitors continued their procession through the congregation, selecting others accused of heresy. Domingo stared at his clasped hands, powerless in his lap. He was spared. The Inquisitors must not know of his secret journeys to the *call*. But he was guilty of exactly the Holy Office's accusation: renouncing Christianity. Meanwhile, Roca prayed three times a day, went to confession several times a week, and gave money to the Church at every opportunity. He was generous, affable. But no one, not even Domingo, protested or stopped the Inquisitors from leading him away.

"He's one of us," his mother said later as they sat at the kitchen table. None of them could eat the cheese and bread she had placed on a plate.

Roca was a *converso*. "But Roca loves Jesus. You've seen his painting in the hallway near my room —"

"It's complicated," Uncle Fernando began. "Some *conversos* do come to believe."

"I thought I knew everything about him," Domingo said. "I am like a son to him."

"You are like Roca's son," Caterina reassured Domingo. "Who do you think betrayed him?" she asked Uncle Fernando.

"Last week he told me the Inquisitors paid a call on him and demanded he serve the Inquisition as a scribe in the prison. He refused."

Domingo tried to imagine Roca sitting in an Inquisitorial chamber, writing down the confessions of those who were being tortured. "Of course he refused."

Caterina laughed. "Domingo, you are so naïve. You cannot refuse to serve the Inquisitors, especially if you are a known *converso*."

"A known *converso*?"

"Families in Girona have known each other for generations. Even if the Inquisitors are from Barcelona, plenty of people in Girona know about Roca's past, and ours as well. Or perhaps they suspected Clara. It only takes one informant."

Someone had betrayed Roca and Clara. Domingo remembered the conversation at the tavern. Was it Carlos? He put his forehead on the table. He had done nothing to save his master.

"I pray Roca and Clara don't give us away," his mother said. "Under torture they may not keep silent."

Under torture might Roca confess that Domingo regularly went out all night?

His mother rubbed her exhausted face. "I'm going down to the cellar to pray for all of us."

The next day, guards marched Roca and Clara down the Carrer de la Força in a bizarre ceremonial parade with seven other *conversos*, most of whom Domingo knew by name. They wore yellow *sambenitos*, robes of the accused, each painted with a picture of a devil being thrown into the flames of hell. On their heads the jailers fastened tall hats decorated with crosses. The Inquisitors led the *conversos* to the Plaça Sant Domènec near the Cathedral, where a stage had been constructed a few days ago. The Inquisition was employing many carpenters. Peasants poured in from the countryside to attend this grisly carnival. Not to appear would cast instant suspicion upon oneself and one's family. The Inquisitors and their staff moved among the populace, noting on a long scroll who was there and who was absent.

Father Hidalgo strode out the door of the Cathedral carrying a cross. He hoisted it high, and the people of Girona swore to defend their faith against heretics. Domingo mouthed the words with his mother and uncle. His mother leaned on him.

Roca, Clara, and the other *conversos* kneeled before Alfonso de Espina, who sat on the platform high above them. The trial itself would not take place until the Inquisitors conducted an investigation in which they interrogated the accused.

Huldah hovered just over Roca's head as the Inquisitors put him in the potro, *the rack, and stretched his limbs. She dipped into his soul just once to read his thoughts. She felt afraid that Roca's extreme pain would entrap her spirit. "If Jesus died on the cross for my sins, I too can withstand pain to protect those I love," she heard him think. Roca's aging body could not survive torture, but they did not extract a confession from him. He died in that dungeon, as did Clara. Perhaps death spared Roca the worst, which was yet to come.*

Three conversos *from the Vidal family and two from the Mercador family were burned at the stake a few weeks later. Again the Inquisitors transported peasants in from the countryside and the townspeople came to watch. A dry wind blew their remains into the* call, *coated the stones with ash. Thus death reunited the* conversos *with their people. In the* aljama *it was the first day of Tishri 5252, Rosh Hashanah, the beginning of a new year.*

As she watched the conversos *burn, Huldah remembered the shrines of Asherah burning long ago, the murdered priestesses. Now Girona's sacred Jewish places would be destroyed, the people exiled once more.*

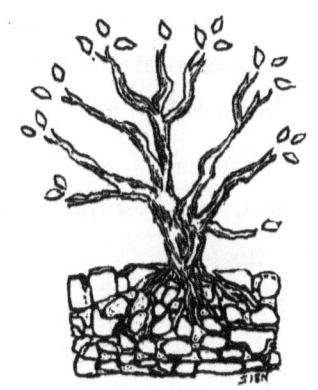

Chapter Fifteen

They first heard the jeers of the crowd during the morning *Torah* service. The scent of burning flesh drifted from the square several blocks away. Raphael gestured at the congregation to remain inside. The men sank into their prayer shawls; the women held each other. The rabbi kept reading from the *Torah* portion:

Abraham gave his newborn son, whom Sarah had borne him, the name of Isaac. And when his son Isaac was eight days old, Abraham circumcised him, as God had commanded him. Now Abraham was a hundred years old when his son Isaac was born to him. Sarah said, "God has brought me laughter; everyone who hears will laugh with me." And she added, "Who would have said to Abraham that Sarah would suckle children! Yet I have borne a son in his old age.

Miracles had happened to their ancestors; perhaps here too a miracle would take place. As long as he led the New Year's Day prayers Raphael remained composed; the words contained his anguish. But then he sat down and Vidal de Porta began the *shofar* service.

Tekiah! The first long blast of the ram's horn shattered his heart. He covered his eyes.

Shevarim! The *shofar* moaned three times, a wounded animal crying to God for redemption. Raphael removed his hands from his eyes and looked at the men around him. Most were openly crying.

Teruah! The *shofar* quavered nine times, a trumpet of war, of judgment. *Rosh Hashanah* was the judgment day for all creatures, not only Jews. It seemed no accident the Inquisitors had selected that day for the execution. On the anniversary of the day God created Adam and Eve, they chose murder.

Tekiah Gedolah! One long, final blast signified that God the King had heard their prayers. It is said the *shofar* will sound when the Messiah arrives; *Shekhinah*, the Divine Feminine presence of God, will return to the Temple; and the Mount of Olives will once more serve as the footstool of God. There the Redemption of the Dead will take place in the End of Days. But that time of redemption felt remote to Raphael.

God spare Amos, he prayed, and then he felt guilty for worrying about Amos while the Inquisitors burned *conversos*. *Rosh Hashanah* was not a time for praying for oneself alone but for the whole community. And that community included both Jews and *conversos*, though he could not pray for the *conversos* aloud.

El Rachamim, Compassionate One, please take their souls quickly so they do not feel the flames. *Melech,* King. Have mercy. Renew our days. Grant us peace.

Later Raphael slumped in front of his hearth. A chill descended from the Pyrenees and penetrated the synagogue walls. Miriam had invited him for dinner, but he wanted to be alone. She insisted he take home dates and figs, sweet foods for *Rosh Hashanah,* but he could not eat. He placed another log on the fire and gagged. The scent of burning wood evoked the smell of the *auto-de-fe.*

This week to come, the ten days between *Rosh Hashanah* and *Yom Kippur,* was a time for deep reflection and seeking forgiveness from those one had wronged. But he could not forgive himself. He served as the rabbi of an embattled community, yet he took enormous risks on behalf of one person. Raphael knew his own motives were not pure. He desired Amos, even if he resisted acting on those desires.

In the past days Raphael again sought admission to the World Beyond. But not since that first night had he floated through the stones to the heavens where the mysterious female voice called him. He pictured a *Dalet,* a door, but the gates remained sealed. He fasted, sang hymns, lay on the floor in the dark, and pictured the letter *Yud* for *yichud,* the unification of all life. He dropped his head between his

129

knees and wept, a practice the Kabbalists said would open a pathway to God.

Now he stood by the stinking fire and shaped his body into the letter *Shin*, a *shofar* to call from exile all of the banished, to gather the world's broken pieces. He spread his arms: Oh, God, bring *shalom*, peace, wholeness. *Shekhinah*, spread your wings and help me. Whatever assistance he could find must lie beyond the *call*, beyond this place.

Raphael had never aspired to be a prophet. Yet these times demanded knowledge of the future, deep wisdom, the counsel of the sages such as Rabbi Akiva, whom he might yet encounter in the starry realm above Girona. Open the gates, he beseeched. But the gates of prophecy remained closed.

Remember what Maimonides wrote in his *Guide for the Perplexed*, he told himself. The great rabbi believed prophecy was attainable if a man eradicated his desire for eating, drinking, and the pleasures of the body. Suddenly he understood the problem. God, sacred one, you deny prophecy to me because of my desires. I wish to enjoy physical acts forbidden by the *Torah*. But God had made him this way; how could it be wrong? No, he must not have such thoughts. He hurried to the *mikvah* and plunged into the water.

In the stones beneath the mikvah, *Huldah felt the pain and sadness of the rabbi as if it were her own.*

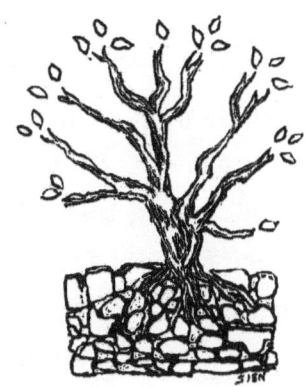

Chapter Sixteen

Miriam peered into the pool of olive oil she had poured onto her best plate.

A line of ragged men and women toiled along cliffs above a violent sea. A child squatted in the dust weeping. A man stumbled and fell onto toothy rocks; the ocean swallowed him. Burning sun blistered lips. It must be summer.

This time she searched for a vision, though lately they came unbidden. "Miriam, child, does something ail you?" Doña Falco had asked yesterday in services, touching Miriam's arm. "You sing beautifully but your voice carries hints of darkness."

"I'm fine. Just a little tired."

"Tired?" Doña Falco leaned closer in the crowded women's section so no one else could overhear and smiled conspiratorially. "Could this mean—"

"I don't think so," Miriam replied. She could not tell Doña Falco she used rue and cohosh to prevent pregnancy. She would not bring one more child into this world, not when she dreamt of the emaciated faces and bodies of Jews, some dead, some alive, fleeing through red deserts, dust and flies sticking to their faces. She thought she recognized people. Her father, her husband? They were changed, skeletal. She could not be sure. She woke screaming and Jonas held her. His bulky arms comforted her, but she could not turn to him for counsel. Not learned like her father, Jonas was only a simple man who ran the butcher shop next to the synagogue. She married him because he seemed kind and they had known each other since childhood. He kept her anchored in this world. Without him, she might drift away to join her mother.

"Miriam, come to bed," Jonas pleaded from the other room.

"Soon," she promised. She heard him recite Psalm 27 to himself: "*Adonai is my light and my life. Whom shall I fear?*"

She listened in tears. Her husband's faith in Adonai was much stronger than her own.

She peered into the oil pool. Clouds condensed over a desolate coast and then cleared. The clouds closed in. She stared into the oil, but it shimmered blankly, just a liquid on a plate now.

She heard Jonas hoist his body into the bed they shared. She would go to him soon. But first she would study for just a few moments. She found her best beeswax candle, the one that shed the brightest light. She wanted to look at the text her father had lent her, Maimonides. She wished she knew someone to study with besides her father. How she envied the young men her father taught, the ones he complained sat silently with bored expressions in the *yeshiva*. What they took for granted. She wished for even one woman friend, her equal in learning, to sit at this table with and study *Talmud* and *Torah*.

Huldah watched Miriam. She wished she could transport her to ancient Jerusalem to study with Batya and Hannah and the other women in her yeshiva. Black-haired and eager-eyed, they had been her most apt pupils in the school Huldah held each morning. She had come to think of them as her daughters, since she had birthed only a son. She had shown them how to interpret and chant the stories, but she had also instructed them in how to repair vellum when it tore and how to make a correction when ink wore thin from age and oily fingers.

Perhaps Miriam sensed Huldah's company, for she suddenly felt less despondent, less alone. At least being childless gave her the freedom to immerse herself in the Hebrew texts few other women could read, she told herself. Rashi's commentary, the *Talmud* — she borrowed many of her father's books. The only books he refused to let her study were the ones by the mystics. She asked him for the *Zohar*, the mystical commentary on the *Torah*, or the writings of the ecstatic Kabbalist Abraham Abulafia, but he shook his head. "This I cannot do. You are a woman. Even

I cannot go so far." When she argued, he remained resolute. He had listed the books she had not read, offered her Maimonides, and proposed they discuss it.

"Miriam," her husband grumbled. "It's late and it's cold. Can a man not have his wife's body to warm his bed?"

"Soon," Miriam called. She wiped the oil off the plate. The next evening would be *Kol Nidre,* the evening service of *Yom Kippur*. The ashes of the *conversos* still clung to the paths of the *call* and the cobblestone road of the Via Augusta leading north to Provence. She thought of her vision: lines of weary Jews, someone's body plummeting into the sea. The sea — *mayim,* water. *Midbar* — wilderness. Her people would be cast out of Girona, as once they had wandered in the desert wilderness of Sinai, crossed the Red Sea. Their ancestors had lived here for more than six centuries. Their days had contained much sorrow, especially in the past one hundred years, which had brought brutal attacks, including the one that stole her mother from her. But the violence had not been continuous. Perhaps it would ebb. She paced in front of the hearth, peering into the fire. The Inquisitor Alfonso de Espina's face appeared in the smoke for a moment, inscribed with hate. Miriam's throat constricted. She could not lie to herself. Something different pursued them now, something unstoppable.

Her father must know what destiny held for them. He seemed distracted, more tired than usual. She worried about him, sleeping in his small room in the cold synagogue, alone. He should come and talk to people more, offer comfort. She had overheard the women complaining that Rabbi Halevi spent too much time studying and meditating.

She crept into the cold bedroom, removed her tunic, and curled against Jonas's warm body. He sighed and reached for her.

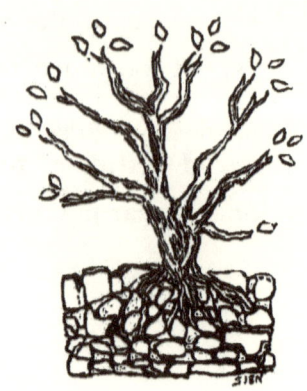

Chapter Seventeen

Domingo dug a deep hole in the clay along the banks of the Onyar River. The shovel scraped against rock. His mother seized his arm and whispered, "Be careful, Domingo! What if someone hears us?" But the night stayed silent as they buried their *menorah* by the river.

Domingo's mother confessed she had hidden this *menorah* in the cellar for over two decades. Now she thought it too dangerous to keep in the house. Domingo would never light these small oil lamps.

Domingo remembered the rabbi showing him the large *menorah* in the synagogue and explaining, "The light of *Chanukah* is the eternal radiance of God, *l'olam va'ed*, beyond time. This primordial light shone at the beginning of creation before the exile from the Garden of Eden. On *Chanukah* we are granted temporary access to that light. If we are blessed, we receive prophecy when we meditate on the flames. Miracles may happen."

Traditionally, each family lit their *menorah* and placed it in a window so the glow could be shared with those who passed by. But most *conversos* concealed their *menorot* from the world. Now he and his mother smothered that potential light in dirt. Domingo lifted the shovel, feeling as though he were burying a relative.

When they returned home, his mother beckoned him downstairs. Uncle Fernando had already gone to bed. The cellar smelled of the onions and garlic Caterina stored in the cool darkness. He and his mother stood in the same corner where his father had once sheltered him under his prayer shawl.

"Amos," his mother said. "Say the Bedtime *Shema* with me. Let's pray for a miracle for our people. I will teach you. I cannot take the risk of going to the *call* now. Rabbi Halevi will understand."

Finally she had called him Amos. She wanted to pray *with* him. He wished he could tell her he already knew the Bedtime *Shema* because Rabbi Halevi had taught it to him. But he had promised the rabbi he would tell no one about their lessons.

"Yes, Mama. I will pray with you." It took Roca's death to bring him and his mother together to pray. True, they had knelt next to each other countless times in Mass, but that meant little to him now. In the damp cellar, he and his mother chanted the *Shema,* and he pretended to learn it for the first time.

Later that night, he lay sleepless in his childhood bed. Nowhere in Girona seemed safe. The Inquisitors had seized all of Roca's property: his house and of course the shop. He would never again sit at his desk under the window across from Roca. They had stolen the astonishing manuscript about the stars. Perhaps it would never be finished.

He could not believe they had tortured Roca to death, Roca of the huge smile and belly laugh and surprisingly delicate hands. At least Roca and Clara had not been burned. So? Was torture a better way to die? He had entered a world of absurd types of gratitude. The smell of charred flesh clung to the air of Girona, especially along the river banks. He had smelled it tonight as he shoveled earth. He tasted ash in his teeth; he still heard the crowd cheer as the priests sentenced the *conversos.* It was not the first time the Inquisitors had arrested, imprisoned, and torched heretics in Spain, but Uncle Fernando said they had never before done so in such a public manner in Girona. His uncle seemed years older. His cheeks, collapsed and gray, sprouted unshaven hair. His mother sat by the hearth with a vacant expression, her garden neglected. He could do little to contribute. Their only income came from his uncle's binding projects. With Roca dead, the only employment for a scribe in Girona was at the monastery, a choice not open to him.

As much as his family suffered, the people of the *call* must be in terror. While the Church attacked only the *conversos* now, at any moment the Inquisitors could incite a mob against the Jews. The bells tolled midnight from the Cathedral. Still, he lay sleepless. Amos willed himself to rise and journey through the passageway to see his rabbi. But he could not. It had been weeks since he had last studied with Raphael. What little Hebrew he once knew had probably vanished. He no longer wanted to practice making the shapes of the letters with his body. His limbs felt as heavy as the stones in the Tower of Gironella, where his family had been imprisoned one hundred years ago.

Chapter Eighteen

From the air, the shape of Spain resembled a bull's hide staked out in the sun. A jumble of mountains forked in all directions across the Iberian peninsula. Huldah soared over the highest peaks, but she could not escape her sadness, the flames, the cries of the conversos burning.

A line of storks passed, their enormous white wings in motion. She remembered the storks raising their young in the crowns of cypress trees in the Holy Land. Then she had longed to grasp what it meant to be a stork, to wing north and south, to know woodland and desert, swamp and sea and steppe. Now she knew, but she felt alone, without a flock.

She sensed the presence of the rabbi, making another one of his ascents.

"Raphael," she called as he soared through the lighted gate formed by the letter *Hey*. Like him, she rode a letter *Yud* but urged hers toward his with the confidence of a queen mounted on a royal steed. He recognized the voice that had called to him weeks ago.

"What kind of being are you?" he asked the wraith-like female figure, "A demon come to torment me for my transgressions?"

She laughed. "I am no demon, Rabbi, only a human soul. You called for help."

"I was looking for Rabbi Akiva."

She laughed again. "Well, the great Rabbi Akiva is busy. God sent me instead."

"Akiva taught *Torah* at a time like mine. I thought he might understand."

"I know all about Rabbi Akiva. Perhaps I can help, Rabbi. Destiny brings a task for us to complete together."

"Destiny?" He stretched out on his *Yud* to listen. "A task?"

She galloped by him sidesaddle on her *Yud*, spun the letter in circles like a fast horse. "Come, Rabbi. Let me show you something."

Suddenly he longed to rest here on his *Yud*, his urgency forgotten. "Can't I just enjoy this view of the lights of heaven?"

"Prophets don't rest. Sit up. Look ahead." She pointed below. "See the moon, which rules our calendar; it has not abandoned you."

She sped off on her *Yud*, gesturing for him to follow. Clumsily he rode his *Yud*, wobbling from side to side and trying to catch up, his feet dangling into space. God, don't let me fall.

"The moon shines into the darkest of prisons, in the bloodiest massacres of the Crusades," she said as he caught up with her. Together they skimmed low over the moon's plains. He hoped he would not crash on the rocks below. But they touched down gently on the moon's surface and stood on a powdered desert surrounded by low gray hills.

"Look. The earth is your chariot, your *merkavah*." She pointed. A luminescent blue and green sphere rose over the hills, just as the moon rose above Girona. "You might be the first living soul to see this. One day men will walk here and look back at this vision," she said, "in body, not as we are here today."

He stared at its beauty, transfixed.

"Who are you?"

"I am a soul come to speak with you." She shimmered at him, a cloud of light in the shape of a woman. Her voice spoke inside him. The accent sounded foreign.

This is the fate my clumsy ascent has led me to, he thought. He had forgotten to protect himself against inhabitation by demons, as the texts advised.

"What do you want?"

"I wish to inhabit you for a while, to share a prophecy. I believe it will help you in this dire time."

142

"Inhabit me?" If she offered help, he was in no position to refuse.

"As an *Ibbur*. Surely you studied this concept in your Kabbalistic texts."

"Yes. Then you are a high soul."

She bowed her head modestly. "I am only a weasel."

"A weasel?"

"Never mind. Would you allow me?"

"What kind of prophecy?"

"Bring the other man, the one you love. Then I will tell you more."

He covered his face and moaned. She knew his deepest secret.

"Don't be ashamed, Rabbi. The love you have is pure, despite what the tradition says. One day this love will flourish openly. Like the moon, it will no longer be diminished."

He looked away and gazed at the earth, huge on the horizon.

"What do you speak of? How can you know such things?"

"Time is not the same for me here in the stones. This period in history offers much opportunity, despite its dangers. So bring the other man."

"Amos is no Kabbalist. Only a few months ago he returned to our people."

"He loves the letters. He longs for God. Bring him. But first, teach him something of the secrets of the letters and creation."

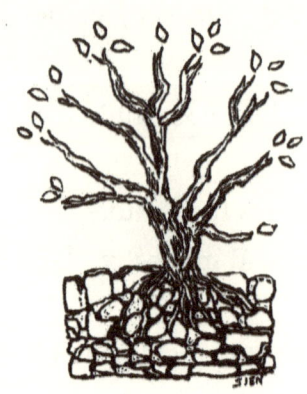

Chapter Nineteen

At last Amos left his mother's house and wound his way through the passages to the *call*. The moon penetrated cracks in the stone walls, which seemed to reach for his flesh. He had felt invincible before Roca's death. Now he trembled as he walked. The stones sighed and moaned, though the night was windless. Tolrana mourned the children she had lost in the Tower of Gironella.

He arrived at the synagogue cold and shaking.

"Rabbi."

The rabbi startled and stood with his arms extended before sinking down again. He looked old, thin. "I've worried about you for weeks." His voice cracked.

Amos stood in the doorway, stricken. The rabbi remained seated.

"They tortured Roca," Amos managed. "He's dead."

"He was like a father to you."

Amos nodded and walked toward the rabbi, arms open.

Raphael held up his hand. "I am relieved to see you. But I must not touch you. It is wrong in more ways than one."

Amos stopped to lean against the wall instead, longing for physical comfort, confused. "Should I leave?"

"Stay," the rabbi said. The moon glowed through the narrow window. "There is a task we must do together. I need you."

"What can I possibly help with?"

"You love the letters."

"Yes."

"They are not just letters. They contain secrets."

"There are already too many secrets in my life. Even the letters are secret from me. I doubt I can remember what you have taught me."

"Oh, you are so young, so new — perhaps you *should* go home," the rabbi sighed.

"No. I cannot go back. I am not the youth you met months ago. Everything is different now."

"Yes. Everything is different." The rabbi released a breath. "Then, please, sit down. There is something I must tell you, Amos. It is strange. I hope I will not frighten you."

"It is not you who frightens me. It is what gathers all around us."

"Perhaps I have discovered some protection. I have agreed to share my body with a spirit who wishes to bring prophecy, to be my *Ibbur*. *Ibburim* are high souls who

145

choose to inhabit an agreeable host for a short time in order to complete an important task that must be accomplished here in the earthly realm."

"What, a demon has possessed you?"

"Not a demon, a benevolent spirit."

"How do you know this spirit means no harm?"

"You must trust me."

"How did this happen?"

"Remember when you discovered me on the floor and could not wake me? That was my first successful ascent. I heard this spirit call me just before you woke me from my trance. This evening I ascended and found her again."

Amos shook his head. "This is a mistake. You can find someone to remove this spirit from you. I know priests can do this. Surely another rabbi—"

"I cannot. She wants the three of us to work on a task."

"She wants to mingle her soul with mine as well?"

"No. I think she needs a scribe."

"But I don't know the letters."

"She promises if you work with us you will immediately speak and write our sacred language."

At that Amos fell silent and sat down by the fire to think. This is what he had wished for: to know Hebrew instantly. This answered his prayers. His language had been stolen from him. But God had heard his prayer and offered this gift in a time of terror that prevented ordinary learning. Amos's eyes rested greedily on the quill on the rabbi's desk, on the books stacked upon the table. Soon he would be able to read these texts.

But perhaps God did not send the *Ibbur*. Perhaps the Devil brought her. Amos's mind flashed on the flaming images of hell depicted in the paintings in the Cathedral and on the robes of the accused. No benevolent spirit would tempt him to make such a pact. The rabbi must be under a spell.

"She wants to help us," the rabbi said. "She says I must teach you the mystical secrets of the letters before you can become our scribe."

"I must consider this carefully."

"But we need to begin tonight. The Inquisitors prepare to burn more *conversos*. There is no time to wait."

"I have to consider this matter."

"Amos, I need you."

Amos walked home pondering. Usually he talked to Uncle Fernando about major decisions. He imagined what his uncle's expression would be if he confided that he was considering making a pact with a spirit so he could write Hebrew. And of course his uncle must not know that he took lessons from the rabbi or that he went to the *call*. His mother was terrified of demons. She did not want him to be a Jew. Besides, he was not a child who turned to his mother.

He could have gone to Roca. He thought again of the stain on Roca's tunic as the Inquisitors had led him away. Roca had always kept himself clean, scrubbed his hands so no ink gathered under his fingernails. They took away his dignity.

"Who is there?" an authoritative voice called. Amos had reached the place where the passage forked. The main passage led under the Onyar River and back to his mother's neighborhood. He could not remember where the narrow one led, though he and Pau had probably explored it when they were boys.

"It's long past curfew, Jew," the voice called.

Amos halted when he saw the bouncing light of a torch. Footsteps approached.

He ducked through spider webs into the smaller passage and pressed himself against a wall. Nearby, water gurgled. Perhaps the river flooded this tunnel. In that case, he would not be able to escape. Something crawled in his hair, probably a spider. He willed himself not to move. A spider bite might not kill him; the Inquisitors would.

The guard stopped nearby. He stank of beer and sweat. Drinking probably helped the man pass the long hours of patrolling this underworld. Amos waited. Something scuttled across the floor. A rat? It sounded large.

"Could have sworn I heard a footstep," he heard the voice mutter.

Perhaps the man talked to keep himself company in the empty passages.

The footsteps finally receded, but Amos waited until the muffled sound of the Cathedral bells told him an hour had passed. For once he felt grateful to those bells for their company. He listened to the water trickle, the rats scuffle. He felt cold and numb. This must be what it was like to be dead, buried under the ground. He was young, but he might not have long to walk this earth. He didn't have time to learn Hebrew through ordinary methods. He would make a pact with the demon and attain his dream. Besides, he could not deny the rabbi his help. Raphael risked so much for him.

Amos arrived at the rabbi's study the next evening just before midnight. His breath came hard from hurrying, and his face looked pinched. He blurted out, "Tell me now. Tell me the secrets of the letters."

"Amos. Has something happened?"

He did not want to alarm the rabbi by telling him of his narrow escape from the guard the previous evening. If he did, perhaps the rabbi would no longer permit him to come.

"No, Rabbi. The times terrify me."

"This is why we must do this work together. There is no time to waste. Come. Sit at my desk, Amos. Let me pour us both some wine." The rabbi had never offered Amos wine before. Raphael's face reddened as he drank. He rose and paced around the study. Amos watched. The rabbi seemed frantic too. Words rushed from his throat.

"*Baruch she'amar vehayah ha'olam. Blessed be the One who speaks the world into being each day through the twenty-two letters. Their shapes represent the paths of creation.*"

Amos sipped wine. This much he knew: he had stood straight and tall as a *Vav*, with the strength of the earth holding him. He remembered how calm he had felt, how steady the rabbi had seemed when he had taught him this pose. Now the rabbi's eyes fluttered as he ventured to teach Amos the secrets of Kabbalah in one night.

"*Olam*, the heavens and the earth; *Shanah*, time; and *Nefesh*, soul, are created and re-created through the sound of the twenty-two letters of the Hebrew alphabet. All of this was recorded long ago in the *Sefer Yetzirah*, a book written in the time of Abraham, brought forward by my beloved Rabbi Akiva, and then refined by the famous Kabbalists who walked these streets in Girona, who breathed letters in this very room."

The rabbi had told him about Rabbi Azriel, about Nachmanides. Maybe their spirits listened now.

"This is enough. As the Kabbalists have taught, I will soon chant the name of God and open the gates of heaven for us. But first—" The rabbi slumped down into his chair and dropped his head between his knees.

"Rabbi?"

The rabbi pulled his head up from between his knees and stared as if he didn't know how Amos had appeared in his study. "Oh, yes. I'm waiting."

"Waiting for what?"

"For the *Ibbur*. She told me that you would come tonight, that we could begin. She seems to know the future. Ah, yes." The rabbi breathed deeply and stroked his Adam's apple. "I feel her right here."

Amos fought an urge to run out of the room.

"On the desk is a scroll of parchment and a newly carved quill," the rabbi said. "Take them." He got up off his stool and stretched out on the floor.

Amos picked up the quill and filled it with ink. His hand trembled.

The rabbi began to chant the name of God — *Yud-Hey-Vav-Hey, Y-H-V-H, Y-H-V-H* over and over, his voice suddenly confident. Amos's breath rose and fell in the same rhythms. The rabbi added the letters for *adamah*, earth — *Aleph, Dalet, Mem, Hey*, in endless permutations. The letters of creation whirled through the moonlit room.

I do love the letters, Amos thought. Beneath the chanting, Amos felt the rabbi's breath and his own breath synchronize. He picked up his quill as the rabbi began to speak.

Rabbi Halevi spoke in a voice no longer his own, a melodic tenor. His facial features softened. Amos stared at the *Ibbur*, fascinated and horrified. He dropped his quill. Ink spilled on the stone floor.

"Good, Rabbi. I see you brought the scribe. Scribe, I trust this is not too frightening."

Amos opened his mouth to speak but discovered he had no voice. He shook his head.

"Very well. The scribe is speechless. Let us hope he can still write. Please have a better grip on your quill this time, Scribe."

He knew this voice. It was the spirit inside the stone wall behind the synagogue. "It's you!"

The rabbi gaped at Amos and said in his own voice, "You know this spirit?"

"Yes, she once told me she was the voice of God."

"I never said any such thing," the *Ibbur* laughed. "You thought God spoke to you directly."

"But you seemed to know everything about me," Amos protested.

"I am fond of you, Scribe," said the *Ibbur*. "You remind me of my son, whom I have not seen in many centuries. But we have work to do. The task we must complete is urgent."

"And I will be able to write in Hebrew?" Amos asked.

"If you allow your hand to trust me, I will speak through it in the Holy Tongue. May we begin?"

"I am ready," Amos said, his hand poised above the scroll.

"I come to you from the World of Prophecy. It is not easy. I feel unwell. What a dense realm. I had forgotten how it feels to live in a body, to walk upon the earth with heavy limbs and constant hunger. But I speak to you with great anticipation. I waited hundreds of years in the stones to introduce this prophecy, and I believe you are the two souls who can help me bring it into your Kabbalah. It must be written down before our people are exiled from this land."

The Jews will be exiled? thought Amos. He dared not interrupt. Still, the *Ibbur* read his thoughts.

"Yes. The time of exile draws near."

"Will we survive that exile?" Raphael asked.

"The knowledge of the Kabbalists will survive, even flourish for a few hundred years," the *Ibbur* prophesized. "The great lineage—the lineage of Isaac the Blind, Nachmanides and the other wise ones—will travel with your people when you leave Spain. At times it will be submerged. For centuries many people will believe everything important is material and nothing else can be trusted." The rabbi shook his head. "No corner of the earth will go untrammeled. Even the moon will be scarred by garbage."

Amos wrote fluidly, joyfully. The holy language flowed from his quill as if he had known it since boyhood. He could write in Hebrew. He was finally a Jew.

"First, you must come to where I lived long ago. I want you to know me, the woman I once was."

As Raphael's *Ibbur*, Huldah could share her memories with the rabbi as if he had been with her in Jerusalem over two millennia ago. They ascended through the roof of the synagogue into the clouds over Girona and then sped across the ocean to the Holy Land, to Jerusalem. Raphael narrated what he saw and Amos recorded it on the scroll.

Huldah had found her cousin Jeremiah in the market, preaching in his usual place near the wine merchants. "Yes, Adonai has also sent me visions of the coming destruction," he had confirmed.

Huldah had stared at the wooden yoke chafing his neck. For her cousin, prophecy offered a kind of delicious agony. It overtook him like a fever.

"We have forsaken the law against idol worship," her cousin had warned. "Adonai will punish us. When the city of Jerusalem is destroyed, our enemies will put a yoke of iron around our necks. In my visions, a pot boils, facing away from the north. Out of the north, evil shall break forth upon all of the inhabitants of the land. 'I am calling all the tribes of the kingdoms of the north,' Adonai has told me. 'And they shall come and every one shall set his throne at the entrance of the gates of Jerusalem, against all its walls around about, and against all the cities of Judah. I will utter my judgments against them, for all their wickedness in forsaking Me; they have burned incense to other gods and worshipped the works of their own hands.'

"Huldah," he had glowered, forgetting for a moment she was his beloved elder cousin, "I know you burn incense to Asherah. You must cease visiting her groves and teaching your students her ways. You cannot be a prophet of Adonai and teach here in His Temple and also worship at her leafy shrines."

"You know I will never forsake Her," Huldah had replied, looking into her cousin's exhausted eyes. "It is not the people's love for Asherah that dooms us to exile from this city."

"Then what must we do to return to the path of righteousness?"

"It is justice we must serve. No woman, no child, no man should go hungry in this land. We must care for the widow and the orphan. Then Adonai will find us worthy. And so will Asherah."

"It is true we must serve justice. But it is Adonai alone we should revere."

Huldah had looked at her cousin, at his matted hair and his worn sandals covered in dust. There seemed no sense in arguing with him. He was too thin. "Come have dinner with Shallum and me tonight. Let us study together. I'll serve warm bread and stew."

"No. King Josiah asked me to visit the Jewish exiles in Assyria, where they suffer in captivity. I must leave immediately and tell them Adonai has not forsaken them." Jeremiah had stridden away from Huldah without saying farewell, his head down.

Huldah had walked toward the Temple, watched a column of smoke rise from the sacrificed animals. Four hundred years ago, King Solomon had built this House of Adonai. His workmen had constructed a room of cedars from Lebanon, a place to hold the Holy of Holies, the Ark of the Covenant that had cradled the Tablets of the Law Moses had brought from Mount Sinai and the Bnei Yisrael had carried as they had wandered in the wilderness. She had longed to see and touch those stone tablets sequestered in the Holy of Holies, a room she, along with most of the Bnei Yisrael, could not enter. She had studied and taught Torah at her school by the Temple's southern gate. She loved words. Words were holy vessels.

She had reached the Temple courtyard and rested under a palm tree, still thinking about her cousin's prophecies. On the imminent destruction of Jerusalem they agreed. Nearby stood the great basin of water representing the primordial sea. It was held by twelve majestic bronze bulls. She had touched the silver *amulet hanging around her neck. It contained the priestly bless-ing of Aaron: "May the Lord bless you and watch over you. May the Lord make his face shine upon you and grant you peace."*

The first ascent went on most of the night. Amos's hand grew tired, but he did not stop. He covered a long piece of parchment with Huldah's story.

Chapter Twenty

Raphael's dreams were no longer his own.

Huldah had left Jerusalem and walked across the valley of Kidron, past the meadows where her students collected sage, rosemary, and other herbs used to cure their husbands and children. The scent of mint wafted from where gazelle stirred the ground. In the spring, pink cyclamen spread their crowns here and poppies poked through grass.

She had climbed past an olive orchard near a buzzing earthenware beehive. The old farmer had nodded his greeting, though he had not interrupted his work of beating the branches to gather the harvest, sending silver leaves spiraling into the air.

Huldah had passed another grove of terebinth trees and thought of what terebinths knew about her people. Long ago, at Mamre, near Hebron, Abraham pitched his tent under terebinth trees. One hot day he sat at the entrance to his tent. Three angels appeared. He thought they were men. He offered them water, bathed their feet, and called into the tent for Sarah to make them cakes of flour. The angels rested under the terebinth trees and ate the cakes. Then they predicted that Sarah, even though she was old, would have a child. Sarah laughed.

Huldah had reached a tower of dark basalt and scrambled up the rocks until she had peered into a deep mouth, a dry cave in the cliff. She had crawled into the cave and mourned for Jerusalem. Far below her, the Dead Sea shimmered. Heavy clouds gathered around, growling. The first rain of the year had been approaching.

One night a stork flew through Raphael's bedroom and deposited a feather on the floor. Another morning his sleeping cloak smelled of sage and unfamiliar herbs. But Huldah had not yet revealed her prophecy. She had said he and Amos needed further preparation before they would understand what she had to tell them. She had spoken of the future and assured him that the traditions of the mystics would endure. But *how* were his people to bring Kabbalah out of Spain? He looked at the dozens of sacred texts stacked on his table. He must save these books. He would ascend and ask her advice.

"That is where you are mistaken," he heard Huldah's familiar voice say. He looked around the room for her.

"You need not make elaborate ascents to speak with me, Rabbi. I am always inside of you. The letters are necessary for you, not for me."

"I can't see you."

"I don't feel like creating an apparition for you today. I am losing patience with you, Rabbi. Why do you continue to deny the love between you and this sweet scribe? You believe your written *Torah* instead of the *torah* of your heart."

"It is dangerous."

"To be a Jew is dangerous. To teach *conversos* is dangerous. Yet you continue to be a Jew and you continue to teach the *conversos*. But you lack the courage to touch this man, even though he has touched your soul."

"I am a rabbi. I must teach and be who I am. I believe in the *Torah*, our sacred law. Love between men is forbidden by this tradition."

"The tradition evolves. Sometimes this love is forbidden; sometimes it is not such a problem. Remember the poetry of your ancestor Judah Halevi, whose poems sing of both God and his love for men. He longed for Zion, lamented his people's suffering during the Crusades, wove together the past and the present in his writing. He loved men and women and did not see this as a contradiction with his faith. You should be proud to be his descendant; don't conceal his book at the bottom of a pile."

"How do you know I hide his poetry?"

"Oh, Raphael Halevi of Girona, there is little I do not know about you, as your soul now intertwines with mine. However, that does not mean I understand your fears or why you persist in denying what you feel."

"Amos is young enough to be my son. He looks to me as to a father, especially because his own died so young. A rabbi should not ask for private affection from his student."

"Perhaps. But Amos is your equal. He is a grown man, not a boy. He has much courage and a gift for language. You and Amos expand the possibilities in your world, open the narrow places that constrict our people. This is part of the prophecy we will bring forth together."

"To be a prophet one must deny the body," Raphael argued.

"Those who think prophecy requires repression of the body are misled by the Greeks."

"You call Maimonides a fool?"

"Maimonides was wise, but about this he followed the wrong path. He was a man of his time. Your beloved Nachmanides criticized Maimonides on this point. We talked about it one night."

"You knew Nachmanides?"

"Not well. But we once enjoyed a delicious discussion in this very room. He put his hands right there, on that wall." She remained quiet for so long Raphael thought she had left him again. He gazed at the wall Nachmanides had touched.

"There is profound wisdom hidden in the body," Huldah finally continued. "The body, the senses, are a *merkavah*, a chariot to be cherished, just like the earth I showed you from the moon. Do not deny your body or the earth it stands on." He felt a light touch on his shoulder and jumped. "Oh, your arm is nothing but skin and bones. The women of the *aljama* love to feed you. Why do you deny your flesh? You cannot live on hard bread alone. I want to enjoy food, even if you do not. Your community may be poor and hemmed in, but surely there must be something to eat: eggs, milk, chard from the garden."

For centuries she had lived in the stones, a human spirit released from the limitations of human existence but denied sensory pleasure. Now she was an Ibbur. *But this rabbi spent all his time indoors, far from the comfort of honeybees and sunlit water. And he rarely ate. She missed having her own body.*

"I no longer find comfort in the physical," Raphael admitted. "Each week the Inquisitors tighten their grip. My sweat stinks. Your presence makes me feel strange and heavy. You have lived a long time without food. I'm sure you don't need it. Better we forget this body. My desires only lead me into trouble."

She remained quiet.

"I liked it better when you showed me how to soar, to commune with the heavenly bodies. Amos could come there with us."

"His faithful pen records what I say. He writes dutifully but sits there longing. He wants you to love him."

"Father?"

The front door of the synagogue opened, interrupting their conversation.

Miriam entered the room carrying a loaf of bread. Snow clung to her frayed woolen cloak. How thin she appeared. Raphael wondered how he had not noticed this before.

God, forgive me. I must pray for the health of my daughter. Winter has not even begun.

Miriam looked around the room, confused. "I heard you talking. Who were you speaking with, Father?"

"I was praying."

"Father, I had another dream." Miriam sat down at the table, still in her snow-flecked cloak, shivering. "Jonas says it means nothing; it is only a sign of my fears."

"Tell me," Raphael urged. Her face, though gaunt, looked luminous. He understood why the women were drawn to her. "You should not bear such dreams alone."

"I dreamt the *call* was deserted. The stone buildings remained, but only empty cavities showed where the *mezuzot* had been pried from our doorposts." Her voice broke. "The *Torah* scroll had disappeared from the ark."

The rabbi lowered his head and sat in silence with his daughter.

"Something even worse. Our gravestones. They—" Miriam swallowed and could not continue for a moment. "They were desecrated, stolen and used for ordinary buildings. I saw one overturned in a courtyard garden. Small fish swam in the hollow once sheltering the bones of Joan Reuben."

Raphael looked at his daughter. He wanted to comfort her, but her visions probably told the awful truth. She deserved his honesty. "You know what this means."

She nodded.

"We are to leave this place, Miriam. Only God knows what will become of us and of the graves of our ancestors. But perhaps all will not be lost," he mused.

She was quiet; then she asked, "Who is that man you study with under the moon?"

What could he tell her?

Miriam interrupted his silence, "Then it's true. I could not believe it, though my divinations do not lie. It is true."

"His name is Amos. He is one of the lost ones, the son of Caterina."

She nodded. She knew Caterina, knew all the *conversos* who came to the *call*.

He tried to explain, but Miriam put her finger on her lips.

"How can you take such risks?"

His daughter was right.

He cut Miriam a slice of bread and handed it to her. "Amos is my student and my scribe. We have a task to do together, something I cannot tell you about."

"Secrets from me?" Miriam burst out. "I thought we kept no secrets from each other. I bring you soup. I clean the fleas from your bed. I'm like a wife to you. Why don't you find a wife, someone who can care for you *and* keep your secrets?"

"You have a husband. I don't need—"

"Who would do it then?" Miriam still held the scrap of bread in her palm, forgotten. "Who will cook, clean for you, mend your cloaks? Oh, I wish my mother were alive."

"Miriam, you are a good daughter. Perhaps Doña Falco can help with these things, even though she has a family. Yes, I see it is too much for you. You are a grown woman with a husband. You will soon, God willing, have a family of your own."

At that, Miriam fell silent.

He smiled. "Be patient. It took a while with your mother. Pray every day that God will give you a child."

"Father, be careful. The Inquisitors know you have taught *conversos* in the past."

"Shush." Raphael looked at her as he had when she was a child. "God will protect me. I do his holy work."

"I lost Mama. I can't lose you too."

After Miriam left, Raphael returned to his desk. Huldah chafed inside him, insisted on his attention. "So now you have denied your love for Amos to your daughter. Coward," she chided. "How will you ever become a prophet?"

"Oh, why do I bother with you?" Raphael exploded. "You aren't helping me save my people. You speak of possible futures and love between two men. Such prophecies are of no use as the good Christians of Girona light pyres. I soar through the heavens while my people starve. Go away. Leave me in peace."

"So you can look for your beloved Rabbi Akiva? We're not done yet. I still haven't given you the prophecy that must be brought into this realm. I hope it will make a difference."

He felt frightened. Would he be able to refuse her anything?

"Rabbi, I'm sorry. I must be more patient. Change takes place slowly in the physical world. When I have transmitted the prophecy, I promise I will depart. I do not desire to remain within you."

Now her shape billowed in the corner among his books. Or perhaps it was only his tired eyes. Yes, he could see her now — a cloud of light in front of the hearth. She created her apparition. She must have forgiven him.

She spun his tomes through the air.

"Careful," he called as she bounced Nachmanides' *Book of Redemption* toward the ceiling. "Those wise mystics taught me how to find you."

At that she pushed the entire stack onto the floor and swirled in circles over the pile.

"What are you doing? The books will be damaged."

She stopped playing with him. Here spoke the grave spirit who soared in the heavens, the prophet who saw beyond this time. "These are the words of men. Where are the words of women?"

He was silent. Finally he ventured, "There are stories of women: Sarah, Rachel, Leah, Judith, Esther —"

She darted across the room and hovered over him, shone her light directly into his eyes. Too bright, too much. He covered his face. "Stop."

"Words *by* women! Not these distorted tales about women as seen through the eyes of men," she hissed. "I thought you were different from the others. You taught your daughter well."

"My daughter had a terrible dream."

"Yes. I sent her this dream." Huldah swooped back across the room to hover above the books and scrolls scattered across the floor.

"Miriam knows you?" He had thought he was the only one who conversed with this spirit. But both Amos and Miriam had encountered her, though not as an *Ibbur*.

"She knows only the dreams, never the source. A powerful woman, your daughter. I enjoy hearing her thoughts in the *mikvah*. She is of my spiritual lineage. Pity you will not let her read the mystics. But she has no need of arcane formulas and diagrams. A simple drop of oil will work for her, or a glass of water."

"Why come to me when you have my daughter?"

"What I have to say must be written so it survives into the future. The writings of a woman do not yet earn respect. So, where is the scribe?"

"He will return tonight."

"Then we must wait. Much remains to tell you both."

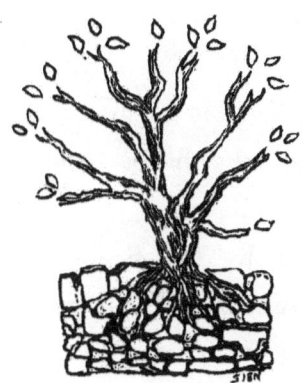

Chapter Twenty-One

Y ou are late. Huldah asked for you!" the rabbi said anxiously when he arrived.

Amos looked at Raphael with his longing eyes.

Raphael stepped forward to embrace Amos.

Amos tried to linger in Raphael's arms, but soon Raphael gently pulled away. Amos stood by himself, his face full of sadness. He was proud to serve Raphael and Huldah as a scribe. Writing in Hebrew was a tremendous gift. But this situation inflamed other desires he wished he did not feel.

The rabbi's blue eyes were large and bloodshot in his bony face as he began to speak in Huldah's voice.

"There is something missing in your Kabbalah," Huldah said. Amos wrote quickly. "A problematic metaphor," she continued. Amos bent over the vellum and tried to concentrate. Spit trailed down the rabbi's beard. Amos wanted to wipe it off but he was afraid to touch him. He felt troubled. Huldah inhabited the rabbi's body more and more fully. After each of these scribal sessions, the rabbi's voice sounded higher. He even smelled different. Amos could swear he smelled of herbs, though he knew the rabbi rarely left the *call*.

Huldah continued. "The *Bahir* first called the *Shekhinah* the Divine Feminine. But this merely reflected human desires. There are other metaphors. Read the *Torah*. There we learn of the seven clouds of glory that followed the Israelites in the desert, God's presence in the physical world, protecting the people. I have always liked that image of clouds filled with light, water, and fragments of earth, ever-shifting clouds transforming into the shapes of animals, faces, doorways, and mountains suspended halfway between heaven and earth.

"So my problem is not with the *Torah*, which speaks of God's Oneness, but with the Kabbalists, who speak of Adonai and his *Shekhinah* and of their unification as *yichud*. This is only a partial conceptualization of *yichud*. The mystic experiences the oneness of all creation. Creation is much more than two. It spins a web between stones and trees, stars and drops of water, lions and deer, even between the myriad invisible creatures inhabiting the soil. It is this complex vision of *yichud* we must come to understand. We need to shed these human images of the Divine that rely on divisions between what is considered masculine and what is considered feminine." She paused. "Scribe, I trust you have written all of this?"

Amos nodded.

She spoke directly to him for the first time since he had dropped his quill: "Scribe, your courage to love those of your sex is a form of desire that is interconnected with the bringing forth of this prophecy: a prophecy of a broader kind of *yichud* not based on metaphors of sexual union between men and women. And your longing for God is a desire intensified because Judaism is hidden from you. Your longings are part of the Divine light concealed in the everyday world. They pour onto the scroll in every letter you inscribe."

He stopped writing. "I—why are you talking to me?" Witnessing Huldah speaking positively of love between men through the mouth of the rabbi disturbed him. But she knew so much about him—his longing for God, his longing for Raphael.

"You are a man who does not let fear of his desires, or of his tears, define him. I applaud your bravery," Huldah continued.

Amos looked down at the scroll, which blurred under his gaze. It made no difference. The rabbi would never change his mind because of Huldah's approval. Nor would Amos ever become a real Jew. Neither of his longings would be gratified. I am a good scribe, thought Amos. I provide skilled hands to record Huldah's prophecies. But I cannot attend a Shabbat service because it is too dangerous for me to be seen. I should not deceive myself. I will never be enfolded into this community. My very presence in the *call* remains a secret, as is my attraction to Raphael.

That night, as Amos rounded a corner of the passageway near the outer edge of the *call*, a thin hand grabbed his arm. He looked into Pau's stunned face.

"I knew it. I knew you came here."

"Pau! Let go. You're bruising me."

Pau dropped his hand but hissed, "You're a Jew. I've suspected this since we were boys. I hoped it was not true. People speak rumors about your family. I did not want to believe them because I cared about you so much. Well, I am glad you did not marry my sister."

"Pau, you are my closest friend. I'm—"

"Such close friends? You haven't talked to me in months. When did we last walk through the valley or share a meal? I haven't seen you since the *auto-de-fe*."

Amos put his hand on Pau's familiar arm. "I'm sorry, old friend. There is much I cannot tell you."

"Did your beloved Roca know about your night in the oak grove with the rabbi?"

Amos stared at him.

Pau examined Amos in silence. Then his expression softened and he said more calmly, "You must stop going to the *call* at night, Domingo. If you don't, something terrible will happen. The Inquisitors are serious about purification of Spanish blood. Father Hidalgo says I must—"

"Inquisitors cannot come between us, Pau. Times will change. It will not matter."

Pau shook his head. "I don't want us to be so different, you a Jew, me a priest. I've known you all my life. I can't bear this. I need—" Pau looked into his friend's sorrowful eyes and his anger blew away. He felt only a desire to be close to Domingo once more, to revive their boyhood passion. He leaned over and kissed Domingo on the mouth and then urged him into a nearby side passage. They lay together. Domingo felt relieved, but he was sad that they could never return to the love they had once shared. This lovemaking was but a ghost, a shadow of boyhood.

Domingo returned home just before dawn, his eyes gritty with exhaustion. He crawled into bed and heard Huldah's voice: "Your longing is part of the Divine light concealed in the everyday world. It pours onto the scroll in every letter you inscribe."

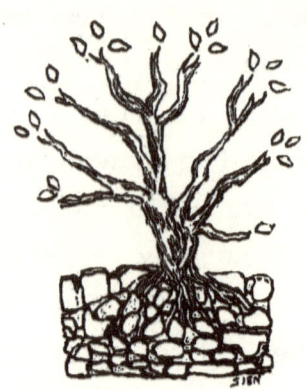

Chapter Twenty-Two

How could she explain yichud — unification with all of creation, all time, *l'olam va'ed?* She tried, but the rabbi had not understood her. *Yichud* was so much more than what happened between two human beings, whether they were men and women joining bodies, two men, or two women. The Kabbalists described *yichud* through human eyes informed by the sexual conventions of their time. Through the stones she understood the interconnectedness of all creation. She would take the rabbi into the stones. He would comprehend everything. Her prophecy would be complete.

"Take my hand, Rabbi," Huldah invited. As they rose, Raphael looked down and was shocked to see his wasted body. Amos sat bent over the desk, his quill in his hand.

Higher, higher they drifted, until they penetrated the stones of the synagogue. He expected to pass through the ceiling into the night sky over Girona, but they entered a cavern filled with light. "Watch out," Huldah warned. A current of silvery Hebrew letters streamed past. "Don't touch them, not even by accident. Prayers must travel directly through stone to God."

"Where are we?"

"Inside stone. I must show you something before it is too late. I believe time is running out."

"On that point we agree."

Raphael and Huldah sailed through the cavern on a steady wind, a wind unlike any Raphael had experienced before: warm, invigorating. He felt more awake than he had in years. He smiled. "Why do I feel so well?"

"We bask in *ruach*, the breath of God. One must swim in these currents to receive prophecy. We are lucky they are mild today."

Waves of sound bounced around the cavern. "May Adonai remember my mother. God, forgive me. *Shema Yisrael Adonai—*"

"Hold tight to my hand. I don't want to lose your spirit here. I'm not sure how strong the bond of *Ibbur* is in this realm."

"Did you get permission to bring me here?"

"Don't ask impertinent questions. Sometimes prophets must take shortcuts. Aren't you the rabbi who seeks adventure? Maybe we'll find Rabbi Akiva."

"Don't tease me." He gripped Huldah's hand. The cavern narrowed; the ceiling lowered. Raphael and Huldah stood on a cobblestone floor in a pool of blue light. "Where are we now?"

"We stand in *Yetzirah*, the realm of the messengers, those of us who transmit the speech of God. This is the sphere of dreams, of creativity, of myth, of archetype, the place where sacred letters form, where angels appear."

"Angels. Will I see them?"

"Oh, I'm sure Gabriel knows we are here, or she would not have let us pass."

"Gabriel, she?"

"She, he—who knows? The Angel Gabriel is neither man nor woman. He cradles me upon his muscular breasts; she sings to me in her sweet baritone."

"Truly bizarre," Raphael murmured.

"This place may seem strange to you as well, but you know it. You dwell here between lives. You just don't remember."

It looks like the streets of the *call*, Raphael mused. Beyond where they stood, wide steps led upward through a twisting corridor and vanished in mist. The air chilled.

"Perhaps we've traveled far enough." Raphael tugged on Huldah's hand.

"Shush," she hissed. "Don't be afraid. Think of your predecessors, the hallowed Isaac the Blind, Nachmanides. How would they feel if you turned back now, Rabbi? How will you live with yourself if you refuse prophecy?"

"I am a novice, a coward. I don't deserve prophecy." He imagined Amos trying to wake him from this deep a trance. As Huldah pulled him up the flat stones into the mist, he tried to calm himself by counting the steps. On the eighteenth step Huldah stopped in front of a smooth wall of rock.

"*Yud. Hey. Vav. Hey.*" Huldah began to chant. "*Yud. Hey. Vav. Hey.*"

"I thought you had no need of letters."

"Quiet," Huldah ordered, and she continued to chant.

Raphael heard his own voice, weak at first and then stronger, join in.

"That's it," Huldah encouraged him, and she squeezed his hand. Raphael realized that the beat of his heart served as the metronome for this chant. The granite split and they peered through an archway to even bluer light beyond.

"What lies through that gate?"

"The light of *Beriyah*: the world of thought, of creation, of revelation. It is beyond speech. This is where we will go to understand *yichud*."

"Why me?" Raphael's legs shook. "Why choose me to receive this prophecy?"

"Girona is one birthplace of Kabbalah. The gate between worlds stands open within the stones of your synagogue. I found you through that gate. You did your part to find me, clumsy as your meditations were. But there is another reason I chose you to receive this truth, the most important reason of all: Amos."

The rabbi's eyes stung from the sulfur vapors wafting into the cavern from *Beriyah*.

"Rabbi?"

He rubbed his eyes and saw Amos standing across the cavern in the yellow mist, looking terrified.

"Rabbi, where are we?"

Raphael spoke to Huldah. "You brought him here. It's too dangerous. How dare you?"

"I swear I did not bring him. Amos's longing transported him through the stones to us."

"He does not know the permutations of the letters, how to ascend."

"Longing is enough. You don't need—"

Amos came closer and broke into their argument. "I sat at my desk and recorded your journey," he said to the rabbi. "But much more time went by than usual. Your face looked white and gaunt. I stared at you as you croaked these prophecies; I feared for you. Next thing I knew, I stood here with you. Rabbi," he asked again, "What is this place? It smells like sulfur. This scares me. Are we in hell?"

"No, Amos. This isn't hell. It is only the scent of the stones as they breathe," Raphael said as he walked over to Amos and embraced him.

Huldah hovered nearby, nervous because she no longer held the rabbi's hand.

Then Raphael kissed Amos on the mouth. It was safe. No one could see them, no one but Huldah. Here, no one would kill them for this desire.

Amos returned Raphael's kiss, his breath deepening. Raphael's lips were chapped but still sensuous. Amos moved his lips to Raphael's neck.

Huldah watched like a jubilant matchmaker. She waited as long as she could and then said, "You desire union not based on the coupling of a man and a woman."

Must she state the obvious? Amos lifted his face from Raphael's neck to stare at Huldah in irritation. "Clearly, we do. Must you persist in sharing your prophecy even now?"

"I am sorry, Scribe. I know how long you have dreamt of this moment. But we have work to do. I am not sure how long we may safely remain in this realm."

Amos shook his head.

Raphael looked as if he were in a daze. He touched his lips. Although he had left his body on the floor of his study, he tasted Amos's mouth as though they had touched each other in the physical world.

"Very well," Amos sighed. "Let us continue. I transported part of my spirit here, but my hands remain poised over the scroll in the study, awaiting your words."

Huldah looked at Amos gratefully.

Raphael stirred from his daze to ask, "Does your prophecy call for the return of Asherah as the wife of Adonai?"

"I did love Asherah," Huldah sighed. "But she remained a human-centered idea of God, as is Adonai, the Lord. Once I dwelled in the stones I understood that these human conceptions of the Divine as husband and wife have limitations. But I am challenged to describe a theology of *yichud* that articulates the ever-unfolding interactions between and within the web of creation, even within the stones you think have no consciousness. I must admit it may be beyond my powers of language to express. Perhaps this is because I am no longer embodied. You both love words. I thought if I took you into *Beriyah*, you could describe this experience on the scroll. Your love unlocks the gates of prophecy. So come. Let us walk through the archway and experience creation as *yichud*."

Raphael, Amos, and Huldah moved through the opening in the rock and into the aqua light beyond. Shapes pulsed around them, trailing threads of light, as if the three of them swam in the half-lit latitudes of the sea. Then the cavern vanished and they entered a grove of gnarled trees. To their right stood a large vertical stone and a bowl smoking with incense. Raphael recognized the shrine of Asherah from Huldah's memories. He looked up. A white bird watched them from a high branch.

"A stork. Don't be afraid. They are magical birds. They carry prophecy. We have returned to that long-ago shrine of Asherah on the Mount of Olives, so you can understand *yichud* through the sacredness of the earth. These terebinths root in soil formed of small particles of stone, enriched by worms and thousands of other creatures. A handful of soil teems with countless tiny animals feasting on the red and yellow leaves shed by the terebinth, the flesh of a gazelle killed in this grove last summer by a hungry young leopard, and even the withered pink flowers of cyclamen. Below the surface, hairy roots of the terebinths intertwine and share root systems, thereby feeding each other. Amos, the mushrooms you search for in the forest are the fruits of a vast underground network living on tree roots, feeding trees. In turn, the trees sustain the mushrooms. Other things related to mushrooms help produce beer and bread, cheese and wine. Creation interacts with itself, mingles and transforms. Raphael, you are thinking, where is spirit in all this?"

"Yes," replied the rabbi. "Where is spirit?"

"Woven into all of creation is spirit, for the world is ensouled. I am your *Ibbur*. We share a body. Most living souls do not share one body but are still interwoven, intertwined, just as tree roots mingle, just as mushrooms and trees nurture each other. And the dead are not really dead. Ask your daughter. She senses the individual soul sparks of departed ancestors in the bodies of those who now walk the streets of the *call*, even sometimes in the fish you eat. Your bodies and the bodies of all creatures on earth are composed of the dust of ancient stars. Minerals in your blood formed inside the core of a star. Consciousness is the ghost of an ancient star, contemplating itself after thirteen billion years."

Amos remembered Ptolemy's map of the constellations and the dozens of meticulous diagrams describing the motion of the spheres. He had faithfully redrawn those illustrations in the margins of the book. How he had labored over that project. Now, as he listened to Huldah, those schematics animated themselves, and just for a moment he felt the heavens move and threads of light connect him to the stars. If only he could return to Roca's shop and examine the *Almagest*. Now he would understand what he had copied. But Inquisitors had stolen both the master document and the unfinished book.

"Enough talking," Huldah said. "I must be aware of my tendency to pontificate. Long ago my students criticized me for this. We are here so you can receive this prophecy directly, record it on the scroll in your own words, share these ideas with the world, and live them by loving each other. Amos and Raphael, please lie down on the earth close together and journey into the soil. This is *yichud*, the prophecy urgently needed in this time of hatred and separation."

Amos stared at Huldah in disbelief. "This is your prophecy, to show us the invisible creatures that make beer and cheese, to bury us alive in the soil amid the mushrooms?" He laughed. "I am sorry, but I must respectfully refuse. The black passageways beneath the *call* are quite enough of an underworld experience. I should like to lie down with Raphael but not—"

"No!" Raphael interrupted. He dropped Amos's hand and backed away from the shrine. "Enough. I cannot go further. I cannot accept this prophecy. I purify myself in the *mikvah* every morning. I do not touch Amos. I must never touch him again." He looked wildly around the grove for someone to rescue him. "This prophecy about *yichud* will not save my people. For too long I have gone on these journeys with you, while outside the synagogue our elders die, our children fall ill. Take us home, Huldah. I only want a prophecy that will save my people from destruction."

"But—this is our destiny, the prophecy I promised you. The soil is but one illustration. I admit my choice of voyages may not appeal to human beings, who fear death. Once again I forgot what it means to reside in a body. We shall find a less frightening journey for you to take; let's say we follow the web connecting an owl to the light of the sun—"

"No," Raphael repeated. "I am not interested in stardust, owls, or worms right now. I am concerned with the health of my people."

"But this prophecy of *yichud*, of the sacred unity of all creation, if truly understood, would render the Inquisition impossible."

"Perhaps, Huldah," replied the rabbi more calmly. "But it's too late for words on a scroll to save the Jews or the *conversos*. Take us back."

Amos stood looking sadly back and forth between Raphael and Huldah. He could still feel the softness of Raphael's beard. He would remember that one kiss for the rest of his life.

As Huldah and the rabbi argued, the shrine in the grove dissolved. Soon they were back in the cavern and then in front of the cleft in the rock, which sutured itself into a mere scratch in a smooth wall of granite. Huldah pressed herself against the rock, silent, morose.

"Huldah, it is not your fault," the rabbi ventured after a few moments. "It is I who have confused talking to you with praying to God. It is my lack of faith."

"Very well, Rabbi," Huldah sighed. "Pray to Adonai. See what your prayer can do for you."

She extricated herself from the wall and stood between Raphael and Amos, holding each of their hands. They retraced their steps in silence through the passageway in the stones and finally into the synagogue.

Raphael's body ached from what had taken place: a battle of two souls inhabiting one body. He moaned on the floor. Amos massaged his ink-stained fingers and glanced at the parchment on his desk. Next to columns of new words, he had drawn a sphere rising above a horizon of gray hills.

"Whatever is that?" the rabbi asked, sitting up painfully to examine the parchment.

"It came into my head during the night. It reminds me a little of Ptolemy's *Almagest*. What do you think?"

Raphael felt faint. Perhaps if he ate something he could concentrate on Amos's drawing. "Amos, let's have a little bread and cheese."

Amos tore off a piece of bread, salted it, and handed it to the rabbi. "Did you eat any supper before I came? You should consume more than a slice of bread and a nibble of cheese. You looked ghastly during this ascent. I was worried about you. Why were you gone so long?"

Raphael stared at him. Amos seemed to have forgotten his journey through the stones. Did he remember the kiss?

"I believe Huldah and I are finished, Amos. She cannot help us in our predicament." The rabbi lay weakly back on the floor and gazed up at the rough ceiling of the synagogue, the stones through which they had traveled. When he closed his eyes, Raphael saw aquamarine light pouring through a cleft in rock. Aged terebinth trees surrounded a bowl of smoking incense. He and Amos had refused Huldah's prophecy. Now who would help him?

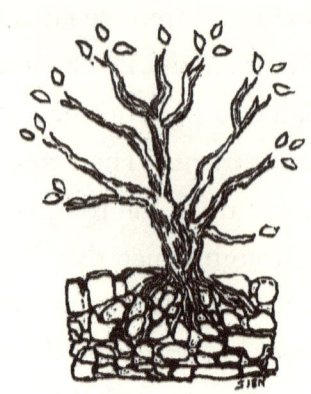

Chapter Twenty-Three

I've been a fool," Huldah said to the Angel Gabriel. "I should never have brought the rabbi to the world of *Yetzirah*. And I never expected Amos to transport himself into the stones."

Gabriel spoke gently to the prophet she had known for centuries, though time moved differently through the stones. "No, not *Yetzirah*. *Beriyah,* the realm of creation, overwhelmed them, Huldah. You went too far. You got impatient. Suggesting a journey among the crawling things that create soil was not a good idea. Amos looked quite enchanted when you told them about the stardust in their bodies. You might have done better to pursue that metaphor."

"The rabbi is impatient. If I were the spirit of Rabbi Akiva, perhaps he would trust my wisdom. He does not want a prophet but a magician. He wants me to foretell the future, find him a safe place to take the Jews of Girona. Or perhaps he thinks I can stop the Inquisition itself."

"You led him to believe your prophecy might hold that power," the angel replied.

"Perhaps I did," Huldah admitted. "But once it could have. I just waited too long."

"Maybe," the angel replied gently.

She wanted to hide inside Gabriel's wings. The angel knew all she had been, the purpose of her soul.

"There is something I've finally gotten permission to tell you, Huldah. That scroll they brought you was indeed an old copy of the book of Deuteronomy. Hilkiah and the other priests knew about this text. Their predecessors hid it in the age of King Manasseh, and generations of priests guarded the scroll until they decided upon the right moment to reveal it to the people. Hilkiah turned the scroll to the text of curses describing God leading Israel and its king into exile. He knew this story would terrify Josiah, who would carry out their agenda to destroy Asherah and strengthen the power of the priesthood. They staged this discovery and used you in their plan."

Huldah looked at the angel sadly. "I suspected this betrayal. It doesn't matter now. That was all long ago. I am not so interested in Asherah. But I cannot explain *yichud* to those whose feet walk the earth. The stones are a text teaching me much about *yichud* I wish to share. Yet my plan is not working. I loathe being an *Ibbur*."

"Come." Gabriel gathered Huldah against her breasts.

"I have disappointed you."

"You acted a bit quickly. But you have accomplished much. Some of the prophecy has been written."

"Yes, Amos wrote Raphael's words down on the scroll faithfully."

"Perfect."

"But I didn't finish."

"It is enough. You planted seeds for a possible future. You have done well, Huldah."

"Thank you. But there is a question I want to ask."

"Ask me anything."

"There's something I don't understand about time. When I lived in Jerusalem, time flowed like a stream from one event to another. Now I glimpse many futures. How do I know the scroll will make a difference?"

Gabriel opened her arms to release the prophet. "There are a myriad of possibilities. Let me show you."

Huldah skimmed above a coastline. Someone had died. An epidemic. A disease had killed them. Whom did she mourn?

Huldah hovered by the shore. She explored an abandoned path, washed out in places, broken. She soared higher, gazing at dry waves of mountains pushing up from the ocean. Smoke rose from a remote valley. No storks soared here in this empty sky.

"In this world, poison lodged in living things, altered the sacred code God encoded in letters at the beginning of creation," she heard Gabriel say. "So little life here."

Huldah bore witness.

"The scroll and its call for a different understanding of *yichud* could prevent this," Gabriel intoned. "Or it may not."

She recognized her city, Jerusalem, built of tawny stone. Far larger than she remembered, it sprawled across hills and valleys. The Temple was still missing. Above the city rose the Mount of Olives, where her husband and son had buried her bones. The Judean hills, parched and stripped of their *tallit* of soil, had been reduced to barren white rocks protruding from chalky dust. No orchards of peaches or apples or almonds perfumed the land. Even the olive trees had vanished. She flew east, surveying her former home, and entered smoke. Wildfires burned uncontrolled; brush exploded in flames. The Jordan Valley pulsed with heat. Even the Dead Sea had evaporated into a bed of salt. She could not bear it and fled to the coast, seeking cool breezes. But there a tempestuous sea seized fragments of volcanoes, hurled them into churning water. Offshore, a canyon swallowed sediment into its dark mouth. Now covered in perpetual smoke, the shaved hills and the sea were gray, the few scraggly plants gray-green. Everything looked muted. God had withdrawn the light from the world.

She skimmed lower to look at a house by the coast. The corpse of a woman leaned against a wall; flies buzzed around it. Huldah went no closer. Below the house, waves boomed against rock. She rested in a patch of herbs. There was no one here to talk to, but at least some drought-resistant herbs had survived. In grief, Huldah remembered the scent of rosemary crushed by sheep hooves in the Judean hills. She recited the names of her favorite herbs like a prayer: poppy, thyme, rue, germander, mint, lemon verbena. Plant names were poetry, brought solace. Pungent bushes endured.

But something terrible had been created in this burning world.

"Huldah!" she heard Gabriel call. "Come back."

Gabriel swooped down, caught her in vast red wings, and carried her into a black sky. They beheld the earth from space, a bubble of light.

"I showed Raphael this vision of the earth," she told the angel.

"There it is, Huldah." Gabriel pointed. "*Yichud*, the unification of creation. It is not the whole cosmos, but it is more than enough for human beings to understand."

"Raphael described this vision of *yichud*. Amos recorded it and even drew a picture of the earth a few nights ago."

"Then you have done well, Weasel. Do not seek to understand time. The scroll is only one variable in the repair of the world. It alone cannot save the world, but it is your unique contribution. You act and, in acting, try to fulfill your destiny."

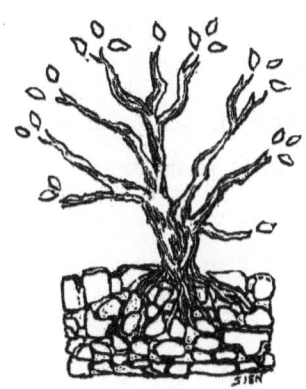

Chapter Twenty-Four

Huldah watched a dream crumble, the last vestiges of *convivencia* in Spain, this country where Jews, Muslims, and Christians had lived for hundreds of years, sometimes in conflict but enriching each other's knowledge and traditions. It had been unlike any other place, a borderland between two continents, bridged by the Jews, who spoke Arabic, Latin, and Greek and, like pollinators, transmitted Arabic culture, science, and philosophy to the rest of Europe. Muslim scholars studied Hebrew and Muslim texts together as brothers; Muslim poets inspired Raphael's ancestor Judah Halevi to write Hebrew secular poetry.

From her home in the stones of Girona, Huldah had explored much of Spain. She had entered the caves of Altamira, marveled at their ceilings painted with red and yellow stags, horses, and boars, thousands of years before anyone had thought of being a Jew, a Christian, or a Muslim.

She had soared through the dripping forests of Galicia and across the luminous plains of Castile, skimmed the beaches along the Mediterranean. Now she watched her dream die amid the flowing fountains of Granada.

On a hill high above Granada stood the Alhambra, an enchanted palace composed of hundreds of delicate red arches and elaborate blue and white mosaics. Water arrived at the palace from the mountains through ingenious aqueducts. Huldah heard that softly flowing water as she haunted the Alhambra in the last week of 1491. If she had possessed a body, she would have washed herself in the warm, perfumed royal baths. She would have sipped from the fountain in the garden of elm and cypress trees, where frogs conversed on lotus pads. If she had inhabited a body, she would have sung that night with the nightingales, inhaled the fragrance of lemons. And watching what happened to the Muslims in Granada, she would have wailed like any mother watching her children die in war.

Abraham Pardo, council member of the *aljama*, stopped Raphael as he walked through the plaza. "Rabbi, have you heard? Granada has fallen."

"When?"

"Over a week ago, Rabbi. The Christian victors have planted a cross and a Spanish flag on Alhambra Hill. The Catholic monarchs, Fernando and Isabella, reside in the Alhambra. The Christians rejoice. They closed the baths, which they call bastions of sexual immorality. They claim the Muslims are guaranteed religious freedom and will be allowed to retain their own laws and their homes and possessions. We'll see how long that promise lasts."

The rabbi retreated to the synagogue. He stood in front of the oil lamp, drawn by its eternal flame. So the Muslims were defeated. It had taken the Christians eight centuries to drive the Muslims from Spain. Now the Jews stood alone as the last enemy, all that sullied the Inquisition's dream of *limpieza de sangre*, purity of Spanish blood.

The words from Psalm 94 came to him: *God, God to whom vengeance belongs, shine forth. Judge of the earth, render justice. . . .* Visions of the royal family dying in their own blood swirled through his head. He could call on a vengeful God to help the Jews.

No. He did not truly want vengeance. He went to his study, drew the wooden shades, lay on the floor, and concentrated on his breath. God, guide me. Tell me how to protect my people. He chanted the *Y-H-V-H*. Silence. Then he heard a familiar voice in the corner of his room.

"Rabbi."

He opened his eyes. Huldah hovered like a large hummingbird above his head. He looked up at her and sighed. "Huldah, why are you still with me? I refused the prophecy you came to deliver."

"We are bound together," Huldah said, extending a wing of light to touch his forehead. "You know Granada has fallen."

"It is terrible."

"I watched it happen."

"Was there much blood?"

"It stains the ground and renders the red stone of the palace a darker crimson."

"Can you forgive me for refusing you?"

"I expected too much of you, Rabbi. I proceeded too quickly. Gabriel tells me I lack patience. Yes, I forgive you."

"I, too, am not patient. I expected you to perform miracles," the rabbi sighed. "But where can we find comfort in this time?"

Huldah stopped hovering and came to recline next to Raphael on the floor. "Remember, you have much to learn from Amos. The body, pleasure, is not to be neglected, Rabbi."

And suddenly Raphael was in Huldah's memories again.

Shallum had prepared to leave the house very early. "By noon it will be hot."

"Yesterday, I heard clouds speaking over the desert," Huldah had told him. "Rain will fall by afternoon."

"Yes, but now it is sweltering. I must gather water for the travelers to drink."

She had not yet spoken to Shallum of her prophecy. Telling him would give the words solidity. Would Adonai and Asherah fault her for wanting to treasure these simple moments for one day longer—her handsome husband biting into freshly baked bread, crumbs in his black beard; sparrows singing in the fig tree outside their house; the waterskins stacked near the front door, ready to be filled with spring water?

Shallum had been a righteous soul who spent his days cleaning and mending the royal wardrobe. He had also provided water to thirsty travelers at the gates of Jerusalem. This generous, holy task had brought him back from death. She would never forget his burial, attended by a crowd of mourners. In the middle of their prayers, trumpets announced an invasion of Jerusalem. The undertakers had hastily dropped Shallum's body on top of the prophet Elisha's grave and fled. As she had watched, Shallum had risen up on his feet. They had said this was her husband's reward because he had restored so many travelers.

At first she had feared making love with a man whose mouth had tasted death. But then Shallum had told her of the light-filled cavern beyond this place, of the angel who had told him his life in Jerusalem remained incomplete. Soon they had been blessed with their son Chanamel's birth. He too had shown a gift for prophecy. As he had grown older, Chanamel had helped his father draw water. Every day Shallum and Chanamel had descended the steps from the Kidron Valley to Dragon's Spring, the city's only source of water. Like Huldah, Shallum had grown old, but he had insisted he had enough strength to draw a bucket up the shaft.

"Huldah, you were restless again last night, calling out in your sleep. Are you well?" Shallum had asked as he had kissed her goodbye. After decades, passion had still blessed their marriage.

"I am well," she had lied.

Shallum had kissed her again and moved his lips to her neck, his hands to her waist. The waterskins waited, forgotten.

After Shallum had left, she had sat by the hearth, savoring his touch.

Raphael opened his eyes to discover Huldah stroking his chest and legs with a ray of light. He moaned as his body responded to her. But she was not a woman; she was a spirit inside of him. He wanted his wife back. He wanted Amos. "Stop," he ordered. "I am not Shallum." He rolled away from her and got up to perch stiffly on the stool by his desk. "I should never have kissed Amos. But let us not speak of it. What will these times bring? Please tell me. You must know."

Huldah rose from the floor, once again grave. "It may not be easy, this exile."

The rabbi slumped over his desk, his head in his hands. "Where will we go?"

"Portugal, Morocco, North Africa, Italy, even the Holy Land. Some of these journeys may be more successful than others. Many people may die. But as I have told you before, I think the wisdom will survive. This is a future I have seen from the stones, one of many possible worlds."

"Stop," Raphael begged. "You tell me about possible worlds. I want to know what *will* happen in *this* one. And what good is wisdom when we shed blood, when Inquisitors tear a people from the land that has sheltered them for six hundred years?"

Huldah moved to his table of books and gently stroked the *Sefer Yetzirah*, the *Zohar*, and then the *Talmud* as if she were blessing each text. "Do you think I know nothing of exodus? I prophesied the exile of the Jewish people from the Holy Land. I watched from inside the stones of the Temple as King Nebuchadnezzar's army sacked Jerusalem on the Ninth of *Av* in the year 586 BCE. What my cousin Jeremiah and I prophesied came to pass, after a siege of eighteen months in which starvation and thirst plagued our people. The army smashed the twelve bronze oxen into pieces and carried them away. They stole the pots, the shovels, the snuffers, the dishes for incense, the candlesticks, the vessels of bronze used for worship, the firepans, and the bowls. Vultures and lions feasted upon the bodies that lay in the street. Seventy years passed. The Temple was rebuilt and then destroyed again. My soul lives in these few stones ripped from the ruin of Jerusalem and shipped across the sea. But the recorded wisdom of your Rabbi Akiva is not a waste. Nor are the tracts of Nachmanides or Maimonides. The writing survives."

"Huldah?"

A bleary-eyed young messenger had stood at her door. He had looked as if he had been roused from bed to work. "The High Priest Hilkiah wishes to consult with you. It is a matter of utmost secrecy. Come to the Temple this afternoon."

"Tell Hilkiah I will come as soon as I can," she had said to the messenger, who had nodded and slouched away.

She had been determined to return to her writing. Surely the High Priest's business would wait a little while. But she had sat looking at the blank scroll, distracted. She had believed that the stories she had learned at the shrines of Asherah should be written down. Texts, language did not belong to Adonai alone. Yet she had struggled with how to transmit in letters the stories she had learned from the terebinth. The visions Asherah had shown her of the future had eluded the page. Perhaps the Divine Mother did not want her teachings recorded on a scroll.

She had sighed and put her quill away, dressed in her best cloak, and walked up the hill to the Temple. She entered the wide courtyard, now baking in the sun. Under one of the huge bulls holding up the bronze basin symbolizing the sea, she had seen Shallum pacing, his eyes scanning the crowd. When he saw her, he had looked uncharacteristically annoyed.

"They told me they sent a messenger. I've been standing here waiting for you in the heat. I'm sure there are thirsty travelers by the gate." He had wiped his brow.

"Why are you here?"

"I am told Hilkiah needs you for a consultation. It would not be seemly for you to be alone with the High Priest and his men. Your husband must accompany you." Shallum's sly glance had told Huldah he had not for a moment believed she would behave immodestly. She had been lucky to have a husband who respected her mind and her common sense.

"What do they wish to speak with me about?"

"That they would not reveal. Another messenger told me to wait for you and bring you to Hilkiah's office. I still don't understand what took you so long."

"I was writing," Huldah had admitted.

"Huldah." The rabbi's voice brought her back to Girona. "I understand how much you value written wisdom. I treasure it too." He felt dizzy from these journeys into Huldah's past in Jerusalem. "To know that the wisdom will survive does offer some comfort, though I worry about what will happen to my books when we leave Girona. But the human souls entrusted to my care, what of their suffering?"

Huldah remained silent. Raphael wondered once more if too much time had passed since she had inhabited a body of her own. She could no longer understand the feelings of the embodied, could only gaze across the vast plain of history. But then Huldah seemed to soften. "I will try to help you. Amos is in danger. Someone may betray him. Someone he has known since boyhood."

"Pau. The young acolyte."

"Yes. Amos must leave Girona."

"But where can he go?"

"That you must arrange. I only know he must leave." Huldah fingered the parchment containing her wisdom. "He could take this scroll with him. Some of my teachings are here. If this much endures, perhaps it will help. Rabbi, I believe we have reached the end of what we can do together. I will leave you now. I am sure you will feel better without me."

"But—"

"Farewell, Rabbi Raphael Halevi." Huldah vanished into the stones.

Raphael sat at his desk, bereft.

"You have to leave. Huldah says you are in danger. She wants you to depart with the scroll, to save it along with yourself."

"I'm not going," Amos stated.

Raphael rose and stood in front of Amos. Amos cupped his hand on Raphael's cheek and leaned forward to kiss him on the lips. He and Raphael had kissed in the stone cavern. But that had been as spirits. Now they would kiss as men.

The rabbi turned his head at the very last moment. Amos kissed air.

The rabbi looked at Amos sadly. "I cannot. I am sorry."

"But you —"

"You do remember," the rabbi said.

"I reread the scroll. It all came back to me."

The rabbi looked at him gravely. "Amos, we must concentrate on saving your life now, all of our lives. Pau may betray you. He saw us in the oak glen. He saw you in the *call* at night."

Amos knew Pau felt neglected, abandoned. But would jealousy drive him to betray his best friend? Pau had always loved Amos's soul, and he had touched his body with familiar and gentle passion. But Pau might have no choice. He wanted to be a priest with his entire soul, Amos reminded himself. He must turn over a *converso* disloyal to Christianity to the Inquisitors. If Pau also told them Rabbi Raphael Halevi taught a *converso*, there would be great rewards. Amos gazed at Raphael. "You are right. I must leave as soon as possible."

Outside it began to rain, lightly and then heavily. An immense storm blew in from the sea. Ice encrusted the streets. The Iberian peninsula choked in dense clouds. It is as if God weeps for our fate, Amos thought to himself as he shivered in his bed in the house with his grieving mother and uncle. But why doesn't He help me, help Pau, help all of us?

"Uncle Fernando secured me a position as a scribe on the first Portuguese trading ship of the season," Amos told the rabbi a few nights later. "The ship's captain is a distant *converso* relative willing to help me escape. In a few days someone could accompany me to the coast, and then fishermen will take me to Barcelona, where the ship is scheduled to pick up a load of Catalonian wood. It will sail down the east coast past Valencia, head along the coast of North Africa, and cross to the Levant to pick up a shipment of pepper and other spices. Do you think I should take this chance for passage to the Holy Land?"

The rabbi rubbed his eyes. "It will not be easy, such secrecy. You will be unable to confide in a single soul. But you must go. What better plan do we have?"

"I'll miss you so." Amos's voice held tears. "I long to remain here with you and depart with the people of the *aljama* when it is time. You will be together, face these dangers as a community. But I must go alone."

The rabbi rested his hand on the top of Amos's head as if he were giving a blessing. "Destiny brought us together; we will see each other again. You know it is not safe for any of us if you remain here. Pau may already have betrayed you." Raphael knew soon the Jews would have to flee as well. He had not told Amos the details of Miriam's visions or his private discussions with Huldah, for he wished not to alarm him. He wondered if he himself would survive the ordeal. "We will meet again in the Holy Land, Amos." The rabbi tried to sound reassuring, but he knew his voice sounded false. "There we will wander the hills of the Galilee, not be confined to rooms. Like Nachmanides and my ancestor Judah Halevi, we will leave Spain and live where Jews belong. 'My heart is in the East, and I am in the uttermost West,' Halevi wrote. 'How can I find savor in food? How shall it be sweet to me? How shall I render my vows and my bonds, while yet Zion lies beneath the fetter of Edom, and I am in the chains of Arabia?'"

"The Holy Land," Amos repeated. "Didn't you tell me an Arab horseman mowed down Halvei as he knelt by the stones of the Wailing Wall?"

"Oh, Amos. You are too good a student. You take everything I tell you to heart. Such misfortune need not befall you. It can be no worse than what we already encounter here in Spain."

What would the Holy Land be like? Amos wondered. It would not be as Huldah had described it. That glorious Jerusalem of the First Temple period no longer existed.

"Listen," the rabbi told Amos. "You have a sacred task to complete. High in the mountains above the Sea of Galilee lies a town named Safed, where soon, according to Huldah, many mystics will gather. Carry the scroll there. Perhaps this is why you are named Amos. Remember, I told you it means 'to carry.' Now carry the scroll to Safed. Someone will care for it, if they are not too disturbed by its content. I think it is best if you do not reveal what the scroll says. Say only that it holds sacred teachings."

Chapter Twenty-Five

Caterina had held her tears. She felt proud of that. Her son must not see her cry. It might prevent him from leaving Girona for safety. She had packed his satchel that morning with all the food she could spare: the last of her ewe's milk cheese, a loaf of rye bread, a chunk of marzipan, two oranges, even a jar of olives.

"It's only for a little while, Mama," he told her. "Until things pass and we are no longer in danger. Then I will return. I will take the next ship back. I promise." He leaned down to kiss the top of her head.

She turned her face away so he would not see her despair. It seemed unlikely Amos would ever return. Somehow she had always known it would come to this: she would cast her son into a world that might burn him for what he was, for what she was as well and could not escape despite all of her lies. She had not protected him; she had fooled herself into thinking that her carefully woven secrets, her buried *menorot* and smothered prayers and songs would shield him from this fate. As an open-hearted little boy, he had thrown himself into a friendship with Pau. If she had raised him differently from the beginning, raised him to understand that friendship between Jew and Catholic meant danger, she might have saved him from this betrayal. Someone, whose identity he could not reveal to her, had told Amos that Pau would report him as a secret Jew to the Inquisition if he did not leave immediately.

"You should leave too, Mama. He may inform on you as well. You and Fernando."

"I will speak to Fernando about it. I promise."

She looked at him, his ink-stained hands, his every curl, the dark eyelashes that shadowed his cheeks. How could she have fought with him, wasted a single moment they had had together?

She held her tears.

"Please, not so tight," Amos begged as the rabbi wrapped the scroll around his waist. It was the only way they could devise to hide the scroll.

"You will depart Girona encased in Hebrew letters, a cocoon from which you will emerge into the Holy Land," the rabbi pronounced.

Amos sighed. "That is very poetic. Meanwhile, I must breathe."

"The scroll is long. If I do not wrap it tightly, it will bulge under your tunic. At least the vellum will keep you warm."

"Yes, and I will smell like an animal hide. A warm animal hide." Amos noticed the rabbi's stricken expression. "Don't be afraid. I will take good care of your scroll."

"It's your scroll, too."

When he finished wrapping Amos, the rabbi lifted his hands and chanted the prayer for safe travel. He put his arms around Amos, held both him and the scroll. Amos's body felt empty. His soul was already prepared for exile.

Lekh lekha — the words haunted the rabbi. And Abraham left and became a wanderer, roamed from land to land, *mimakom lemakom.* Perhaps Amos would find a new life across the seas and his soul would strengthen on this journey. But he could be killed. By urging Amos to leave with the scroll, did he not cast him out to die alone? *Take your son, your favored one, whom you love, Isaac. Sacrifice him as a burnt offering on one of the mountains.* Or perhaps Amos resembled Ishmael, cast out in the desert alone to die. Cast out, sacrificed — maybe Amos embodied both of these biblical sons woven together into one. But Raphael must be honest with himself: he would be relieved to have Amos out of his presence, far away, so that Raphael would no longer be tempted to perform acts of abomination.

He tried to push these thoughts out of his mind, embraced Amos, and said, "Soon. Soon in the Holy Land."

Just after sunset on the fourteenth day of the month of *Adar,* Raphael pronounced the blessing for reading the Scroll of Esther. *"Baruch atah Adonai Eloheinu Melech ha'olam asher kidshanu bemitzvotav vetzivanu al mikra megillah. Bless You Adonai our God, King of the Universe, who sanctified us with his commandments, and commanded us to read the Book of Esther."* He began to chant the story of Purim.

The congregation listened raptly to the story of Jewish victory over oppression in Shushan in the Kingdom of Persia long ago. During a royal feast, King Ahasuerus ordered his wife, Vashti, to parade before the guests. She refused. The king's advisors warned that her disobedience would inspire other wives to defy their husbands. Ahasuerus removed her as queen and banished her from the kingdom. He held a beauty contest to replace his wife. Esther, the niece of a pious Jew named Mordechai, won the contest. However, the king did not know Esther was a Jew, for her name was not Jewish. The king married Esther, the secret Jew, and made her his new queen.

Mordechai sat at the palace gates and refused to bow to the king's advisor, Haman. Haman plotted to kill Mordechai and built a gallows to hang him on. His hatred grew each day as he passed Mordechai, who would not lower his gaze. Soon Haman wanted to kill all of the Jews. "A certain people scattered abroad and dispersed among the peoples refuses to assimilate and might someday become a threat. They should be wiped out now," he complained to King Ahasuerus, who ordered the "certain people" destroyed without finding out who they were.

When Mordechai discovered this plot, he told Esther, who asked him to proclaim a three-day fast among the

Jews. Esther revealed to the king that she was a Jew and her people were the "certain people" Haman desired to destroy. When the king heard this, he turned on Haman and ordered him hanged on the gallows he had originally built to hang Mordechai. The Jews were saved, and everybody celebrated.

Purim is a carnival of hilarity and drinking. The commandment is to drink so much one can no longer tell the difference between Haman and Mordechai. Nothing is as it seems. Miriam borrowed an elegant robe from Doña Falco and paraded through the room as Vashti. Abraham Falco dressed as Mordechai. Inside the small synagogue in Girona's *call* in March of 1492, only a few months before the expulsion of the Jews from Spain, enforced hilarity careened into hysteria. The people became drunk, loud, desperate. Will Esther appear and save us from Fernando and Isabella? Raphael wondered. He wished he were not the rabbi so he could lose himself in drunkenness like most of the congregation.

Purim was also a day to give charity to the poor. Almost all of the citizens of the *call* were poor now. Still, people brought dates or boiled eggs or fried pastries called Haman's Ears to give each other. The children busily darted about the room delivering baskets of treats. Doña Falco collected alms.

Huldah watched the carnival with fascination. This festival commemorated an event after her time on earth. She marveled at all the drinking and felt relieved not to be inside Raphael's body as he imbibed so much wine. No longer an *Ibbur*, she could depart Girona. But she did not want to leave. She loved these people. And the pastries were so like the cakes she had once baked and brought to the shrine of the Queen of Heaven. Some things had not changed so much after all.

Raphael drank his third cup of red wine. He swayed on the raised platform in front of the congregation. The words of the story crawled across the scroll. His body burned. He felt faint in the airless room. "Cursed be Haman," the rabbi shouted. On cue, the congregation jeered and stomped their feet. On the bottoms of the soles of their shoes they had written Haman's name, so when they stomped, they blotted out evil. Since the name of Haman appears fifty times in the book of Esther, the rabbi's reading was interrupted constantly. Each time, he paused and waited for the loudest men in the front row to stop shouting. The Law demanded that people hear every word of the story.

"And Esther's ordinance validating these observances of Purim was recorded in a scroll," the rabbi concluded, to cheers from his congregants. He glanced up to see a tall and muscular version of Esther, masked and in a purple cloak, standing at the back of the room. Amos, dressed as the wily and beautiful queen, waved at the rabbi and pointed to the scroll hidden around his belly. Raphael paled and lifted his cup for another draft of wine. When he looked again, Amos had vanished.

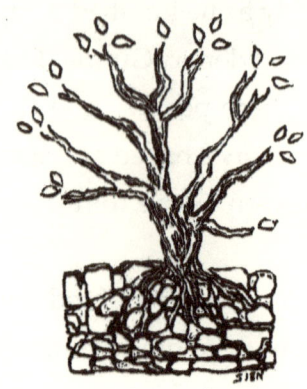

Chapter Twenty-Six

The scroll chafed his skin and rubbed welts on his stomach. Amos had taken the letters into his body; now his belly was branded with Huldah's words. He dared not remove the scroll, even when he slept, for the Hebrew letters would betray his origins. He tried to imagine the embrace of the scroll around his waist as the arms of Raphael. He thought of the rabbi as he had last seen him at Purim, flushed with wine, his voice hoarse and slurred as he had read. Amos hoped that in the wild celebration of Purim no one had wondered about the identity of the elegant queen in the back of the room. It had been worth the risk to set foot in the rabbi's synagogue during services just once before he had left Girona.

His memories formed another kind of scroll: Pau chasing him through the green meadows of Sant Daniel, laughing as they rolled down hills together, their cloaks decorated in grass and the petals of red poppies; Pau eating dinner at his mother's table, savoring her Friday night stew; Pau taking him to the monastery to show off his latest scribal masterpiece; he and Pau rising before dawn to admire the stars above Girona. Now Pau might betray them.

"You have a chance, Amos, the chance I always wanted for you," his mother had said.

And so, the night after Purim, Amos left Girona and the Jewish world he had only just discovered. He met a surly man, another friend of his uncle's, who waited on his donkey at dawn. The man would not reveal his name. "Better we know nothing about each other so I will have nothing to tell an Inquisitor if I am questioned." He carried a long knife to protect them from robbers.

They rode silently on the two-day journey to the coast, on a muddy path through hills crossed by rivers still swollen with winter rain. Sometimes the road disappeared altogether in the mud. Domingo feared that the man might abandon him in one of these bogs. He had stopped thinking of himself as Amos as soon as he had left Girona. It was too painful. If his name meant "to carry," that was only a curse. They spent the night in a primitive tavern that served only wine, and bread on a large wooden platter. The travelers speared slices of bread with knives they used both for eating and to defend themselves on the road. The man forbade Domingo to talk to anyone, lest they remember him if the Inquisitors questioned them later.

Domingo felt reluctant to part from the man when they reached the fishing village on the coast, even though his presence brought scant comfort. He was from Girona, someone who at least knew Uncle Fernando. But after Domingo met three friendlier men, daring cod fishermen who thought it an adventure to smuggle him in their boat south to the great port of Barcelona, he felt less lonely, though he did not like how the sea tossed them back and forth. The men looked sympathetic when he vomited the salted fish they gave him for lunch. "Here, young man," one offered, "take my clean cloak and keep your eyes on the horizon while we move. You will feel better."

"What's Barcelona like?" he asked, trying to distract himself from his lurching stomach.

"Oh, it's quite something. Huge, it is. Over forty thousand souls. Mules and horses carry the citizens about the city. The streets are much cleaner than you'd be used to. Drainage pipes take wastes to the sea. Almost every house boasts its own well."

Domingo's spirits rose. Perhaps this would be a grand adventure.

They arrived in Barcelona's sheltered harbor, a bay surrounded by low cliffs. Domingo felt sorry to say farewell to the fishermen but relieved to walk on land again. He passed the Royal Shipyards, where loud hammering hurt his ears. Dozens of men were building a huge caravel. The scents of clean split wood and burly, sweating men enticed him. He could stay here, blend into this bustling city. But

Uncle Fernando had warned him that close connections existed between the priests of Barcelona and the priests of Girona. If someone recognized him, he would put the rabbi and his own mother and uncle at risk.

So he found Captain Joaquin on the docks, and their caravel departed a few days later: thirty sailors, the captain, and Domingo, who served as the captain's personal scribe. His gift with letters was wasted now in making banal lists of goods. He felt exiled from everything and everyone he knew. No one knew his Jewish name; in fact, using a Jewish name would mean death. God allowed the Inquisition to torture men like Roca, women like his mother. He could not believe in such a God, be He Hebrew or Christian. There were no speaking stones here, only water, salty water, tossing the boat up and down, and he had nothing to eat but stale biscuits, mushy lentils, and salted fish. Domingo watched the gray sea, nauseated.

A voice inside him taunted: Did the rabbi and Huldah truly want to keep him safe or just their precious scroll? Who really cared about him? His mother and Fernando, to be sure, but soon they might be dead. He had escaped danger on this ship, but he felt more alone than ever—lonely and longing for a God he wasn't sure he believed in.

Domingo attempted to hold his hand steady on the ship's log, but the violent motion of the waves jerked the boat back and forth, spattering the ink. It had been early in the season to set sail. But Captain Joaquin was greedy, eager to be the first ship to catch the spring winds that would blow them across the sea to the Levant. So waves soaked them when they visited the lavatory near the bow of the ship. Domingo's scalp itched from an infestation of lice. He should have shaved off his curls before embarking on this journey. Now the rocking of the boat made using a razor unsafe.

Among the crew he remained a stranger. He spent his days with the captain, updating the log, keeping detailed records as they sailed southward and stopped at coastal towns. At meals he hunched over, wrapped in the scroll, itching. None of the men tried to befriend him. That was fine. He had no desire to become close to anyone. The captain, an olive-skinned man with a face scarred by pirates, was the only person who knew Domingo's true identity. Despite his warrior countenance, his eyes were kind. "He too has Jewish blood," Uncle Fernando had said. "But you must never speak of it."

"We will detour to Gibraltar," the captain confided to his scribe. "The men will curse me. It means a long journey to the west, but Gibraltar is too important to bypass. It's the gateway to North Africa and to Portugal and countries on the Atlantic coast to the north. The Spanish sailors prefer the Inner Sea, the warm bathtub of the Mediterranean. The open Atlantic makes them nervous. They call it the Ocean Sea. We real men of Lisbon have no such womanly fears." Captain Joaquin's green eyes watered as he peered across the horizon. "I long to see what lies beyond the Azores. There is a captain who plans a voyage across the ocean this

August. I waited too long. He has no more need for men to captain his ships. What an adventure that would have been for us to make together, Domingo." The captain draped his arm around Domingo's shoulder jovially.

Domingo stiffened. Such gestures reminded him of Roca. He did not want a father in Captain Joaquin. Still, he owed the man his life, so he forced himself to smile.

In Gibraltar, Domingo and the captain completed their paperwork and then visited a tavern near the docks. "Did you hear that the King and Queen have decreed that the Jews have three months to leave Spain?" one sailor shouted over the din. He held his mug up for a refill of wine. "Or be killed by the Inquisition."

"Better off without that bunch of greedy tax farmers," replied another. He belched. "Let us celebrate. Spain will soon be a Christian country."

Domingo nearly choked on his wine as the men at the table guffawed. He was afraid his face would betray him. He and Captain Joaquin did not look at each other. When they left the tavern and returned to the ship, they did not speak of what they had learned, but Captain Joaquin touched Domingo's arm as they parted for the night.

That night Domingo lay awake. He remembered the meditations Raphael used to communicate with Huldah. Perhaps she could help him, bring news of home. *Y-H-V-H.* He chanted the name of God silently. But Huldah did not appear. Instead he saw the rabbi burning in the Plaça Sant Domènec, praying to God as the flames consumed his beard. Rats swarmed the synagogue. A cross desecrated one wall of the sanctuary, and where the Eternal Lamp once burned: empty darkness. He lay shaking, smelling the stale sweat of the sleeping men around him. Perhaps this was not a true vision but a demon taunting him. *Shema Yisrael,* he prayed, and he asked for the protection of the angels. Finally, he fell asleep.

The next day, a letter from the shipping company was delivered. Domingo read it to the captain, "'Proceed to Lisbon.' That's all it says. No explanation." The captain shook his gray head. "Gone are the days when a captain was the master of his own ship."

At the news that they would sail up the Atlantic coast of Portugal, most of the crew disembarked to look for positions on ships heading east to the Levant. The captain recruited new sailors, burly Portuguese men who stank of fish and whistled ballads as they coiled rope. Domingo could scarcely understand their songs: Catalan and Portuguese differed more than he had realized. Huge waves broke over the caravel, soaking the men in brine. He could have left with the rest of the crew in Gibraltar, but it seemed easier to stay with Captain Joaquin. He really didn't care where he went or even if they sank. "Lost souls," the rabbi had once called the *conversos.* Now Domingo understood what Raphael had meant.

He longed to write the Hebrew letters forbidden to him. The letters formed the building blocks of creation. Through them he had crossed into the Jewish world—letters, light, ink, wisdom swirling in that tiny room in Girona, now impossibly far away. The scroll was all he had left of that life.

They reached Lisbon. Above the port, a great walled city of towers, cathedrals, and tiled roofs clambered up seven steep hills. The crew would take leave in Lisbon for a week while the captain took care of business. He paid them wages for the voyage thus far.

On shore, Domingo wobbled back and forth, still feeling the deck shifting beneath his feet. He ordered sweet rice and grilled sardines from a woman selling food on the docks. After eating he felt better but still encumbered. He labored along the wide banks of the Tagus River, swaddled in the scroll, sweating in the heat. He watched two men on a salt boat unload ceramic jugs filled with pale crystals. At another pier, a bare-chested, muscular man repaired a gouge in a ship, pounding heavy planks with gusto. He smiled at Domingo. Gulls circled above the docks, dove to snatch stray scraps of grilled fish, squabbled over their prizes.

The scroll tightened around Domingo's ribs after he ate. He had forgotten what it felt like to be unbound and unchafed, to expand his stomach under a loose tunic. His eyes followed a mongrel dog as it wandered through the shipyards and turned to trot through the gate of the city.

As he watched the dog, a thought came to him: he could stay in Lisbon for a few months. The Inquisition did not rule Portugal. Here no one would persecute him. The journey back to the Straits of Gibraltar and east to the Levant would still be possible later this summer. The captain could hire another scribe in a city of this size. He should explore what opportunities Lisbon might hold for him. But he could not walk around strangled by the scroll. Surely someone would keep it for a few months. Perhaps a synagogue?

Domingo hiked uphill from the docks, breathing heavily, unused to exertion. He counted the coins in his pouch. He came upon a fruit vendor and bought an orange, signaling his wishes with his hands. Its tangy juice after so many weeks shocked him. He had forgotten about sweetness. Juice dripped down his chin and onto his filthy tunic. He craved more. He rushed to another fruit stand and bought himself dates, olives, and a lemon, paused a few feet away, popped the dates two at a time into his mouth, spat out the pits. He devoured the olives, savoring their salt. Finally, he sucked on the juice of the lemon, cleansing his mouth. A dark-haired man strolling by stopped to stare at him open-mouthed. Domingo smiled, bit into the lemon again, licked his lips clean of salt and juice. He had been delivered from the sea to this hot and golden city of citrus and handsome men. He wiped his mouth with his sleeve and strode uphill through shady streets lined with stately chestnut trees.

After some inquiries involving much pointing and the few words of Portuguese he had learned from the sailors on Captain Joaquin's ship, he found the Jewish quarter. In the narrow streets that reminded him painfully of Girona's *call*, Domingo located the synagogue. He crossed a courtyard landscaped in oleander bushes, their pink blooms glowing against slate gray tiles. He stood near the door wiping the sweat from his brow.

A cat the color of sandstone watched him from the shade under the oleander. Domingo touched the *mezuzah* on the doorpost and then kissed his fingers. He longed for Raphael. The cat left the shadows and twined through and around his legs. Domingo reached down to scratch its head and then brushed his hand over the whiskers on his own face. During the weeks at sea, shaving had been impossible. Ripe odors wafted up from where the scroll coiled around his stomach. What would the rabbi think of this dirty sailor? He could only imagine the stink that would emanate from the vellum when he finally unwound it from his body. But he could not wear this scroll for one more hour.

Domingo entered the synagogue and paused to let his eyes adjust to the darkened interior. He walked down an echoing hallway to the rabbi's office and knocked. He felt almost overcome with emotion. If this were Rabbi Halevi's door, Domingo would gladly study *Torah* and serve as a midnight scribe for Huldah's prophecies. He would ask for nothing more this time. Instead he waited alone in this strange and seductive city, at the door of an unknown rabbi.

A short man with red-rimmed eyes opened the door.

"Rabbi?"

The old man peered up at the hulking young man in his doorway. "*Sim.* I am Rabbi Zarco."

"Rabbi, I am Domingo Fontclara. I have traveled far and bring you greetings from Rabbi Raphael Halevi of Girona." Domingo spoke in Catalan, hoping the rabbi would understand him.

"Ah. Gi-ro-na." The rabbi drew out the word as if Domingo were delivering something delicious to eat. "Girona. *Misticismo. Por favor*, come in. Sit." The rabbi wheezed.

But Domingo remained standing in the doorway. "Rabbi, I beg your forgiveness for my appearance." He pointed at his ragged clothing. "I must not enter your room of sacred texts in this condition. Just now I disembarked from a ship." He shook his head and held his nose. "We sailed for weeks. I have found no time to visit the baths—" Domingo stopped. His voice cracked as he glimpsed the Hebrew texts that lined the bookshelves. He wanted to touch the letters on the spines of the books. If only he had taken the time to build Raphael beautiful oak bookshelves like these. He could almost hear Huldah speak through Raphael's mouth. He had traveled across the Iberian Peninsula to stand in a room so like the one he had fled. His fingers traced the shape of an *Aleph* in the air.

The rabbi looked at him curiously.

"I am a scribe." Domingo clasped his hands and smothered them behind his back.

"I understand. You feel *amor* for the texts."

"*Sim*. I come bearing a sacred scroll from Rabbi Halevi, one I smuggled out of Girona."

"A scroll? Indeed."

"Yes, Rabbi Zarco. I wonder if you might keep it while I am in Lisbon. I may be here a few months."

The rabbi nodded. *"Por favor*, come in."

"Perdoe-me," Domingo said, beginning to remove his woolen tunic and then his linen undertunic. He hoped the rabbi was old enough to lack a sense of smell. He unwound the scroll from his waist, winced as the vellum pulled away from his chafed skin. He stared down at his pale, soft belly. Red welts cut into his flesh. How ugly! What man would want him like this?

He took a deep breath and pushed out his belly, not caring what the rabbi thought. At last he could breathe. He moved the scroll over to the rabbi's desk, unrolled and examined it. Sweat stained the manuscript, but most of the letters were intact. He had used his best ink for this scroll.

The rabbi walked over to the table and looked at the scroll with interest. Domingo heard Raphael's voice: "I think it is best if you do not reveal what the scroll says. Say only that it holds sacred teachings." Too late. Rabbi Zarco was already reading the text.

"Certo I will take care of it," he said in a constricted voice, looking strangely at Domingo. "It will be safe here. You have my word."

As Domingo put on his filthy clothing once more, he glanced one last time at the scroll. Should he entrust it to this foreign rabbi? He had been alarmed to realize he could no longer read some of the words. Without Huldah's help, his knowledge of Hebrew withered. So Hebrew forsook him. He no longer possessed the gift he had desired. Everything had been taken away. He thanked Rabbi Zarco and turned to leave.

Amos! the scroll pled with him as he departed the office. He ignored its call and strode down the hallway, past the main sanctuary of the synagogue, free of the burden he had carried for so long. He pulled the front door open. Now the cat sat in the sunny center of the courtyard, its blue eyes beholding him steadily, calmly, exactly the way Raphael's eyes had that first night long ago. It padded over to him. Domingo bent down to run his hand over the cat's back. But suddenly it too seemed part of some malevolent force to seduce him back into the Jewish world. Perhaps it was no accident that he met this cat the color of Girona's stones. He remembered another cat that had kept him company as he had communed with the voice in the stone wall of Girona's synagogue, the voice that had turned out to be Huldah. Well, he was finished with cats and *Ibburim*. He withdrew his hand, ignoring the animal's plaintive cries, and hurried across the courtyard toward the dazzling feast of a city beyond.

Domingo shut the iron gate and inhaled the orange-scented breeze. The dim passages under the *call*, his mother's secrets, the desperate rabbi, Huldah with her strange prophecies, the Inquisitors — all of it he now regarded as a grave he had escaped from. Even the letters had branded his stomach, nearly strangled him. Now he would live in a city where the language was unfamiliar. So? He was a healthy young man in a port city promising adventure. Domingo bounded up the hills of the city, intoxicated by his freedom.

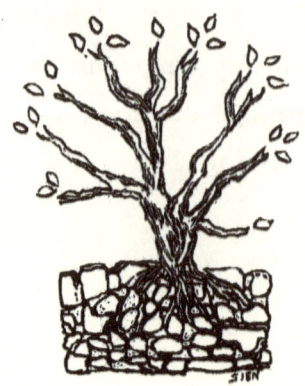

Chapter Twenty-Seven

I think we should move to Perpignan," Isaac Falco said at the rabbi's table. The Council of the *Aljama* had asked him to talk to Rabbi Halevi about the future of Girona's Jews.

"Perpignan seems not a bad choice."

"Yes. As part of Roussillon it remains under the control of the French king, therefore not subject to the Edict of Expulsion. It's familiar, nearby, only a three-day journey if we have the strength to travel there."

"If we have the strength indeed. Many people cannot walk that far."

"We can find mules and horses to carry them. Our relatives in Perpignan will help their brethren. Our communities have intermarried. It won't be so difficult to start over there."

"Of course. But how long will Roussillon remain safe? There are rumors King Fernando wants the territory back from the French king. I would prefer somewhere more secure."

"And where would that be? Where else can we go?" Falco looked at him in despair.

"I don't know," the rabbi conceded. "Portugal is a natural choice for Jews in Southern Spain. But this far north—"

"To reach Portugal from Girona entails a grueling journey to the west, across deserts and mountains, or boarding a ship and sailing far to the south, through the Straits of Gibraltar and up the Atlantic coast. It is a long way."

"Perhaps Italy or the Ottoman Empire will accept us. We could set sail from Barcelona."

The two men fell silent, looking at each other. There were no easy answers.

"Rabbi, I keep praying that God will save us from this terrible edict," Falco finally said. "Perhaps the Inquisitors will not enforce the edicts in Girona because the *call* sheltered King Fernando and his mother during the civil war, when Fernando was a little boy."

"No," the rabbi sighed. "The King may hate the Jews of Girona all the more for witnessing his childhood vulnerability and also for knowing he is part Jewish."

Falco sat chewing his nails. One of his fingers bled from his efforts. His confident bluster had disappeared. "Rabbi, have we made the right decision in not telling the people what is to come?"

Raphael could not sleep that night. He wondered if he should lead the people to the familiar town of Perpignan or some faraway, perhaps safer land. How vast the world, how few places for a Jew.

"The world is indeed vast, but it is all connected. Africa begins at the Pyrenees," he heard Huldah's voice say. "In this Spanish borderland, between Africa and Europe, Muslim, Christian, and Jew once mingled in relative peace. All of that is coming to an end. Such a tragedy. Spain will mount an empire, but without its Jews and Muslims it will become a backwater."

"Huldah, I thought you had left me."

"I no longer reside in your body. But may I visit from time to time, Rabbi Raphael Halevi? I enjoy conversing with you."

"I don't know. You tell me things I do not want to know, can do nothing about. Leave me alone right now, so I can sleep."

"You weren't sleeping."

"Sleep doesn't happen instantly, especially when one has much to ponder. Don't you remember being incarnate?"

"Not too well," Huldah admitted.

"It's too late now anyway. I'm awake." His head hurt. He sat up and peered around his room.

Instead of the gauzy apparition he had become used to, now a lifelike, beak-nosed woman with long russet hair and black eyes smiled at him from the corner of his bedroom. Was this how she had appeared as a prophet in Jerusalem?

Huldah stopped grinning. "One day humankind must grow beyond empires, Rabbi. I have seen burning landscapes in the future I pray you never witness. But all possible realities must be accepted. Gabriel tells me I must practice detachment."

"Detachment? The Inquisition feeds us to its pyres and you speak of detachment. I cannot detach. I must choose a new country for the people of Girona."

"Some choices create an entirely new world; some make only a small difference. We don't always know which choices matter. You will make the best choice you can, and the history of the Jews will continue, regardless of the Expulsion. "

"Then the prophecy will not stop the Expulsion."

"You are right. It is too late for a prophecy on a scroll to halt what already consumes the soul of Spain. In this coming age of violence and destruction, other peoples shall be massacred, faraway landscapes desecrated. Spain will rule an empire extending over five continents. But perhaps the prophecy will make a difference in some future time."

The rabbi sat in his bed holding his head in pain.

"Oh, why do I share these horrors with you?" Huldah lamented. "I have trouble discerning what I must tell you and what I should keep to myself. I make mistakes."

For the first time, Raphael wondered if Huldah came to him for comfort. Perhaps she just needed a rabbi. Once she had seemed invincible, a timeless being sent to help him. Now he recognized her desperation, her loneliness.

"If I knew how to save your people, I would. Do you still think me a demon?"

"No, I don't think you a demon. I'm sorry I ever said that." He felt a rush of sympathy for her, a soul who knew past and future but remained powerless to avert catastrophe.

"Not entirely powerless, Rabbi," she said, reading his thoughts. "There are ways to preserve the best parts of some pasts and try to create the finest of all possible futures. Long ago, when I lived in the Holy Land, I listened to the words of many prophets. But only those words written down survived. Jeremiah has his book. Isaiah and Amos have theirs. But where is the book of Miriam, the book of Deborah? The letters persist. The letters are the sturdiest *merkavah*, the most robust chariot of all. They carry messages through time. Have you heard about the new books printed with metal letters instead of copied by hand?"

Amos had raved about the printing presses and bemoaned the fact that Girona was too small to support one.

"Printing is much faster than writing with a quill. Copies can be made quickly, distributed widely. It is not all bad, this moment in time. You are also witnessing the dawn of the age of books. Much wisdom will be discovered in those books, which will travel far beyond the monastery. Pray to God the scroll Amos wrote for us survives and more copies are created on these printing presses."

"How is he?"

"I cannot reach him. Amos's mind is closed to me."

"But he hasn't died?" This possibility had occurred to Raphael, yet he felt he would know if Amos had died.

"I don't think so. But I fear he has lost himself."

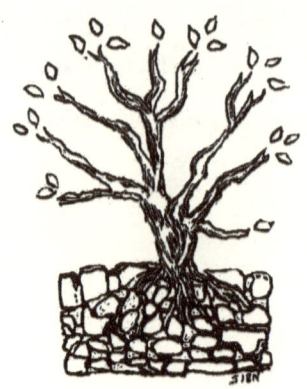

Chapter Twenty-Eight

Domingo quickly located a job copying Latin books for Mario, a Christian publisher. Mario ran a cluttered, dirty shop. The eyes of the workers burned from overwork and poor light. But Domingo preferred to work in this place that bore no resemblance to Roca's shop in Girona. Mario was a curt man who wasted no time befriending his scribes. He would not try to become a father to Domingo.

Weeks and then months passed. Domingo strode with confidence through the crowded streets of Lisbon. Feasting on fresh codfish and eggs, filberts and walnuts, figs and dates, the sweetest pears and the juiciest oranges, Domingo vibrated with health, caught the eye of many who saw him swagger by. Here there was still no Inquisition, although some feared the Inquisitors would control Portugal. In that case, Domingo thought, he must enjoy freedom while it lasted. Then he could retreat to the Holy Land and become a Jew once more.

Jew, Christian—what difference did it make as long as one survived? He would always be a stranger, neither Catholic nor Jewish. A man not circumcised, who as a child had never chanted the prayers, watched his mother light Shabbat candles, or recited the mourner's prayer for his father—such a man could not take on the mantle of Judaism without forever feeling like an impostor, or at least an outsider. He walked through this glorious city as a man without faith, a man who had now lost even his mother tongue, Catalan.

All Domingo knew for certain was that he desired other men. To express those desires demanded little facility with Portuguese, for the language of touch was universal. Now he could explore his attractions around the docks and streets of this port city. Certainly, acts between men were forbidden. In Portugal King Alfonso had decreed that sodomites should be burned. Domingo must be careful to avoid the police and clergy. But here no mother begged him to marry, no childhood friend wished he would become a priest. Women eyed his muscled shoulders, but he wanted men. They discovered each other on the hill behind the castle, in the privacy of the woods, in the baths, or in particular taverns near the docks.

Although he avoided the Jewish quarter, on his adventures after work he met Lorenzo, a lute player from Seville, who told him, "The deadline for the Expulsion has passed.

Thousands of starving, ill refugees from Castile are arriving in Lisbon."

He had seen these refugees but turned away in fear. They might recognize him as one of their own. Now Lorenzo lay in his bed. Should he offer him food, a place to stay? His wages were enough to support two.

"We paid the Portuguese government eight *cruzadas* per family so we could cross the border," Lorenzo explained. "Those who can afford to pay more, one thousand *cruzadas* per family, will be allowed eight months in Portugal. Then we too must move to other lands. I'm lucky my family has the money to buy this time while we decide where to go next. Temporary refuge is better than no refuge at all."

"What happens to those who cannot pay?"

"They live in filthy *barrios* at the edge of the city and work as hired laborers for little money."

"Have you ever met refugees from Girona?"

"Girona is far away."

They fell asleep holding each other. In the morning Domingo awoke to find Lorenzo already gone. He sighed with relief and then felt ashamed of his reluctance to help Lorenzo. He wondered if he was unable to be close to other men because of Pau, whom he had once trusted completely.

Fall rains eroded the hills of Lisbon, filling the streets with brown mud. Toads hopped on steep paths. He assumed that the Jews of Girona had secured passage on a boat. Domingo had not forgotten his promise to carry the scroll to the Holy Land, but now the journey must wait for spring.

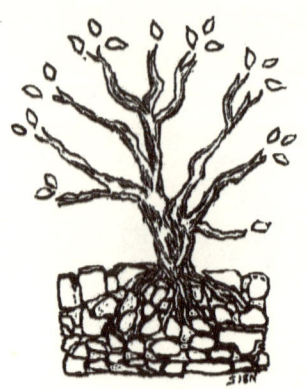

Chapter Twenty-Nine

Seven candles flickered, lighting the faces of Miriam and Jonas, Raphael, and Don Isaac and Doña Hannah Falco. Miriam sank into her chair. For days she had labored, searching for and sweeping every crumb of bread out of the cupboards and off the floor and then burning them in the hearth. She had fetched special Passover dishes out of the cellar. She and Hannah had baked flat sheets of *matzah* and fashioned a Passover meal from meager supplies. Hannah had surprised her with eggs from their last few chickens, and almonds for a nut cake. It had been years since she had baked her mother's cake.

She swallowed a wave of nausea and then stole a look at Jonas to see if he noticed. Her waist had thickened; her breasts felt swollen and heavy. Perhaps Jonas thought she feasted in the kitchen, as if stores of food remained in the house to get fat on. Still, she participated in the deception, telling him she needed to immerse herself in the *mikvah* each month because it was her bleeding time.

At night she lay awake, wondering at her decision to bear a child now, as the moment of their exile drew near. Perhaps this was how she resisted despair, her act of faith in some future. Miriam saw everywhere the face of the red-haired baby girl who would be born into this broken world. She beheld her in flickering candlelight, in glasses of water, in dreams, even in patterns of crumbs she swept out into the street. A daughter. Her husband and her father would rejoice, even over a girl. But it was too soon to tell anyone. She suspected that Hannah Falco noticed her condition but guarded her secret. Hannah understood. They must not attract attention from the evil eye.

Miriam had insisted her father visit the hospital during the past few weeks. "Enough studying and meditation, Father. Give the people your heart, your kind eyes." Miriam sang to the women, while the rabbi sat by the bedsides of the men. Though neither knew when the Jews would be forced to leave, they understood that the date approached. The old people of the *aljama* seemed to recognize what was about to transpire. Some simply walked to the hospital, lay down, and succumbed to fevers. Their souls recognized that their bodies would not withstand the journey to come.

Now Miriam sat next to Jonas at their table laden with Passover dishes. Her father raised his cup of wine from the bottle they had saved for this occasion. They knew it was unlikely they would drink wine at this table a year from now. *"Zeman cheiruteinu,"* Raphael chanted. "To the season of our liberation."

Her father spoke of this as the season of freedom. Miriam licked sweet wine from her lips and winced.

Raphael smiled at her across the table. "Daughter, perhaps soon a child will ask the questions in our family."

Miriam struggled to keep her face expressionless. Did her father know, or did he just express a wish? He could not have guessed, not when her husband remained ignorant. Or perhaps her father was not as oblivious as she sometimes thought.

Last night the spirit woman had appeared to her again. In her dream they had traveled together through a sky filled with Hebrew letters, *Alephs* and *Gimels* and *Heys* and *Bets*, like stars. "These are the pathways of creation, Miriam," the woman had said, pointing.

"I know," Miriam had answered. "I want to walk those pathways to God. I want to study the teachings in these sacred letters. But now, God willing, I will have a child to care for, this baby girl. I feel the texts recede from me with each week of my pregnancy. I feel dull. Perhaps someday the letters will return to me."

"In this time, few honor the mind of a woman, Miriam, even one as remarkable as yours. Still, you must study as much as you can. And teach your daughter, even if Jonas does not approve. Also, you must share the other traditions with her, the wisdom passed down to you from your mother."

"Miriam." Her father's voice interrupted her reverie. "Since we have no child yet, beloved daughter of mine, please recite the Four Questions for us."

Isaac Falco cleared his throat and frowned. "Rabbi, it is our tradition to have the entire table recite the questions. Why have only a woman recite them? A woman's voice should not be heard alone. It is immodest."

"With all due respect, Don Falco, the voice of my daughter is holy and precious to me. Besides, her Hebrew is impeccable." The rabbi's voice was firm as the stone walls of the synagogue they had thought would be theirs forever.

"As you wish, Rabbi."

"How is this night different from all other nights?" Miriam chanted. Her father recited the story of the ten plagues God unleashed on the Egyptian people to demonstrate his power so Pharaoh would let the Jews go. A river of blood. Swarms of frogs, lice, dog flies encrusting the eyelids of the Egyptians. Boils erupting on their feet, locusts, darkness—Miriam shuddered and placed her hand over her belly. God protected their ancestors and delivered them from slavery. She needed His help now. She was pregnant, weakened. Her baby might die. She understood the terror of the women who begged her to save their children.

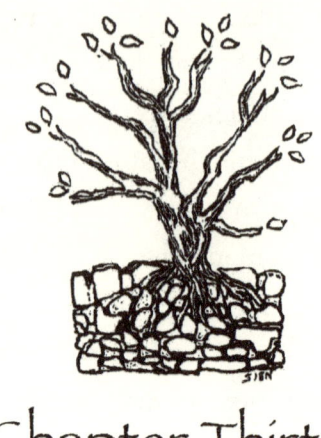

Chapter Thirty

On April 30, 1492, as the Christians counted the days, as the grass greened on the conical mountains around Girona, Juan Estrella, a young notary from Barcelona, rode into town and knocked on the synagogue's door. "Are you Rabbi Raphael Halevi?"

Raphael clutched the doorpost, his hand touching the *mezuzah*. God, this is the moment Huldah spoke of. Grant me strength. "Yes. I am the rabbi here."

The notary thrust a roll of parchment into the rabbi's hands. Raphael opened the message and read:

Thus the great damage caused to Christians by their participation, connection, and conversation with the Jews has been discovered. It is clearly demonstrated that Jews always try by all means at their disposal to destroy and draw away the Christian believers from our Holy Catholic Faith, to separate them from it, to bring them near to their faith by initiating Christians into their rituals and religious customs by organizing assemblies in which they read to them and teach them and their children, providing them with books from which they could read and recite their prayers and announce their fast-days, gathering together to read and study the stories of their Bible, announcing to them the festivals before their celebration, informing them of what they have to observe and do, giving them from their houses the unleavened bread and ritually slaughtered meat. Therefore we have agreed to order the expulsion of all Jews and Jewesses in our kingdom. Never should any of them return and come back. If they are found living in our kingdoms and domains they should be put to death. And we command and forbid any person or persons of our said kingdom to presume publicly or secretly to receive, shelter, protect, or defend any Jew or Jewess, under pain of losing all their property, vassals, castles, and other possessions.

It was as bad as he feared. He lowered his eyes to pray. The notary coughed. Raphael raised his eyes and looked at this chubby young man who must bear terrible news to the Jewish communities of this region. *El Rachamim*, Compassionate One. Help me to have compassion for this young man's soul. These edicts are not his invention. He is but a poor notary doing his assigned task. Raphael straightened in the doorway. "I will deliver the edicts to my people. You be well and be careful on your difficult journey." The notary nodded gratefully and left.

Raphael retreated to his study. He sat down to reread the official document. There seemed to be no way to soften the harshness of this news. He listened for Huldah, but she did not speak. He chastised himself: once more he sought Huldah when he should turn to God for guidance.

Raphael lowered himself onto the floor and squashed his face into hard stone. God, why have you forsaken us? he cried in the *Tachanun* prayer. Adonai, have mercy on me. I am unworthy. I humble myself before you. None of my knowledge, my texts, my prayers tell me how to help my people now. Huldah cannot assist me. My life and all of our lives are in your hands, God. I am as dust, as nothing, before you. He wet the stones with his tears.

He lay prostrate. This moment tested his faith. The long road of exile after the destruction of the Second Temple had brought them to this town where two rivers met, where Kabbalah flourished. Huldah had reassured him that Kabbalah would travel to the Holy Land. The received tradition would continue. God would protect them. And if he died on this journey to Perpignan, he would die knowing that like his beloved Rabbi Akiva, he refused to deny God or *Torah*. He taught all those who needed him.

Calmly he rose from the dust to search for his daughter. The two of them would convene the community. Miriam could read the decree to the women; he would tell the men.

A great wailing filled the synagogue. A few men blamed the edict on the empty royal treasuries depleted by the war against Granada. "Do they really think we are so wealthy that they will stuff their treasuries with Jewish possessions when they expel us?" scoffed Josep Saporta.

"This is only one more of their distorted ideas. They think we are all rich," Rabbi Halevi responded. "But perhaps we should ponder our future, rather than why our life in Spain draws to an end."

Most of the congregation looked at their rabbi's exhausted eyes and understood that he was doing the best he could.

"The deadline is the eighth of *Av*. We have three months to sell our houses and leave Girona. We are allowed to take only what we can carry in a cart."

"Where will we go?" a woman asked.

"My father has made arrangements with the rabbi in Perpignan," Miriam answered. "We will find enough mules to carry us."

"All of us?" another woman asked.

"There are over sixty individuals," said another.

"My uncle is too old to make such a journey," protested a third.

"My son is just a baby," sobbed another. "He is too young."

Miriam tried to calm the people. "We will prevail."

"What do your dreams say, Miriam?" Rosa asked.

"That we will survive." She did not share her vision of emaciated men and women falling into the sea. "We come from persistent people. Yes, Girona has been a refuge. But we have known hatred here. Do not forget those we lost to the sword or the stake. Long ago we came from the Holy Land and made our way to Spain. God has a plan for us now."

Late that afternoon Raphael walked slowly up the western face of Montjuic, the Mountain of the Jews. The community owned this sacred spot between two rushing streams where the Jewish dead of Girona were buried. The rabbi opened the cemetery gate and picked his way between the graves, some of them ramshackle and untended. He spoke to his ancestors. "So our long respite in Girona comes to an end."

"It has not always been easy, Rabbi," a male voice replied. Raphael looked around. He was the only living soul wandering here. He passed the burial site of Rabbi Azriel and the other members of his circle. These Kabbalists had lain prone on graves at midnight, wept, sought wisdom from *Ibburim*. "Rav Azriel, I did find an *Ibbur*, but even this holy prophet cannot help me with the journey we must make."

"We will come with you," said a voice, and then another from higher on the mountain and another, until from the entire cemetery spoke spirits offering to accompany them. "Remember us when you touch the stones of Perpignan. All stones are connected. You think we need remain here? Travel is easy for us."

"Yes, all you must do is remember us," advised another voice.

"Zachor, Remember" echoed across the mountain.

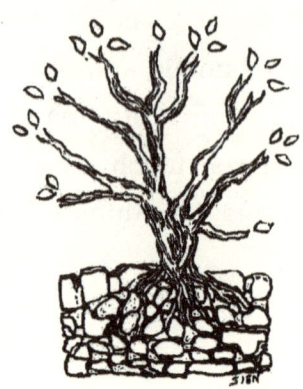

Chapter Thirty-One

Now it was Raphael who walked through the secret passageway in the middle of the night on this most dangerous of journeys, his satchel heavy with sacred texts. Since the Edicts of Expulsion, the guards had strictly enforced the curfew. If they caught him, the penalties would be severe.

"Fernando," he whispered as he tapped on the window of the house he had visited before only in dreams. Amos had described the building to him so clearly that he was sure he knew which room the bookbinder slept in. He hoped Amos's uncle slept lightly, for he could not chance a second knock. It was a windy night. To a passerby the first knock might pass as the scratching of a tree branch.

"Who's there?" a gruff voice whispered. The window opened a crack. "Identify yourself immediately."

"Raphael Halevi, the Rabbi of Girona. Caterina has spoken of me, I'm sure."

"A moment," the voice replied. "Come to the back door, by the garden."

The rabbi tiptoed around the side of the house, his feet sinking in the dark soil. He smelled onions from Caterina's garden.

He waited by the back door. In a few moments a heavy, unshaven man ushered him inside. "Quiet," he ordered even after they sat at the oak table in the kitchen. "Caterina is asleep. She does not sleep well, ever since—"

"Domingo left," the rabbi finished for him.

Fernando looked at him suspiciously. "How do you know my nephew?"

"Perhaps it's better for all of us if we don't discuss that. Better not to have too much information in case—"

"The Inquisitors interrogate us." This time Fernando finished the rabbi's sentence. "Very well. So, tell me. What brings you here in the middle of the night to disturb our sleep?"

Raphael's mouth felt dry. "My books," he croaked.

Fernando rose to pour the rabbi some wine.

"Thank you," the rabbi said. He hoisted his satchel from the floor and placed it on the table between them, taking care to move the wine far to one side. He took out several of his most precious manuscripts. "My books," Raphael repeated. "I must save them from the Inquisitors. We will not be allowed to carry them when we leave for Perpignan. I cannot leave them here to be burnt as heretical texts. Some of these books are hundreds of years old, the writings of the first Kabbalists of Girona. Perhaps Isaac the Blind was right. We should never have written down the secrets of Kabbalah."

Fernando examined each text carefully in silence. The rabbi watched. He saw the brusqueness disappear from Fernando's face as the bookbinder realized the preciousness of what he read. Raphael listened to the wind outside the window. It carried summer's warmth. In other years, this wind had invited joy. Now it only reminded him that soon they must depart Girona.

Fernando finally spoke. "How many more?"

"About a hundred, some more valuable than others, some more sacred." He thought of the volume of Halevi's poetry. Maybe he could carry just that one to Perpignan. Nonsense, he chided himself. He could not risk carrying any text, let alone one with blasphemous content. He focused on the bookbinder's whiskered, serious face. "Will you help me?"

"Help you save sacred books from the fires of the Inquisition?" Amos's uncle sighed. "I don't see that I have much choice. I love books as much as you do. It is of course risky. But we have seen that hiding does not guarantee safety. It did not help Roca, did it?" He regarded the rabbi steadily. "Do you judge us *conversos* for forsaking the faith?"

Raphael's eyes met his. "No, I do not. The choice was made for you a century ago. It has not been easy for you either. It is not my place to judge you."

Fernando seemed to believe him. "I have an idea. Come." He rose and led the rabbi into his workroom. "See how a binding is composed of layers and layers of paper?"

"Yes," the rabbi said, not understanding.

"I could build bindings out of your sacred texts. No one would know the bindings of the notarial registers of Girona conceal pieces of the writings of the *Talmud*, Rabbi Azriel, and Nachmanides. I just received a large job binding receipts for the city."

"But—"

"Yes. The texts would have to be dismantled, separated into fragments."

He must cut his sacred books into pieces to save them.

Fernando regarded Raphael gently. "Is it better to let them burn?"

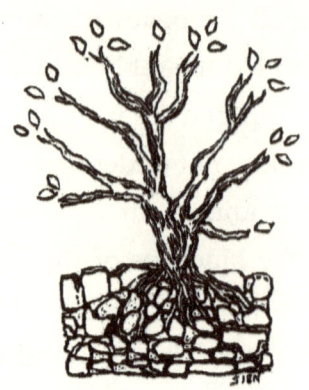

Chapter Thirty-Two

The month of *Av* arrived and with it the dry cough of the Saharan desert. The *xaloc,* an unsettling wind, sprayed Girona with red dust. How apt, thought Raphael as he packed the *Torah* scroll of the Girona synagogue. Perhaps I should wish for a plague to save us.

They had sold the hospital, the *mikvah,* and the synagogue and paid the exit tax that would allow them to leave Spain. Now the rabbi wandered for a last time through his home. His bony, freckled hands touched the walls he had entered in his meditations. These stones had witnessed generations of anguish and joy, absorbed the prayers of this community, provided a home for Huldah and her prophecies. Across Spain, the Church altered Jewish houses of prayer into churches. These stones might become *conversos.*

He must save them from this fate.

Raphael clutched a rough-hewn stone near the hearth. He would tear these rocks away and return them to the earth. He could not allow them to belong to another religion, especially the Church driving them from this land. He was the last rabbi here. He scraped at the surface of the wall with his fingers. He wished to dismantle this building with his bare hands, to carry every stone to Perpignan on a mule. They would reuse them to rebuild a house of prayer in that new home.

Amos would have turned his muscle to this task. But Amos was gone. The work fell to Raphael alone. He pulled a stone, felt it loosen. Dust filled his eyes and mouth. He couldn't see to continue. He wiped his face with his tunic and regained his senses. His knuckles were scraped, bleeding. What am I doing? I do not need stones to find God. God is not absent in the synagogues of Perpignan. Our brethren there will enfold us, welcome our prayers. The rabbi rubbed his beard against the place he had clawed; then he kissed the wounded stone like a fallen prayer book. He glanced around the empty building one last time and fled through the front door into the dry windy day.

Outside, he paused only to pry the *mezuzah* and the tiny prayer scroll it contained from the doorpost. He rested his fingers in the empty slot for a moment. How vacant it felt, as empty as Amos's body the last time he had hugged him. Miriam had dreamt of blank spaces that had once held *mezuzot*. God, help me to find a building in a new land on which to place this *mezuzah*, a holy place for my people. Guide us safely to Perpignan.

Raphael gave the keys to the cemetery to Joan Sarreira, a nobleman who had always treated the Jews of Girona well.

"I promise to care for the keys, Rabbi," Don Sarreira said. "I hope you will all return soon."

"Perhaps," the rabbi replied, but he knew this was what Huldah called an improbable future reality.

In exchange for their property, the Christian townspeople paid some of the people of the *aljama* only a handkerchief or a few loaves of bread. Others were treated more fairly, receiving donkeys and mules to carry their bundles and trunks north. Some who believed this madness would pass and they would return buried their possessions instead of selling them. A few swallowed gold coins because they were not allowed to carry currency.

On foot and on mules and donkeys, around twenty families gathered outside the north gate of the city the next morning. Some brought fragile carts into which they piled blankets and iron kettles, crockery, linen, sacks of food, mattresses.

The Inquisition had granted Rabbi Halevi and the Council of the *Aljama* permission to bring the *Torah* scroll and a few other sacred objects from the synagogue with them to Perpignan. Anything made of gold or silver must be left behind. They sold the Eternal Lamp and the *menorah*.

The Jews trudged away from Girona, sweltering in their hooded cloaks, past gardens glowing with dark purple eggplants and fragrant with basil and rosemary. A small peasant boy ran up to Miriam with a basket of grapes and peaches. This one act of kindness made her sadder.

Raphael watched Miriam and Jonas walk ahead of him on the old Roman road. His daughter was very pregnant. Jonas placed his arm around her protectively. Their love had grown. Seeing them, Raphael felt joy. Their family would continue. He thought of the faith that had brought his people out of Egypt to cross the Sea of Reeds. Now another Exodus.

He must not think of the ruthless world into which they were cast, or of the hungry wolves haunting the country-side. And demons, demons in the forests. He must protect his people from them. He remembered the words of Rabbi Akiva: *Do not exclaim, 'Water! Water!'*

He closed his eyes and sensed righteous spirits hover-ing over them, keeping their promise to accompany the line of Jews struggling through the heat, already thirsty. Water! Water! No, I must not think . . . Protect us now, dear ances-tors. We are in your hands and the hands of God.

Huldah had shown him the blue globe of the earth ris-ing over the plains of the moon. Now his people walked north on that sphere. If they slipped off onto the starry quilt where once he had ridden the letter *Yud*, they would land in *Yetzirah*, the realm of angels, where Huldah told him they all had lived before they were born into this harsh world. Perhaps death was not the worst thing that could befall them.

The screech of a falling cart interrupted his thoughts. Someone's donkey brayed and kicked. A child cried, sat down in the dirt to protest. Everyone stopped walking until the cart was righted, the child soothed. Then they continued north. A few Jews from smaller villages surrounding Girona joined their sad procession.

It took them one week to reach the border town of Cervera, where the Pyrenees dwindle and dip their feet in the sea. The mules and donkeys were thirsty, so wherever they encountered a stream in the dry hills of Roussillon, they paused to water the animals and fill waterskins for themselves. As their procession passed through villages, people stared and whispered to each other. Castles and monasteries guarded the tops of the hills and scrutinized the ragged band of Jews.

From a mountain pass, Raphael looked back at his people, shabby in their tattered robes, limping on blistered feet, faces coated in the red dust from the *xaloc*, but persisting, as Jews had always persisted, in believing in the possibility of a new beginning somewhere else. Nachmanides had argued that the Messianic age would soon arrive, but two more difficult centuries had passed. Perhaps this exile from Sepharad represented the birth pangs of the coming Messiah, Raphael mused. For a moment he thought he heard Huldah laugh.

As they traversed a narrow path above the sea, Leah Mercador stumbled. Her husband, Daniel, reached for her and missed. They cried out and plummeted into the ocean.

Miriam watched, horrified, as her vision in the pool of oil on the plate came true. They disappeared into the waves. Jonas and two other men searched for a few hours along the beach to the south, but they could not find the bodies. Raphael wanted to lead a brief memorial service, but the Council of the *Aljama* said they must continue their journey after saying only the mourner's prayer, the *Kaddish*. "Rabbi, the living shall soon become the dead if they do not sleep with a roof over their heads," Isaac Falco insisted.

Miriam tended to the sick, but her herbs made little difference. "It's more *espanto*," she moaned. She cast pinches of sugar to the side of the road to appease the spirits. She called on the archangels Michael, Gabriel, Uriel, and her father's namesake, Raphael, for protection. Miriam tried to create an imaginary house for her people, a house of spirit to shelter them.

Finally they stood on a hill overlooking Perpignan. The red-tiled roofs of the houses below radiated promise in the late afternoon light. They cheered and prayed their thanks to God as they descended to the town. Many fantasized about the stews and cheeses they would feast on that night, the relatives they would see.

Raphael wondered at his own lack of appetite. He had passed through hunger and pain into some realm beyond the material. At least he no longer worried over his feelings for Amos. Raphael had achieved the purity he sought. He felt no desire. The bones in his hips dug into the ground at night. He refused the dry bread Miriam offered. It only scratched his throat and made him cough.

Huldah must have shifted her attention to someone willing to further her task. Her prophecies were a distant memory. Now his life consisted of dust, exhaustion, and grief. He felt lost without the stones of Girona, his well-worn copy of the *Talmud*, the sprawling fig tree in the synagogue courtyard, the scent of the Onyar wafting up the canyons of the *call*, even the relentless rhythm of cathedral bells—all that was familiar to him. This was exile.

Still, he was a rabbi. He must not collapse now, not while his people looked to him for hope.

Raphael struggled through the gates of Perpignan and into the central plaza of the city. He would have fallen had Jonas not supported him. "You're nothing but skin and bones," Jonas said. Raphael did not answer but silently thanked God for bringing his people here safely.

He swayed back and forth between Jonas and Miriam. "We must go to the *call* and speak to the rabbi at once. Everyone else can wait here. I am losing my strength."

"Father, first rest a while," Miriam pleaded. "The meeting with the rabbi can wait a few hours."

"No, we must not delay."

Raphael, Miriam, Jonas, and Isaac Falco walked through the streets of Perpignan. The town looked remarkably like Girona, which felt comforting at first. But as they completed this last leg of their journey, Raphael wondered if they had made the right decision. The people here looked thin. Some glared at them resentfully. Miriam tripped over a dead rat lying in the street. The buildings wavered in front of Raphael's eyes.

They reached a quiet courtyard cooled by a fountain. Raphael sat gratefully on a stone bench. "We're nearly at the synagogue," Isaac Falco said. "Let us continue."

"We must rest a moment," Miriam insisted.

From the bench, Raphael peered through a gap in the buildings. North of the city rose tawny mountains wooded with oak and beech trees, much drier than Girona. They had walked so far the climate had changed.

"You were lucky," Rabbi Cohen told them when they sat in his study. "Other Jews arrived here infected with plague. We could not accept them."

"What happened to them?" Raphael asked. Sweat shone on his face and he tried to suppress his shivers. He must not appear weak and sick to this well-dressed rabbi. He did not want pity, nor did he want the rabbi to think the people of Girona bore disease.

Rabbi Cohen shook his head. "They were cast away to search for a home. Many will die."

This is how you treat the stranger? Raphael nearly said, but he held his tongue. He must not anger this young rabbi on whose fate his community depended. "May their memory be for a blessing. We beg your kindness."

The rabbi waved his hand expansively. "No need to plead. We are happy to make room for our brethren, though the housing may be crowded. How many are you?"

Raphael counted, subtracting the names of those who had died along the way. "Fewer than fifty. Thank you, Rabbi. We are grateful. Only some need roofs over their heads. Others have relatives who will take them in."

This conversation used the last of Raphael's strength. He released the feeling of responsibility that had driven him here, and when he tried to rise to leave, his legs would not cooperate. "Forgive me. If I could only close my eyes for a few moments—I am very tired."

"Of course. Rest. Let me call my wife, Reyna," Rabbi Cohen said. "She will see you to our guest room, where you are welcome to sleep as long as you like."

A little while later, Reyna showed Raphael upstairs to a room with a soft bed and a quilt of feathers. Raphael nodded his thanks. He closed his eyes and prayed the *Shema* through blistered lips. Thank God here no mule tossed him back and forth, no dust choked him, no one fell into the sea.

Miriam and Jonas looked at Raphael sleeping. "I don't like his appearance," Miriam whispered.

Jonas stroked her hair. "A good night's rest will help your father. Let us return to our people to tell them the good news."

In the morning Reyna brought Raphael tea, but she could not wake him. When Miriam arrived to check on her father, Reyna said, "He has not stirred since I left him yesterday. I fear it's the *espanto*."

Miriam felt cold as she climbed the stairs to her father's room. She added up all he had been through. How much could one old man endure? She too had withstood much, but she held the hope of new life within her. Her father had no certainty in his life, not even the promise of a position as a rabbi in Perpignan. Only his sense of responsibility must have kept him from collapsing on the road.

Reyna climbed the stairs to stand with Miriam over Raphael's emaciated body. "We must take him to the river and immerse him."

So the wife of the rabbi was also a healer. Miriam shook her head. "He is too weak to be moved. Can you fetch me a fistful of salt? And water."

Reyna brought a large vessel of water and a small pottery bowl containing sea salt. She also gave Miriam a black-handled knife. "My mother did these rituals with great success. This was hers."

Miriam nodded her thanks. She began to sway and chant in Hebrew. As she chanted, she dipped the knife in water and gently touched its handle to the top of her father's head, his throat, his stomach, and finally his groin. Perhaps the trouble lay there. She wished he had remarried.

Reyna held the bowl of salt and circled Raphael's body. Then Miriam took the salt and poured it into the water. "As this salt dissolves into the water may whatever has harmed my father dissolve." She handed the bowl to Reyna. "Please.

Take this to the sea. The waters of the earth are vast and can endure everything." She choked back her tears. "They can swallow so much more than my father could."

Miriam remained by her father's side for an entire day and a night. He did not awaken. His eyes flickered and his limbs twitched, but he did not speak. Finally Reyna put her arm around Miriam. "You know what you must do," she said in a low voice.

Miriam nodded. "*Saradura*. It is the only thing left."

Saradura, the ritual of enclosure, was performed under the most desperate circumstances, after everything else had failed.

"You must put out the fire," Reyna said. "I will warn the neighbors."

The Jews of Perpignan had somewhat reluctantly offered refuge to the people from Girona. Now the Gironese would cause even more disruption. The neighbors would have to move out of their houses for three days, in case whatever demon possessed Raphael took up residence in their homes instead. Word would travel through Perpignan's *call* that the rabbi from Girona was possessed.

Reyna rushed back into the room a few moments later. "My neighbor Ahava reminded me you cannot do *Saradura*." She pointed at Miriam's protruding belly.

Miriam put her hand there. She had forgotten. A pregnant woman should not expose herself to demons. She must care for the little girl inside of her. She might already have put the child at risk during these past few days. "But my father—" Miriam protested.

"Miriam, we will do *Saradura*. Return after three nights. It is Rosh Hodesh, the women's new moon holiday. The timing is perfect."

"Such kindness. And we have only just met."

"We are family. Only mountains separate us."

Reyna and Ahava cleared the garlic, onions, and fish from the house, brewed a tea of marjoram, and rubbed it on Raphael's body. Ideally, he would have drunk this tea, but he remained unconscious. The second night they dabbed sugar mixed with rosewater on his lips, in hopes of sweetening the disposition of the spirits. The third night they rubbed him in honey. Raphael lay wrapped in white linen sheets. The two women prayed for their own safety, for now they were *asolombradas*, shadowed, in the presence of evil spirits.

"Where do you think his spirit is?" Ahava whispered to Reyna, watching the skeletal rabbi on the bed.

"I don't know. I don't like how still he is."

"Tomorrow is the last day. We will bathe him in rue to wash away the shadow fallen upon him. He will rise. I know he will."

"He is a man devoured by shadows," Reyna said as the two of them fell asleep on a mat in the corner of the room. "I pray for his soul."

"You chose well for your people, Rabbi," Huldah praised. "You even saved the *Torah* scroll. I am quite proud of you."

"It's you," Raphael said. "You and your prophecies. I thought you were finished with me. What do you want from me now, Huldah? I have no scroll, no scribe. I am broken." Raphael tried to look at Huldah, but instead he saw his body lying below him, emaciated and still. "Am I dead?"

"Not quite yet," she answered, laughing that infuriating laugh he remembered. The familiarity of her laugh conjured the world he had lost, and he understood that Huldah had come to help him make his final ascent. He looked to his right and glimpsed her swirling, graceful form. She spun a tendril of silky light toward him. He grasped it gratefully and entered her world.

"Come," she said. "I will find him for you."

"Find who?" They soared through the walls of the enclosed house, past the two sleeping women who guarded his body against demons. "Demons indeed," Huldah muttered. "You're just finished here." As they rose above Perpignan, Raphael looked down at the town where his people would try to make a new home. "Look." Huldah pointed to Miriam, perched below them on a flat rock by the sea. Raphael's sigh swirled down to where she sat, and caressed her hair. She looked up in wonder. It was the last time he would touch his daughter.

"Find who?" he asked again. Huldah would not answer. "Is it Amos? Do you know where he is?"

"No," she admitted. "I have been searching."

High above the Inner Sea they traveled, Huldah cradling him like a child. They ascended through the layer of clouds surrounding the earth like a gauzy *tallit* and finally out into the starry darkness, until once more they skimmed the surface of the moon. He felt no fear this time. Below them he heard voices. A circle of souls sat on white glowing rocks, earnestly studying *Talmud*. He drifted lower and heard the voice of Rabbi Akiva.

Huldah carried Raphael's spirit to the surface of the moon and let him go.

In the morning the rabbi's body was cold. Ahava and Reyna brought Miriam the news of her father's death.

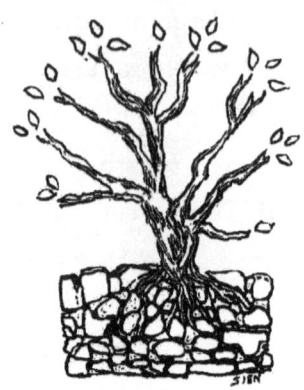

Chapter Thirty-Three

Empty of people but strewn with worn clothing, with broken pots and plates. Empty of human voices but echoing with the cries of gulls dueling over scraps of bread left by the Jews. Empty even of the cluck of chickens. Empty of prayer. Empty of song. This was the *call* Caterina walked through in the late fall of 1492. She placed her fingers in the hollow grooves where a few months ago the *mezuzot* had been torn from the doorposts of houses.

At the door of the synagogue she paused, remembered the night her son had discovered her at services. Thank God Judith had not lived to see this: the *auto-de-fe* and now the Expulsion. She pushed open the door and walked through the dusty interior of the chamber where once she had prayed with the Jews and found acceptance despite her apostasy. The room was dark, the flame of the Eternal

Lamp extinguished. This place was an empty womb, and her womb too felt empty. She had lost her son.

She looked at the vacant ark that once housed the *Torah* scroll. At least the rabbi had carried the *Torah* to Perpignan. She and Fernando should have joined the journey north. "But we are Christians," Fernando argued. "It is Jews they are after. As long as we do not practice Judaism, we will stay safe. Our choice is clear." He had looked at her sternly. Did he know she would never completely give up her faith? "Besides," he boasted, "I have well-paying work here binding the notarial registers for the city. I have finished more than a dozen volumes in just the last few months since the Jews left. There are too many bookbinders already in Perpignan. They do not need one more."

She ventured down the hallway and into the room where Halevi kept his sacred texts. No books remained on the time-scarred table. She was sure there had been dozens of them. The rabbi could not have carried them to Perpignan.

Footsteps outside, voices. It was too late to run. She looked around the room, at the solid desk where generations of rabbis had sat pondering the sacred texts, at the stone floor now dusted with the red powder of the *xaloc* that penetrated these ancient walls, at the two fragile stools still sitting companionably in front of a hearth gone cold. For a moment she thought she heard women's voices out in the main hall of the synagogue, raised in song. Perhaps these were the voices she had heard before. She had nothing to fear from their spirits. But then Pau and Father Hidalgo stood in the doorway staring at her. Pau had tears in his eyes as the priest arrested the mother of his best friend, the boy he had loved.

Chapter Thirty-Four

Reyna kissed Miriam's cheek and left the room. With her help, Miriam had given birth to Sima, the red-haired baby girl, whose name meant "treasure." It had been a long and difficult birth. Exhausted by grief over her father's death, Miriam had lacked the strength to push. Still, with Reyna's expert use of herbs and incantations, both baby and mother had survived.

How could she ever repay the kindness this woman of Perpignan had shown her, tending first to her dying father and then to her? Reyna was the sister she had always longed for. God had sent her a dear friend in these terrible times. She felt grateful even in her grief. Perhaps Reyna would study *Talmud*. She had confessed she read some Hebrew in addition to knowing women's wisdom. Oh, what a dream that would be, Miriam thought, smiling to herself as she drifted into sleep with Sima on her chest — to have a study partner.

As Miriam closed her eyes, Sima appeared as a tall young woman with luxurious red curls and thoughtful green eyes. The two of them sat at a kitchen table arguing intensely about a passage of *Torah*. Late afternoon light poured through a window, illuminating a blue bowl filled with oranges, setting them on fire until it seemed they would rise and spin around the room like planets. *Torah*, the oranges, the light all filled her with joy.

Huldah finally found him, the converso *cast off from all he knew. He lay sleeping, mouth open like a child's, limbs entwined with another's. Amos had helped her record the prophecy. Now she must bring him more sorrow. Huldah smoothed his forehead as Caterina must have long ago, entered his dreams, and told him of the rabbi's passing.*

Domingo awoke alone in the chill of early October. The man he had met at the tavern the night before, the skinny man who reminded him just a little of Raphael, must have left. All the men departed during the night, afraid to wake in the honest light of morning and talk. That suited him fine. He desired only pleasure. He had learned to avoid the taverns with sailors who hunted for men like him, beat them, pushed their bodies into the Tagus River.

He stirred in his bed, scratched his belly, and stretched his limbs. Then he remembered. He had dreamt of Raphael. So peaceful he had looked. Domingo smiled to himself, comforted by this image of Raphael. He closed his eyes and reentered the dream. He saw Raphael's body, skeletal and still. The rabbi no longer stirred.

Domingo's eyes snapped open to his empty room in Lisbon. He lifted his fist and hit the wall. Grief erupted from his belly, where once he had carried the scroll like an unborn child.

His hand ached. He sank onto the bed and remembered all he had left in Girona — his mother, his uncle, Pau. He had even lost his name, the name he had cherished, the name Raphael had called him by. His feet traveled once more through the passageways under the *call* and up the spiral staircase to Raphael's room, where he recalled the deep attentiveness no other man had shown him. He thought of his mother. She had tried so hard to protect him, and she had shown him such care even in the fragrant dishes she had cooked. And he thought of Huldah, who had told him that his love for the rabbi demonstrated courage.

He lay flat on the bed. Only one thought remained. He cared about nothing else. He rose and went in search of the scroll.

Morning sun streaked the walls of Lisbon with warm light, cruelly promising redemption. Domingo rushed down streets lined with olive and pear trees, opened the iron gate to the synagogue, and strode across the courtyard, pausing only to kiss the *mezuzah* on the doorpost.

He passed the ark cradling the *Torah*, hurried down the hallway in search of the old rabbi, and raised his hand to knock. Before his fist met wood, the door opened.

"What do you want this early?" the old man growled. He didn't recognize Domingo. Then, noticing Domingo's swollen face, he asked more gently, "Did someone die?"

Domingo shook his head no, then yes, and then no again. Someone had died, but this was no time to mourn Raphael. He would find no comfort here.

"If no one died, then, young man, what brings you here so early?"

"You remember me. The scroll. I've come for the scroll. The one you kept for me."

The rabbi's eyes widened. He slipped past and walked quickly toward the main chamber of the synagogue. Domingo followed. "I know you remember me. The scroll I brought you last year. The teachings from the rabbi of Girona."

The rabbi mounted the platform by the ark and glared at him from its safety. "Lies!" he barked. "That scroll was impure. It spoke against the law of Adonai. Such transgressions it condoned."

Domingo stood in front of the rabbi. His voice shook. "What did you do with my scroll? Did you burn it?"

"It contains the name of God. Do you think me an Inquisitor, that I could burn God's name?"

"Where is it?"

"I buried it," the rabbi admitted. "The earth will purify it. Such teachings should not be written down. The sages have taught us—"

"How—dare—you—" Domingo mounted the platform. He would choke this man who had buried the precious wisdom of Huldah, all that remained of Raphael. "Where did you bury the scroll?"

"In the earth. I will not tell you where."

Domingo lifted his hands to reach for the rabbi's throat.

Then he felt a tendril of light touch his forehead. His eyes fell on the ark, the ark that cradled the *Torah* with the sacred letters. He dropped his hands and sobbed. He had been about to commit murder in the synagogue, in front of the scroll of the Law Raphael had held holy, in the name of the prophecy they had helped bring forth together. He backed away from the rabbi and fled into the streets of Lisbon.

By the Tagus River he sat down, despondent in the morning mist. A gull circled his knees begging for scraps, but he paid no attention.

Huldah sat beside Amos, but he could not see her. Thank God she had helped prevent him from committing murder. She wanted to do more for this young man with a broken heart who had helped her. The scroll would never travel to Safed, but it lay safe in a genizah, *a crypt for worn-out Hebrew manuscripts. It was forbidden to dispose of writing that contained the name of God. Conditions in this particular* genizah *were dry. The scroll might last hundreds of years. She finally had her own scroll of prophecy, the Book of Huldah She felt so grateful.*

"Beloved one," she said. "You have been brave."

Did he hear her, as he had heard her once through the stones? He did not seem to.

Amos rose to wander along the river, to mourn the man he loved.

Shema Yisrael Adonai Eloheinu Adonai Echad, she *heard him pray.*

He chanted the only prayer he could remember, the one Raphael had taught him.

She followed as he climbed the stairs to his small room, sat at his desk, and picked up his quill, his hand shaking. She would not help this time. He must find his own voice.

Shin, Mem, Ayin, he *wrote in beautiful calligraphy. Shema. Listen . . .*

She watched, exultant.

Perhaps through the letters he would find his way back to his people.

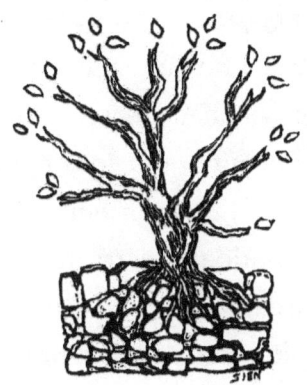

Chapter Thirty-Five

Huldah guarded the scroll in the *genizah*, the crypt where the old rabbi had buried it under the synagogue. Sweat from the *converso's* body had erased some of the letters from the scroll even before he entrusted it to the rabbi who read the words and pronounced them an abomination before God. Even in the dry *genizah*, time chewed at the edges of the scroll. Still, some text could be deciphered. Huldah refused to lose hope.

While she waited, she was not idle. For five hundred years she listened to the prayers of *conversos* in cellars and attics, including those who dared light *Shabbat* candles, if only in their hearts. Spain and Portugal no longer had rabbis or synagogues, *mikvahs* or kosher butchers, Jewish books or songs. Soon the people could pray only from memory — a few words of the *Shema* or the *Kaddish*. Many no longer recalled the dates for *Yom Kippur* or *Purim*. Even if they knew those dates, they could not fast without attracting the attention of a neighbor who might betray them to the Inquisitors. But those who no longer prayed in Hebrew still exhaled the prayers of their hearts into the wind blowing across Spain and Portugal and into the stones. When the *conversos* were betrayed by their neighbors and prosecuted by the Inquisition, Huldah heard them cry. When several thousand were murdered in Lisbon in the great riot of 1506, she mourned. She listened to their prayers and recounted them to the Angel Gabriel, who carried them to God.

Strange and new practices interwove Judaism and Christianity, customs such as not eating pork for forty days before Passover. People rose in the morning to pray the Our Father, washed their hands, and then whispered what Jewish prayers they remembered. Some believed in personal salvation through Moses instead of Jesus. Huldah looked upon these new ideas with fascination.

She had followed Miriam, Jonas, and Sima as they had fled across the Mediterranean from Perpignan to Salonika in the Ottoman Empire (later Greece), where they and their descendants lived in relative safety for hundreds of years until the Nazi invasion, when most of the Jews of Salonika died in Auschwitz or Bergen-Belsen. A few endured by immigrating to Israel or the United States. Ironically, a few hundred survived by returning to Spain.

Deep in the stones, Huldah sensed the shock waves from the radioactive explosion at the end of World War II. This was not the vision of *yichud* she had longed for, this unification in destruction. Then she felt the stones around her shift restlessly as they guided her toward her destiny once more.

Rabbi Ilana Abulafia lay on her bed in a high-rise hotel near the Lisbon airport, exhausted from her long flight. Her mother had exclaimed with excitement when Ilana had told her over the phone that she wanted to trace her Sephardic roots, to research and travel the circuitous path that had brought their family from Spain to Salonika to Monterey, California. Her mother had confided that she had been doing her own research on the Internet. "We had an ancestor who was a rabbi in Girona. Maybe you should go there."

It had taken a few months to arrange, but Ilana had obtained a sabbatical from her congregational job and booked a cheap flight with an overnight layover in Lisbon. The day after tomorrow she would fly to Girona. She smiled, settled under the down comforter, and fell asleep.

In her dream she rose above the bed through the fiberglass ceiling and the roof of the corporate hotel. She soared over the red-tiled buildings of Lisbon, higher than the jet that had swooped over the Tagus River to deliver her to this marvelous bed of feathers. There among the stars she floated. Far below her lay the Iberian Peninsula, the city lights twinkling islands between black patches that must be mountains.

The sky came alive with constellations of Hebrew letters. She recognized *Bet*, for *bereshit*, creation, the earth, the body; *Pey*, for the mouth speaking prophecy; *Lamed*, for *lev*, heart; *Gimel*, for *gilgul*, the wheel of souls circling through time. The letters aligned themselves into a long ladder uncoiling toward the city below. Without fear, she lowered herself rung after rung, followed the *Aleph-Bet* from heaven to earth.

Ilana, whose name meant "tree," carried in her roots the lineage of Rabbi Raphael Halevi; of his daughter, Miriam; of Miriam's daughter, Sima; of Sima's daughter and all whose feet walked the earth in the next five hundred years. Ilana carried the exile of her people from Spain and Portugal; the conquest of peoples and continents; the chemicals in the food people ate, the radiation, poisons altering the code of life itself. And the ghosts of the six million who rose into smoke, lost to the world forever — she brought them with her as well.

The next morning, rain soaked the streets of Lisbon's Juderia. Ilana entered an antiquarian Jewish bookshop and stood awkwardly in the doorway, her plastic raincoat shedding a puddle of water on the floor. She glanced around for a hook to hang the raincoat on. There was none. "*Perdoe-me*," she said to the old, whiskered man regarding her from a stool behind the cash register.

He studied her with a peculiar expression on his face and said in English, "You want perhaps the English bookstore? It is down the street."

"No, I — I love Jewish books."

He pointed at the coat rack behind the register. "You can place it there."

She removed her floppy rain hat. She fought the impulse to apologize for her bare head. Of course the book-man would see her as immodest. Because of the rain she had not worn one of the colorful Tibetan-style hats she used as a religious head covering.

"Miss, do I know you from somewhere? Have you visited Lisbon before?"

"No. It's my first time here. I am only in Lisbon for one more night. Tomorrow I fly to Spain to research my ancestor. His name was Rabbi Raphael Halevi. You must be an expert on Sephardic history. Perhaps you have heard of him. I believe he lived in Girona just before the Expulsion."

The man rose from his chair and limped to the front of the counter. He stood in front of her, anxiously gripping his cane. "Are you a rabbi?" he whispered.

She looked around the empty shop. Why did he whisper? Was there something secret about being a rabbi? Oh, she chided herself. Of course. She was a *woman* rabbi. She always forgot that that was a conversation stopper. But wait. How did this bookman know she was a rabbi? She hadn't even asked for a book of Hebrew text. She had said only that she liked Jewish books and her ancestor was a rabbi.

"Yes, as a matter of fact I am. I am Rabbi Ilana Abulafia."

"Abulafia," he exhaled. "There was a famous Jewish mystic with that name."

"I know. I have studied him. But he is no relation I know of."

"Ach, the mystics are not for women—" he began; then he caught himself and cleared his throat. "But the ancestor you spoke of. It *was* Halevi of Girona?"

"Yes," she answered, feeling warm with excitement despite her damp clothes and hair.

"Then I have something for you to take to the Jewish museum in Girona," the bookstore owner told her. "Come, come, old man. It has to be her," he said to himself. He seemed to have forgotten that she was waiting there. "She must be the woman in my dream."

"Dream?" Ilana repeated. Hadn't she also had a strange dream last night?

"Last month this dream," the old man confessed. "Then again last week. Again on Monday, then once more on Wednesday. My wife says I need to listen to this dream. She's tired of me yelling in my sleep, yanking the covers and waking her up. A dream of a woman from America, red-haired, holding a scroll. Now I understand. The Halevi scroll. I should have guessed there was some connection. It arrived the same day I first had the dream. So. Come."

He limped down the narrow aisle stacked high with old Jewish books. Ilana followed.

In the back room lined with shelves piled high with Hebrew volumes, the bookman picked up a scroll sitting on top of a stack. "Let's take it to where there is some space to look at it, better light."

He carried the scroll over to a table, pushed aside a stack of leather-bound tomes to make room, and unrolled the scroll with skillful hands. Dust wafted from the scroll like breath. The vellum was stained, the letters almost completely faded in some sections. Ilana leaned over and tried to read it.

"Parts of it seem to be missing. And oh, so much decay. It doesn't smell good after hundreds of years in a *genizah*. It must be taken care of. Here in Lisbon we have no Jewish museum. In Girona the Jewish museum will know how to restore it and then translate the text. Besides, it belongs in Girona."

"A *genizah*. This was found in a *genizah*?"

"Yes. Here in Lisbon. Not far from this shop, actually. They are excavating for a new shopping mall. They found more than a dozen crumbling *Torah* scrolls along with it. I shipped the *Torah* scrolls to the Israel Museum in Jerusalem. But this scroll I began to read because I saw the name Halevi. It's a famous Sephardic family, Halevi. You must have heard of the great Judah Halevi."

She nodded.

"But this Halevi—true, he led his people to safety in Perpignan. But that refuge only lasted one year, until September 1493, when King Fernando took Roussillon back from France and they were expelled again. Some of them made it to Salonika."

"Yes. That's where my great-grandparents came from. My parents fled the Holocaust—"

The bookman nodded absently. He did not seem interested in the story of her family. "Perhaps it was not such a wise choice your ancestor made, to go to Perpignan. Before they left for Salonika they had to turn over to the Inquisition even the *Torah* scrolls they saved from Girona. They lost everything.

"Now this scroll surfaces in the *genizah*. Today only three hundred Jews live in Lisbon, though thousands more carry Jewish blood in our veins. Only a couple of us have any expertise in Hebrew manuscripts. So I called my friend Elka, a professor from the University of Barcelona, to examine it. Despite the stains, she deciphered the scribe's name: Amos Fontclara. She believes this Fontclara is the Christian scribe Domingo Fontclara, who skillfully copied many manuscripts in the late fifteenth and early sixteenth centuries in his distinctive style. He lived to be quite old, right here in Lisbon. It is quite possible that Amos Fontclara and Domingo Fontclara are the same man, since Domingo Fontclara lived in Girona before he came to Lisbon and was rumored to be from a *converso* family. I have to agree that the colophon on this scroll looks like Fontclara's. His name is on many classic Christian texts in the rare books room of the National Library of Portugal.

"Together we translated a bit of the scroll. Such odd ideas in Halevi's writings—" The old man broke off and muttered to himself in Portuguese as he rerolled the scroll. Ilana thought she understood the words: *unnatural, fruta*.

"What odd ideas?"

"Lady rabbi, don't ask me questions about this scroll. Elka wanted to take it to Barcelona, but I told her I wanted to study it first and then send it to our colleague at the Jewish Museum in Girona. Please take it safely to Girona. I will give you the necessary paperwork and tell you who to see at the museum." He scribbled a name on the back of his business card and handed it to her. Then he ushered her through the shop.

He swaddled the scroll in sheets of plastic and then a garbage bag to protect it from the rain and thrust it at her. The scroll felt surprisingly heavy. Sadness emanated from it, as if it were an orphan or a grieving widow she held in her arms.

Ilana turned to leave.

"One more thing, Rabbi," he said. She paused in the doorway of the shop. Suddenly he seemed not to want to let her go.

"Have you heard that archivists just discovered thousands of fragments of medieval Hebrew manuscripts hidden in the bookbindings of notarial registers in Girona?"

"No—"

"They found them when the registers were being rebound. It's another kind of *genizah*. Some of the fragments date back to the fourteenth century, only seventy years after the golden age of the Kabbalistic school in Girona. There are works of *Midrash*, commentaries on the *Talmud*, liturgical poetry by Judah Halevi and others, philosophical texts, as well as more ordinary things like notes from the meetings of the councils of the *aljama* and marriage contracts. There is even a record of Girona's last synagogue and how it was sold. These fragments were found in the municipal archives and the archives of the Diocese in Girona."

"Really? In Girona."

"Yes. Ask about them when you visit. I'm sure there are writings from your ancestor."

Ilana stared at him. "How can manuscripts be hidden in a binding?"

"In those days they didn't have cardboard. They made hard covers for books by gluing together layers and layers of paper. Now, poof! A miracle. They dissolve the glue with hydroalcoholic solution and with patience separate the pages. Sometimes they disintegrate, but they can be, how do you say it, reconstructed? An expensive process, but it can be done. What a treasure. I've been wanting to go see them myself, but you see, with the bad leg . . . If you find out more about the Hebrew fragments, let me know."

Ilana cradled the scroll against her belly and stumbled out of the bookstore into the wet street. She felt dizzy, dazed. She found a café and ordered strong coffee, bread, cheese, and olives. She closed her eyes.

She saw a small, dim room. Stones, ancient hand-hewn stones. Hands, a young man's ink-stained hands. Pools of moonlight falling on the scroll. And letters, Hebrew letters.

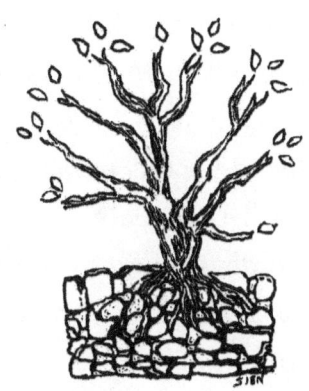

Author's Note

Kabbalah of Stone is a work of fiction, although I have based it on extensive research and followed historical events as closely as possible. A wealth of material was available to me through my affiliation with the University Library of the University of California, Santa Cruz. Much of what I read became compost for this novel.

There was no Rabbi Raphael Halevi of Girona, but many rabbis like Halevi had the difficulty of serving their people during the final, waning century of Jewish life in Spain between the persecutions of 1391 and the Expulsion in 1492. The Jews of Girona did move to Perpignan and were forced to leave there in 1493. From Perpignan, many Gironese Jews journeyed to Salonika.

Huldah is one of the four women prophets in the *Tanach*. She is mentioned in the books of 2 Kings (22:14–20) and 2 Chronicles (34:22–28), though little is known about her prophecies or her life. I am especially indebted to

Diana Edelman's article "Huldah the Prophet—of Yahweh or Asherah?", Raphael Patai's *The Hebrew Goddess,* and William Dever's *Did God Have A Wife? Archaelogy and Folk Religion in Ancient Israel* for this new interpretation of Huldah's ideas. My novel is partially a response to William Dever's challenge to develop new Jewish theology based on the archaeological evidence of Asherah unearthed in the Middle East in the past couple of decades.

For the character of Miriam I am indebted to Isaac Jack Levy and Rosemary Zumwalt Levy for their excellent study *Ritual Medical Lore of Sephardic Women: Sweetening the Spirits.*

To those wishing to study Kabbalah, including the meditations on the Hebrew letters or the concept of *Ibbur,* I recommend the texts in my bibliography. It is with the deepest humility (and some trepidation) that I contribute my ideas about *yichud* as an ecological and nondualistic consciousness.

Glossary

Adonai: One of the names of God, literally meaning "My Lord."

Aljama: The governing structure of the Jewish communities in Medieval Spain (the Council of the Aljama), or the community itself.

Angel Gabriel: The archangel who serves as a messenger of God.

Asherah: An agricultural/fertility goddess worshipped in ancient Israel, probably up until the sixth century BCE, during the time of the prophet Huldah. According to William Dever, Raphael Patai, and others, Asherah was "associated with living trees and hilltop forest sanctuaries, and could sometimes be symbolized by a wooden pole or an image of a tree" (Dever, 102). In the *Torah*, sometimes the word *Asherah* is used to refer to the goddess and sometimes it refers to the tree or pole that marked her shrine, and there is a great deal of scholarly debate about these various meanings. Dever argues that "this tradition concerning a goddess became anathema in time, however, and was perpetuated only in veiled references in the Hebrew Bible, in later Jewish tradition, and in Jewish and Christian versions of the Hebrew Bible." (See part VI of Dever, "The Goddess Asherah and Her Cult.")

Auto-de-fe ("act of faith"): The ritual of public penance of heretics or apostates condemned by the Spanish Inquisition. It involved a Catholic Mass, prayer, a public procession of those found guilty, and a reading of their sentences. In Portuguese this was known as auto-da-fé.

Bahir or **Sefer Habahir**: An anonymous book of Jewish mysticism attributed to Rabbi Nehunya, who lived around 100 CE. In about 1174 CE the *Bahir* was published by the Provence school of Kabbalists. .

Brit: A Jewish baby boy's circumcision ceremony that symbolizes his covenant with God.

Call: The Jewish Quarter of Girona and other cities in Catalonia.

Conversos: Spanish or Portuguese Jews who converted to Catholicism (in many cases these were forced conversions). The word *conversa* is used to refer to women who are *conversos*.

Ibbur: A positive form of spirit possession whereby a righteous soul decides to occupy a living person's body, usually with their consent, and usually for an important task. The word literally means "pregnancy." This concept is part of Kabbalistic thought.

Isaac the Blind (1160–1235): A Kabbalistic thinker from Provence, France, also known as Rabbi Yitzhak Saggi Nehor.

Juderia: The Jewish quarter in Portugal and in Spain (*judería*), except in Catalonia, where the word *call* is used.

Kabbalah: Arthur Green, one of the great contemporary scholars of Kabbalah, writes in *Ehyeh: A Kabbalah for Tomorrow*, "Kabbalah is the ancient Jewish tradition of esoteric wisdom. The word *kabbalah* means 'the received,' that which has been handed down and received by us from prior generations. These age-old traditions are said to originate in divine revelation and are thus 'received' ultimately from God." Meditation is a central practice of Kabbalah, particularly meditation on the Hebrew letters. Some of the first Kabbalistic texts were written by Rabbi Azriel, Rabbi Ezra ben Solomon, and other followers of Isaac the Blind, who emigrated from Provence, France, to Girona, Spain, in the late twelfth century, forming what is now known as the "Gironese Circle." Nachmanides continued their work in the first half of the thirteenth century. These writers connected their ideas to much older forms of Jewish mysticism such as *Merkavah* and *Hekhalot*, which date back to a thousand years earlier. After the expulsion from Spain, Kabbalah did flourish (as Huldah predicted!) in the Galilean town of Safed, as well as in parts of the Ottoman Empire.

Maimonides (1135-1204) (Moshe ben Maimon, also known as the Rambam): A rabbi, physician and philosopher in Southern Spain, Morocco, and Egypt during the Middle Ages.

Merkavah: A first-century CE Jewish mystical movement based on the book of the Prophet Ezekiel. The *Merkavah* was the chariot of God that Ezekiel saw in his vision.

Mikvah: A bath sourced in spring water that is used for the purpose of ritual immersion by either men or women.

Nachmanides (1194–c.1270) (Moshe ben Nahman Girondi [of Girona], also known as the Ramban): A Catalan rabbi, philosopher, rabbi, physician, Kabbalist and biblical commentator.

Tallit: The Jewish prayer shawl.

Talmud: A record of rabbinic discussions pertaining to Jewish law, ethics, customs, and history, a central text of Rabbinic Judaism.

Torah: The most holy of the sacred writings in Judaism, divided into the five books of Moses, whose names in English are Genesis, Exodus, Leviticus, Numbers, and Deuteronomy.

Yeshiva: A Jewish school that teaches *Torah, Talmud,* and other sacred texts.

Yetzer Hara: The inclination to do evil.

Zohar: An important work of Kabbalah that is a mystical commentary on the Torah. It first appeared in Spain in the thirteenth century and was published by a Jewish writer, Moses de León. De León ascribed the work to a rabbi of the second century, Shimon bar Yochai.

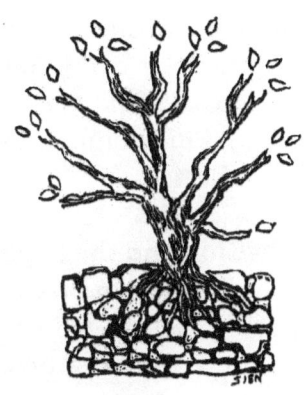

Bibliography

Judaism and Jewish History

Caputo, Nina. *Nahmanides in Medieval Catalonia: History, Community, and Messianism.* Notre Dame, IN: University of Notre Dame Press, 2007.

Chajes, J. H. *Between Worlds: Dybbuks, Exorcists, and Early Modern Judaism.* Philadelphia: University of Pennsylvania Press, 2003.

Dever, William G. *Did God Have a Wife? Archaelogy and Folk Religion in Ancient Israel.* Grand Rapids, MI: Wm. B. Eerdmans, 2005.

Edelman, Diana. "Huldah the Prophet — of Yahweh or Asherah?" In *A Feminist Companion to Samuel and Kings,* edited by Athalya Brenner, 231–250. Sheffield, England: Sheffield Academic Press, 1994.

Gafney, Wilda C. *Daughters of Miriam: Women Prophets in Ancient Israel.* Minneapolis: Fortress Press, 2008.

Heschel, Abraham Joshua. *The Prophets.* New York: Harper & Row, 1962.

Patai, Raphael. *The Hebrew Goddess.* 3rd enl. ed. Detroit: Wayne State University Press, 1990.

Roth, Norman. *Daily Life of the Jews in the Middle Ages.* Westport, CT: Greenwood Press, 2005.

Simms, Norman. *Masks in the Mirror: Marranism in Jewish Experience.* New York: Peter Lang, 2006.

Trachtenberg, Joshua. *Jewish Magic and Superstition: A Study in Folk Religion.* Philadelphia: University of Pennsylvania Press, 2004.

The Inquisition and the Expulsion of the Jews from Spain

Gerber, Jane S. *The Jews of Spain: A History of the Sephardic Experience.* New York: Free Press, 1992.

Gitlitz, David M. *Secrecy and Deceit: The Religion of the Crypto-Jews.* Philadelphia: Jewish Publication Society, 1996.

Lazar, Moshe, and Stephen Haliczer. *The Jews of Spain and the Expulsion of 1492.* Lancaster, CA: Labyrinthos, 1997.

Melammed, Renée Levine. "Sephardi Women in the Medieval and Early Modern Periods." In *Jewish Women in Historical Perspective,* edited by Judith R. Baskin, 128–149. 2nd ed. Detroit: Wayne State University Press, 1998.

Melammed, Renée Levine. *A Question of Identity: Iberian Conversos in Historical Perspective.* New York: Oxford University Press, 2004.

Netanyahu, B. *The Origins of the Inquisition in Fifteenth-Century Spain.* 2nd ed. New York: New York Review of Books, 2001.

Sachar, Howard. *Farewell España: The World of the Sephardim Remembered.* New York: Knopf, 1994.

Jewish Mysticism/Kabbalah

Dan, Joseph. *Jewish Mysticism and Jewish Ethics.* Northvale, NJ: Jason Aronson, 1977.

Firestone, Tirzah. *The Receiving: Reclaiming Jewish Women's Wisdom.* San Francisco: HarperSanFrancisco, 2003.

Green, Arthur. *Ehyeh: A Kabbalah for Tomorrow.* Woodstock, VT: Jewish Lights, 2003.

Green, Arthur. "Shekhinah, the Virgin Mary, and the Song of Songs: Reflections on a Kabbalistic Symbol in Its Historical Context." *AJS Review* 26, no. 1 (2002): 1–52.

Idel, Moshe. *Kabbalah: New Perspectives.* New Haven, CT: Yale University Press, 1988.

Kaplan, Aryeh. *Meditation and Kabbalah.* York Beach, ME: Samuel Weiser, 1982.

Kushner, Lawrence. *The Book of Letters: A Mystical Alef-Bait.* New York: Harper & Row, 1975.

Novick, Rabbi Leah. *On the Wings of Shekhinah: Rediscovering Judaism's Divine Feminine.* Wheaton, IL: Quest Books, 2008.

Schneider, Sarah. *Kabbalistic Writings on the Nature of Masculine and Feminine.* Northvale, NJ: Jason Aronson, 2001.

Scholem, Gershom. *Jewish Gnosticism, Merkabah Mysticism, and Talmudic Tradition.* New York: Jewish Theological Seminary of America, 1960.

Scholem, Gershom. *Origins of the Kabbalah.* Princeton: Princeton University Press, 1987.

Schwartz, Howard. *The Four Who Entered Paradise: A Novella.* Northvale, NJ: Jason Aronson, 1995.

Winkler, Gershon. *Magic of the Ordinary: Recovering the Shamanic in Judaism.* Berkeley, CA: North Atlantic Books, 2003.

Wolfson, Elliot. *Circle in the Square: Studies in the Use of Gender in Kabbalistic Symbolism.* Albany: State University of New York Press, 1995.

Gender and Homosexuality in the Middle Ages

Burger, Glenn, and Steven F. Kruger, eds. *Queering the Middle Ages.* Minneapolis: University of Minnesota Press, 2001.

Cohen, Jeffrey Jerome, and Bonnie Wheeler, eds. *Becoming Male in the Middle Ages.* New York: Routledge, 1999.

Eisenberg, Daniel. "Homosexuality." In *Encyclopedia of Medieval Iberia,* edited by Michael Gerli, 398–399. New York: Routledge, 2003.

Greenberg, Steven. *Wrestling with God and Men: Homosexuality in the Jewish Tradition.* Madison: University of Wisconsin Press, 2004.

Grossman, Avraham. *Pious and Rebellious: Jewish Women in Medieval Europe.* Waltham, MA: Brandeis University Press, 2004.

Hadley, D. M., ed. *Masculinity in Medieval Europe.* New York: Longman, 1999.

Karras, Ruth Mazzo. *From Boys to Men: Formations of Masculinity in Late Medieval Europe.* Philadelphia: University of Pennsylvania Press, 2003.

Leneman, Helen. "Reclaiming Jewish History: Homo-erotic Poetry of the Middle Ages." In *A Mensch Among Men: Explorations in Jewish Masculinity,* edited by Harry Brod, 143-149. Freedom, CA: Crossing Press, 1988.

Levy, Isaac Jack, and Rosemary Levy Zumwalt. *Ritual Medical Lore of Sephardic Women: Sweetening the Spirits, Healing the Sick.* Urbana: University of Illinois Press, 2002.

Roth, Norman. "A Note on Research into Jewish Sexuality in the Medieval Period." In *Handbook of Medieval Sexuality,* edited by Vern L. Bullough and James A. Brundage, 309-314. New York: Garland, 1996.

Girona

Alberch i Fugueras, Ramon. *Jewry Guide of Girona.* Girona, Spain: City Council of Girona, 2005.

Ayats, Gerard Roca, and Nuri Ros Rué. *42 Magical Stories "Legends of Girona."* Girona, Spain: Fundació 60, 2007.

Berthelot, Martine *Jewish Route Narbonne-Girona.* Association SOURCES, 2002.

Escribà i Bonastre, Gemma, and Maria Pilar Frago i Pérez. *Documents Dels Jueus De Girona (1124–1595)*. Girona, Spain: Ajuntament de Girona, 1992.

Graves, Lucia. *The Memory House*. Port Jefferson, NY: Vineyard Press, 2002.

Klein, Elka. *Hebrew Deeds of Catalan Jews/Documents Hebraics de la Catalunya Medieval: 1117–1316*. Barcelona: Societat Catalana d'Estudis Hebraics; Girona: Patronat Municipal Call de Girona, 2004.

Perani, Mauro. "Short Studies." In Proceedings of the International Congress on "New Discoveries in the 'European Genizah.' From Bologna to the Gerona Archives: Prolegomena to a Scientific Inquiry," 21-22. Jerusalem, December 12, 1999.

Sureda i Jubany, Marc. *Guide to Girona Cathedral*. Madrid: Ediciones Aldeasa, 2005.

Feminist Theory and Philosophy

Anzaldúa, Gloria. *Borderlands/La Frontera: The New Mestiza*. 2nd ed. San Francisco: Aunt Lute Books, 1999.

Barad, Karen. *Meeting the Universe Halfway: Quantum Physics and the Entanglement of Matter and Meaning*. Durham, NC: Duke University Press, 2007.

Photo by Daniele Basilio

About the Author

Irene Reti is also the author of *The Keeper of Memory* (HerBooks 2001), a memoir about growing up as a child of Holocaust refugees who kept their Jewishness a secret. She directs the oral history program at the University Library, University of California, Santa Cruz, and has a BA in environmental studies and an MA in history from UC Santa Cruz. Irene is a member of Chadeish Yameinu, the Jewish Renewal Community of Santa Cruz, California.

www.ingramcontent.com/pod-product-compliance
Lightning Source LLC
Chambersburg PA
CBHW021509240626
47154CB00002B/564